give me a SIGN

give me a SIGN

ANNA SORTINO

putnam

G. P. Putnam's Sons

G. P. Putnam's Sons
An imprint of Penguin Random House LLC, New York

First published in the United States of America by G. P. Putnam's Sons,
an imprint of Penguin Random House LLC, 2023

Visit us online at PenguinRandomHouse.com.

Library of Congress Cataloging-in-Publication Data
Names: Sortino, Anna, author.
Title: Give me a sign / Anna Sortino.
Description: New York: G. P. Putnam's Sons, 2023.
Summary: Seventeen-year-old Lilah, who wears hearing aids, returns to a summer camp for the Deaf and Blind as a counselor, eager to improve her ASL and find her place in the community, but she did not expect to also find romance along the way.
Identifiers: LCCN 2022042512 (print) | LCCN 2022042513 (ebook)
ISBN 9780593533796 (hardcover) | ISBN 9780593533819 (epub)
Subjects: CYAC: Deaf—Fiction. | Blind—Fiction. | Camps—Fiction. | Camp counselors—Fiction. | American Sign Language—Fiction. | Interpersonal relations—Fiction.
Classification: LCC PZ7.1.S6796 Gi 2023 (print)
LCC PZ7.1.S6796 (ebook) | DDC [E]—dc23
LC record available at https://lccn.loc.gov/2022042512
LC ebook record available at https://lccn.loc.gov/2022042513

Printed in the United States of America

ISBN 9780593533796
1st Printing

LSCH

Design by Nicole Rheingans
Text set in PT Serif

For my twin, six years younger

NOTE

To distinguish between spoken English and American Sign Language, I've italicized when characters are communicating with sign.

There's no guarantee that children with hearing loss will be provided access to sign. A range of communication styles exist, such as Sim-Com (simultaneous communication of both sign and speech), PSE (a hybrid of ASL and English grammar), and SEE (verbatim English), as well as regional dialects, notably BASL (Black American Sign Language). Many signs don't have direct English counterparts.

Thus, italicized wording in this novel is *not* a literal translation of ASL. It's Lilah's internal interpretation of what's being signed.

CHAPTER ONE

No one knows my deafness as well as I do. There isn't a single test that can truly get inside my head and understand how I'm experiencing the world. Doctors, parents, and strangers like to chime in with their assumptions. But after seventeen years, *I'm* still figuring it all out.

My annual audiology appointment is every January. My mom and I are driving through melting mounds of snow to get there. She won't let me do this alone because she doesn't trust me to be on top of things, especially after I got my fall semester report card this morning.

"We agreed you could stop using the FM system so long as your grades didn't slip." It's not the first time we've fought about this wireless device I'm supposed to use in class. My mom stares straight ahead as she drives down the highway, and I have to crane my neck to read her lips. "Are you proud of getting straight Cs, Lilah?"

"Half of my teachers practically refused to wear it anyway," I mumble. "It's too much of a hassle."

"Then you have to remind them to use it." She sighs, and says something about "——— outlined in your IEP."

"It *isn't* in there?" I ask, not sure I'd heard correctly.

"It *is*," my mom repeats, turning to face me. "So you need to use it. We didn't pay for it to sit in a case all year."

I wanted high school to be different, but these past few years have been rough. When my teachers use the FM system, it brings their voices directly into my hearing aids, making their words louder but not necessarily clearer.

All these necessary accommodations bring attention to me, which I hate. So instead of pointing out that I need closed captions whenever we watch a video, I sit there quietly. I don't catch most of what's being said, and I fail the quiz on the material afterward. Plus, teachers accuse me of "talking during class" whenever I try to ask the person next to me to repeat what the assignment is—after struggling to follow the lesson in the first place. So, I get another bad grade. Every day is exhausting.

"And you've been skipping your group meetings with the hearing itinerant?" my mom asks.

Those are . . . not fun. An hour each week, I'm forced to learn how to "advocate for myself," which often boils down to a reminder to sit in the front row.

"How am I supposed to get better grades if I'm pulled from class?"

My mom can't think of a response to that one. She clenches her teeth and turns carefully into the hospital's salt-covered parking lot.

We wait in the lobby for my audiologist. A toddler fitted with two large hearing aids runs across the room. His parents are trying to hide the fact that they're observing me closely. I'm used to the stares, especially here, since I'm one of the oldest patients at this children's center. It's possible this kid and his family have never seen someone my age with hearing aids before. They wonder what he'll be like when he grows up. When I was young, I didn't really know any older deaf people, either.

Until I went to summer camp.

My audiologist brings us back for my hearing test, and I take a seat in an office chair positioned in the middle of the dark-gray enclosed sound booth. This space doesn't exactly scream comfort.

To the outside observer, this may seem a strange little room. There's a creepy animatronic monkey on the shelf in the corner, with its cymbals hanging lifeless since it's used when testing little kids. The wide metal door to my right seals this chamber shut.

I wish I were alone. Instead, my mom sits on an identical chair against the back wall, holding her purse, silently observing. I steady my hands together in my lap, resisting the urge to crack my knuckles.

My audiologist, Ms. Shelly, a cheerful presence throughout the years, has me remove my hearing aids. They're now sitting on a tissue at the side table to my left. She leaves the booth and takes a seat in the other side, looking at me through a small window. She turns on background clatter and loud crashing sounds, supposedly reminiscent of daily life surrounding me, as I struggle through the chaos to decipher words she says into a microphone.

"Say the word 'baseball.'" Ms. Shelly's voice is initially set loud enough to rival the noise.

"Baseball?" I answer, my voice funny in my throat. I suspect I whispered my response. People tell me I speak too loudly, but whenever I'm focused on the volume of my voice, it comes out too quiet.

I cough to clear my throat, wondering why I'm nervous. I've done this every year of my life. It's nothing new.

"Say the word 'hot dog.'"

"Hot dog!" *Whoops*, sort of yelled that one. I need to settle into a happy medium.

The chair scratches my thighs as I shift to relax my shoulders and stare ahead. But my audiologist is holding an envelope over her mouth so I can't read her lips. She keeps gradually lowering the volume now, so it's projected at a level that isn't necessarily comfortable or effortless to hear. "Say the word 'ice cream.'"

"Ice cream." I'm still confident enough in the words to repeat them.

But it gets more difficult. Ms. Shelly increases the background noise, and I almost can't tell if she's still speaking. She's being drowned out by the roar. From the familiarity, I recognize, "Say the word ———." Yet I can't make out the rest.

I scrunch my nose and tilt my head to the side. Definitely didn't catch this one. It was . . . no. I'm supposed to give my best guess, but I can't even think of a word similar to what I heard. A hint of frustration rises within me.

It's my hearing being graded, not me.

This is the point in a typical conversation where I'd proclaim my most often used word—"what?"—as many times as it'd take for a person to get their message across. It's best when someone can switch up their wording to help me along. The greater the context, the more likely I am to pick up on what I'm missing.

However, right now, there is no context. Only background noise and an elusive word. At least this is better than the frequency test. I swear by the end of that one I'm imagining beeps that don't exist.

I give up and shrug. What's another failed test at this rate?

Ms. Shelly continues. Another twenty or so words later, she finally puts down the envelope and gives me a smile while shutting off the background noise and returning her voice volume to full blast. "Great job, Lilah. We'll move on now."

She enters my side of the booth, her laminated ID badge dangling from her neck, and sticks various diagnostic tools in my ears and on my head. Throughout several rounds of different examinations, I suppress the urge to compare this to an alien abduction.

When it's all over, Ms. Shelly returns and leads us out of the soundbooth and over to her office, where I usually get fitted for new earmolds and have my hearing aid levels adjusted. We take a seat around a small side table. My mom pulls her chair forward so they can crowd together over my results. I sit back, a little anxious, though there hasn't been any reason to be yet. My hearing loss, which I've had since birth, isn't supposed to be degenerative.

My mom frowns at the printout. I scramble to push in my hearing aids, looping the backs over and behind my ears. Wearing them helps, but they're never going to be a perfect fix. What people don't understand is that when I'm wearing my hearing aids, there's still a lot that I miss. And without them, there's still a lot I *could* catch by relying on lipreading and deductive reasoning.

We peer at the audiogram as my audiologist points to the zigzag lines trailing downward along the bottom half of the graph. The results for my left and right ears are close together, a fairly even loss across both sides.

"So we have a small dip since last time," Ms. Shelly explains seriously, but then she smiles. "I wouldn't be too worried about it."

"All the more reason for her to use her accommodations for school," my mom says.

"There is a newer FM she might prefer." Ms. Shelly reaches back to her desk to get a pamphlet for my mom, bypassing other ones that showcase different hearing aid brands or earmold color options. "Look how cool! It's sleek and modern."

But I don't care. While they discuss the pros, cons, and *cost* of a newer model, bemoaning the lack of insurance coverage, I stare back at the audiogram. I've always wondered what an additional loss would feel like. I'm not upset about it. If anything, I'm annoyed it's not more significant.

To hearies, that may seem weird. I can't really express why I feel this way, other than it might be nice to not stay caught in between. Like, if I had to choose between being fully hearing or fully deaf, I'm not certain my decision would be obvious.

And maybe, if the loss were profound, my family would be forced to finally take learning American Sign Language seriously. I'd seem "deaf enough" that my classmates would truly understand my need for all those school accommodations, rather than silently judge and question me. Because right now, they know I'm not hearing, but I don't fit their expectations of deafness, either.

It's a strange realm, here in the middle.

Since I'm overdue for a new set of hearing aids, Ms. Shelley gets out the supplies to create earmold impressions. I sit still as she squeezes cold pink goo into each ear. In a few weeks, I'll come get the molds and processors when they are ready and assembled. It will take wearing them awhile for my brain to adjust to the latest technology and for the world around me to sound like I'm used to.

I'm not ashamed of my disability or anything like that. What bothers me is trying to fit into the hearing world. That I'm constantly the odd one out, the one who always has to explain or adjust.

I can think of *one* place where I didn't feel this way: Gray Wolf, a summer camp for the deaf and blind. I stopped going after eighth grade, since leaving for an entire summer didn't really fit into my plans once high school began. But it was a unique place where I didn't have to explain my hearing loss to anyone. And it was my introduction to sign language and Deaf culture.

I'm starting to really miss it.

CHAPTER TWO

Two months later, our school has a half-day Friday to kick off spring break. My friends and I are sitting at a metal table outside Mackie's. We're enjoying the spring weather, which is unseasonably warm for the Chicago suburbs. I gather my long brown hair and tie it up with a purple ponytail holder. We're trying to figure out how to start off our vacation, but hunger and exhaustion from a morning full of exams has us parked here for lunch.

Kelsey takes a big bite of her chicken sandwich, putting a hand over her mouth to finish speaking while she chews.

"What?" I ask, leaning forward. It's times like these that remind me how much of my hearing is supplemented by lifelong lipreading skills.

"No," my other friend Riley says. "Not that one."

Kelsey takes a big drink of water and tucks her blond hair behind her ears in a feeble attempt to stop the light breeze from blowing it in her face. She hasn't repeated what she said yet. I've hardly touched my cheeseburger and have to swat away a pesky gnat that won't leave it alone. I turn to Riley instead and ask, "What'd she say?"

Having someone else repeat for me helps sometimes. Even if they aren't any louder, I might understand them better if they are closer to me, enunciate more clearly, or have more familiar lips.

But Riley doesn't echo exactly what Kelsey said. She unbuttons her shirt, tying it around her waist to sit cooler in just her tank top, and reaches for lotion from her bag to soothe her dry, white knuckles. "We're trying to figure out what movie to see. It's too hot to hang out outside."

I knew that much. What I still don't know is what movie options are being discussed.

"Is there even a showing soon?" Kelsey asks. Both girls pull up their phones to check the times, so I do the same but get sidetracked on Instagram.

In the midst of a Deaf-identity crisis after my audiology appointment, I've recently started following a ton of ASL accounts to restore my diminishing sign language skills. Fortunately, I remember a bunch from my time at Gray Wolf, but the reality of how much I still have left to learn is hitting hard. At least I know enough that I can determine if an account has a fluent Deaf teacher or an unqualified hearing person giving inaccurate lessons.

Even though I remember summer camp being a welcoming place for kids from all backgrounds, it can be hard to reconcile that with what I've seen on the internet—people arguing over speech, sign, culture, devices, and more. Sometimes it can seem like all I truly know is that I'm *not* hearing. I could spend days scrolling through conflicting takes of people within the community debating semantics as I settle deeper and deeper into impostor syndrome. People give too much power to labels. It can feel exclusionary, whether intentional or not.

"How about something"—Kelsey says—"like, uh . . ."

"What?" I ask again, my mouth jumping to the word before my brain can piece together that she said "like, uh" and not "Li-lah." I shake my head in response to the blank stares from my friends. "Never mind. You two pick. As long as it's something fun."

"Okay, let's do the superhero one," Riley says.

My burger is cold, but I take a few final bites. Kelsey always sits up front in Riley's car, so I climb into the back and stare out the window the entire way, since it's impossible to hear them over the noise of the vehicle and the radio.

At the Regal, Kelsey and Riley buy their tickets. When it's my turn, I step forward and say, "The same one they got."

The guy at the booth nods. I reach for my wallet once the price lights up on the register and slide the cash beneath the glass. He gives me the change and says something I don't catch. But my friends have stepped toward the door and are scrolling through their phones.

"What was that?" I ask him.

He repeats what he'd said, but I can't hear it or read it on his lips since he's behind a computer screen.

"I'm sorry, what?" I point to my ear and then the glass. I try to get my friends' attention.

Kelsey steps forward. "What's up?"

"Can you tell me what he's saying?" I ask, gesturing back to the window.

But the worker rolls his eyes, pulling the ticket from the printer and handing it to me. He dismissively waves me away as he tosses the receipt in the trash.

"Never mind," I tell Kelsey as we head inside the building. Of course it was about the receipt. I should have just defaulted to "no, thanks" and moved things along for everyone.

At the snack counter, Kelsey gets a slushie and Riley asks for Junior Mints. I don't want to spend more money, but I'm starving and will need popcorn to get me through the next three hours of explosions and indecipherable dialogue. There's no way I'm renting a pair of those sticky and hideous captioning glasses that theaters offer as an excuse to not put captions on-screen. They're the last thing I want on my face when I'm out with my friends. The machine doesn't work most of the time anyway.

While waiting for me to get my food, Kelsey and Riley run into some other kids from our school, so they once again aren't with me to repeat anything the cashier says.

"One medium popcorn, please." I hand over the money to the girl behind the counter, who then asks me something.

"No, thanks." I smile. I don't need the receipt, so I'm not going through that whole ordeal again.

She turns around to fill the container, and then hands it back to me along with the receipt. I walk away and grab a handful. Crap. What I'd said no to was the butter.

I join my friends, too irritated to bother figuring out what everyone's discussing, especially since there seem to be two separate conversations happening across the circle.

I nudge Riley. "Hey, should we get to our seats?"

"Yeah, sure," she says, turning to get Kelsey. "Let's go. I don't want to miss the trailers."

Riley and Kelsey lead the way to our seats and sit side by side, leaving me at the end of the row. "Do you mind if I sit in the middle?" Still standing, I offer up my snack. "I can share."

"That's okay," Kelsey says, staying in her spot between Riley and me. "I'm so full."

The lights dim and the first trailer starts. "Ah yes!" Riley points to the screen, saying something excitedly toward Kelsey and me.

I plunk down and stuff my face with popcorn.

A few times during the movie, I nudge Kelsey and ask, "What'd they say?" But she either repeats it staring straight at the screen or whispers it directly into my ear. Neither works, because I can't hear her when she's facing forward or read her lips when they're beside my ear.

Ah well, whatever. The superhero is saving the day; that much is obvious.

~

"You've been quiet," Kelsey tells me once we emerge from the theater back into the daylight. "Are you all right?"

"Yeah," I say, attempting to shrug off the listening fatigue. I'm exhausted and ready for a nap. "Do you guys want to do something next week?"

"Sure," Kelsey says. "I just can't on Monday 'cause I'm going into Chicago to interview for that summer internship."

"Right, I almost forgot!" Riley says. "That would be so cool if you got that."

"Nah, I mean, it's mostly just answering phones and things like that." Based on the way Kelsey talks about the job, it must be a cool position. I remember her mentioning it before, but I wasn't able to catch the company's name. "There're several positions. You both should apply, too. We could take the train into the city together all summer."

"I wish," Riley says. "But I'm not about that office life yet. I'm going back to the coffee shop and teaching dance lessons."

We stop in front of the car. For a moment, I wonder if I'll get the passenger seat this time, but we all climb back into our usual spots. When the engine starts, so does the loud music. Riley looks over her shoulder to tell me something.

"What?" I ask. "Can you turn off the music real quick?"

Riley lowers the volume. "Do you think you'll apply for the internship?"

What I really want to say is that answering phones and taking coffee orders both seem like impossible tasks to me. Instead, I say, "Actually, I may see if I can get a job as a counselor at this summer camp I used to go to . . ."

Hmm, I don't know where that came from. I mainly said it so I wouldn't have to explain to my friends why I didn't want to go for the internship, but there could be something to this idea.

"Oh, that's fun. What kind of camp is it?" Kelsey asks. "I used to love theater camp."

"Well, it's like, um, a Deaf camp," I say, nervous about how my friends will react.

"Death camp?" Riley blurts out.

"No . . ." I say, grazing my fingers along the side of my head to reveal one of my purple hearing aids. "Deaf."

"I always forget you have those," Riley says. "Like, you don't sound deaf. You know what I mean? Have you seen"—she gestures to the side of her head, and I already know what she's going to say—"one of the head things that, like, fixes your hearing? Why don't you get that?"

"A cochlear implant? No." I don't have the energy to explain further. "That's not exactly how that works."

"That'll be fun, though," Kelsey interjects, probably sensing my irritation with Riley's response. "It'd be amazing to spend the whole summer outside. Promise me you'll have a summer romance."

"I don't know about that . . ." I say, amused by the possibility.

"We'll miss you all summer," Riley says. "We'll have to do some major catching up when ———."

I don't catch the rest but get the gist. Sure, I'll miss the pool parties and sleepovers. Having to jump through hoops to feel included? Yeah, I won't miss *that.* Going back to Gray Wolf would be an easier time, at least in terms of accessibility.

My friends turn the music back up and we drive off. I'm left staring out the window . . . again.

I watch the trees as we go by, still wondering where this counselor idea came from but growing more confident about it by the minute. I have been wanting to practice my ASL. And getting away from my family for a bit might be nice, especially since my mom thinks I should study over break to get my grades back on track next year.

But will it be weird going back to Gray Wolf after all this time? It's a pretty small camp. Will anyone there remember me? My counselors all seemed so much older and cooler, though they were probably around my current age.

The idea is at least worth a Google search to see if they're hiring soon.

CHAPTER THREE

Okay, the Gray Wolf web page hasn't been updated since the nineties. I've literally never seen a site this old before. It only has a home page with the name of the camp, the address, and an office number.

Ugh, I don't want to struggle through a call. How have they seriously not included a contact form yet? I could ask my mom to do it for me, but how would that look, trying to apply for a job by having my mother place a phone call for me? Someone needs to fix this website, like, yesterday.

I give up and scroll through Instagram, where I've been paying more attention to posts from people I went to camp with. People I haven't seen in ages—like Ethan, who was a first-year counselor during my last summer at Gray Wolf three years ago. When I see his photo holding up a staff polo, I actually stop to read the caption announcing that he's just been promoted to assistant director for this summer.

Ahh, I feel weird messaging him. But I *do* want to apply for a camp job, and he might be able to help. What's the worst that could happen? He could just ignore this message if he has no idea who I am. But I remember him being really friendly and outgoing, so it's worth a try.

Lilah: Hi Ethan! Congrats on the new job! You probably don't remember me, but I used to go to Gray Wolf and was actually wondering if there are any counselor positions to apply for this summer. I didn't see anything on the website.

I hit Send. Time to Google search for some ASL lessons and confront how much I actually remember. Languages can be "use it or lose it," and sign language is no different. Eventually, I find a Deaf-taught series on YouTube and am relieved at how much vocab I remember. I race through the first few lessons at 2x speed, since I'm already confident in the alphabet, colors, numbers, family members, and so on.

I'm watching the video, practicing, when a notification pops up.

Ethan: Of course I remember you. We'd love to have you back! And yeah . . . we need a budget to update that site. What's your email? I'll share it with our camp director, Gary. We'll be looking soon.

"Yes, yes, yes," I say to myself, quickly typing out and sending my email address. This is all going so well! I really didn't expect my plan to come together this easily.

Lilah: Thank you so much! And congratulations again :)

~~~

For the next several weeks, I constantly refresh my email. There's less than a month left of school, and my friends have already lined up their summer plans. My mom's got it in mind that I'm going to do summer school to help fix my grades. I haven't told my parents about Gray Wolf yet, because have I even applied, really? All I did was give Ethan my email address. There hasn't been any sort of interview, and summer is already right around the corner.

So far, I've resisted the urge to message Ethan again, since that may come across as desperate. If they haven't contacted me by now, maybe they don't plan to. Who am I to skip several years of camp and think I can waltz back in and get the job? If Ethan remembers me, he must also know I wasn't fluent in ASL. Is that one of the job requirements?

Maybe I got my hopes up too high about being a counselor this summer.

Whether or not I get this job, I want to improve my ASL. So I pull up the video lessons again. I've reached the point where the signs are half familiar, half brand-new. Like, when it comes to weather signs, I totally know words we'd have used at camp, like "rain," "wind," or "lightning." But I've never seen "hurricane," "earthquake," or "drought" before.

My eleven-year-old brother plops down on the couch beside me, still in his jersey and cleats from a soccer game he had this morning.

"What are you doing?" Max asks, wiping the sweat that drips from his short brown hair down his tanned neck.
~~~

"Ew, go shower." I scrunch up my nose.

Max stares at the vocabulary video that's paused on my screen. "Do I need to ———."

"What?" I look back toward him.

"Do I need to know all this?"

My brother has the same kind of hearing loss I do, though one of his ears reaches further down the severe category. But we have hearing parents, and like most other deaf and hard of hearing kids, we've been raised with the goal of being hearing-passing. As far as we know, our hearing loss is genetic, even though there's no apparent family history of deafness. But we didn't have any childhood illnesses or head injuries, either. We were simply born with less hearing.

"If you want." I shrug. Max has never been to Gray Wolf, so his exposure to sign language is even less than mine. Instead of ASL lessons, Max and I got years of speech therapy. Which is fine, I guess, but why not both? "I learned a ton when I first went to Deaf camp."

"You learned there?" he repeats to confirm he heard correctly.

"Yeah."

He nods, furrowing his eyebrows. "I don't know. Do you really have to go for the whole summer?"

"Well, it's two months. There's still some time at home."

"Not much . . ." He scrunches up his mouth, probably thinking about his friends and sports that usually occupy the school break.

"Why?" I ask. "Do you want to go to camp?"

This summer was going to be my thing, but I guess it won't be the end of the world if my brother is there, too. Especially since if he learns sign language, it'll be easier to use it at home.

"Did you like going there?" he asks. "Or was it like school, where you had to do a lot of learning?"

"Max, it's fun! There's a lake and a pool and all sorts of outdoors stuff. I think you'd like it."

"Cool. I don't know, maybe. I'll ask Mom." He finally leaves and, fortunately, so does the smell.

~~~

I'm home alone Saturday morning, attempting to focus on a particularly tricky ASL lesson about grammatical sentence structure. I *have* to look busy when my parents get home from Max's soccer match; otherwise they'll ask why I'm not studying for finals. But of course, I keep getting sidetracked on social media.

My phone gets a notification right before my parents and Max walk in the door. No way is this what I hope it is . . . It's an email, and I do a double take when I read who sent it.

Gary@CampGrayWolf.com

Saturday, May 25, 9:46 a.m.

Dear Lilah,

Sorry to be emailing so late! Ethan has nominated you to be a junior counselor this summer, and we'd love to have you on board. Can you be at training on June 1? Campers will be there from Sunday, June 9, through Saturday, July 27, and there's usually a day of cleaning and counselor celebrations afterward.
~~~

There's a weekly stipend of $250/week, which we know really isn't much, but obviously room and board are all free. You don't incur many expenses when enjoying the great outdoors at summer camp!

Let me know.

Gary
Director, Camp Gray Wolf

I have to reread the email several times to get over my surprise. I got the job? I'd almost given up on the possibility. I have to be there in a week—the day after school lets out. Am I ready? I wish I had more time to brush up on my ASL.

"Don't you need to be studying for finals?" my dad asks, walking over to the couch and glancing at my laptop screen.

"Actually . . ." I say, noticing the skepticism on his face. "Well, yes. I need to study. *But*—I just got a job for this summer."

"A job?" my mom calls from the kitchen. "What job? You were supposed to take classes over the break."

"I don't want to do those . . ." I look back at the email to confirm once again that it's real before telling my parents. "Junior counselor at Gray Wolf. It'll be all of June and July."

"Hmm . . ." my mom says. It doesn't seem to be what she expected. But I can tell the wheels are turning in her brain. "That does leave a few weeks in August to prepare for the new school year."

"Sure, I guess," I say. A few weeks is better than a whole summer of homework. "So, can I go?"

"Yeah." My mom gives me a sly look. "And Max did just ask me about maybe going this year, so we'll send him, now that you can keep an eye on him."

"Right," my dad agrees. "We always meant to send him."

"He does have a busy June," my mom says. "I wasn't sure if it would work, but especially with you working there, they'll probably be open to taking him late."

Somehow my new job has now become about Max? Whatever, as long as they let me go. "I have to be there next Saturday."

"That's fast. But we can make it work." My mom nods. "Proud of you for finding a job."

"Yes, great work," my dad adds. "I'm sure it'll be a great time."

"Yeah, yeah," I say nonchalantly but filled with so much relief. I get to go be a counselor, hanging out with the college kids. I text my friends to share the excitement.

I'm already starting to feel a little overwhelmed. Sure, I know the sign language alphabet backward and forward, am decent with numbers, and still have a good grasp on camp-related vocabulary—enough to hopefully discuss the lunch menu or the activities schedule or the weather. But I'm not fluent enough to handle complex subjects like dreams and goals or life and love—the type of things I'd probably talk to the other counselors around the campfire about.

But I got the job, so they must think I'm qualified. I just have to put aside the creeping impostor syndrome that has me wondering . . . what if I struggle in the Deaf world as much as I do in the hearing one?

CHAPTER FOUR

I've never driven this far by myself before, but the three hours to the campgrounds at the Illinois-Wisconsin border are a breeze. My parents were worried about this old Civic making the journey, and reminded me several times that I'll have to run the car periodically throughout the summer or else I may not be able to get it to start for the way home.

But I don't worry about any of that as I blare music and bask in the sunshine warming my sleeveless arms.

The GPS tells me it's only a few more minutes, but it's nearly impossible to find the small arrival sign in the forest along the country road. In fact, I drive past my destination and have to make a hasty U-turn. I go slow down the long dirt entryway and approach the campsite as my stomach flutters. It's an unceremonious arrival site, just a patch of gravel and a few parked vehicles. But I know what's waiting beyond the path through the trees. My nerves dissipate at the sight of Ethan waiting for me.

"Lilah!" he shouts, his arms outstretched as I park and climb out of my car, beaming from ear to ear.

"Hey, Ethan!"

"You've grown, like, a whole foot since I last saw you, and that's not saying much because you're still so short." Ethan tackles me with a hug. I smile, having almost forgotten how Deaf people tend to make a lot of visual comments about appearance.

It's such a relief to see a familiar face at a familiar place. Ethan's been at camp forever, climbing the ranks. He looks older, too, and absolutely in his element here. He's Latino, short and stocky, and wearing bright-yellow socks with gigantic smiley faces patterned all the way up to his knees. His T-shirt spells out "Deaf Pride" in ASL lettering, and his dark-brown hair is long and shaggy, falling over his two silver hearing aids.

"It's great to be back," I say. "Anyone else I'll know back this year?"

"Hmm, did you ever meet Natasha? We've got several former campers on staff."

"Maybe?" I shrug, glancing at a pale freckled girl who just walked over to stand beside Ethan. She is wearing a long-sleeved black shirt despite the heat. I can't place why she looks vaguely familiar.

"Oh, this is Mackenzie," Ethan introduces her. "She's one of our new counselors this year."

"*You're L-i—h, right?*" she signs.

"Yes." I nod. I only caught a jumble of letters that started with an *L* and ended with an *H*, but I assume she spelled my name.

"She's an interpreting major," Ethan adds, answering the question he knows is on my mind. "So, do you still use the ASL you learned here?"

"*I maybe remember some,*" I sign to his delight, since he's the one who taught me much of what I know from way back when. This is a strong start . . . but I also practiced this sentence over and over in my head on the drive here.

"*Perfect.*"

We both grab my stuff from the car and head into the campsite.

"Wasn't there a welcome archway?" I point toward the path that leads to the entrance. There used to be a tall wooden board with a giant gray wolf—a friendly-looking painting that peered down at everyone passing through.

"It had to come down last year," Ethan says sadly. "After that big storm."

Without the sign, now it looks like the campgrounds have a secret magical entrance, where tall evergreen trees surround a rickety wooden footbridge that crosses a small creek. Even the temperature changes as we go over the water, though I've probably got the shade and cool breeze to thank for that. The dirt path before us stretches on until it divides into two at the clearing, forming a circle that hugs the entire perimeter of Gray Wolf's fields and open space, splintering off toward the cabins, the dining hall, the dance barn, the pool, and the lake. It's all the same—but changed. This place has fallen into some disrepair, but the charm is still there.

I wipe sweat from my forehead, glad I don't have to lug my things for much longer. Mackenzie walks alongside us. She waves to get my attention.

"*Where do you go to school?*" she signs, extremely slowly, over-mouthing the words with her lips. "*A deaf school?*"

"Mainstreamed," I tell Mackenzie, not able to sign back because I'm carrying stuff. "You can just talk to me right now. Dramatically mouthing kind of butchers the ability to lip-read. And I don't always use sign, so you don't need to." That might be rude of me to say, but she could benefit from the explanation. "When talking to just me, at least," I clarify.

"I see," she says and signs, finally using her voice. After a pause, she again speaks slowly to keep pace with her hands. I turn back to watch her lips. "But it's best to always sign anyway, so other people around can see and join in the conversation if they want. Like how other hearing people could join us talking."

I frown. "I'm not hearing."

Mackenzie doesn't address this and keeps walking behind Ethan.

"I thought most everyone here would sign. But so many people speak." She momentarily occupies her hands fixing her red braids.

I'm sure one of her professors sold her on this summer gig as a great way to practice sign. She's being showy with her ASL, which she probably only just started learning. Granted, that's more classes than I, with a hearing loss, have ever had the opportunity to take.

"Well, we new people have to stick together," she says and signs.

I take a deep breath to stop myself from correcting her again and telling her I'm not "new" here. I need to practice, but Mackenzie isn't my ideal partner.

Ethan can sense my frustration and gives me a knowing smile as he comes to my rescue. "Lilah was a camper here for many years. And hopefully will be back now for a few more."

"That'd be great," I say, wondering about his use of the word "hopefully." Is becoming a senior counselor after being in the junior role *not* a guarantee? Maybe that's when there's an actual interview or something.

"Well," Mackenzie says and signs. "Since you're a junior counselor, I hope you'll be assigned to help my group. We can learn together. It's such a beautiful language. And it's so special to be able to help deaf people."

"Mm-hmm," I say, relieved to have arrived at the cabins.

"When you get a chance, you should check out my YouTube channel," Mackenzie adds. "I practice and interpret songs."

Yikes. That's why I recognized her! She's one of those hearing people doing ASL videos. I watched about ten seconds of one and knew right away it wasn't something I should learn from. Based on her absurd number of followers, I doubt others realize that.

I pretend I don't hear her and follow Ethan into one of the small red wooden cabins, where I get to drop my bags. If I packed too much, it's all in an effort to get through the summer with minimal laundry runs.

"Didn't there used to be more cabins?" I ask Ethan.

He nods. "We lost one last year. The roof caved in over the winter from that big snowstorm. It'd already taken some major wind damage before that, so it was a lost cause. Enrollment is down anyway, so we have to make do without it."

It's a bit musty here, being the start of the season and all. I quickly choose a free top bunk.

"All the counselors will be staying here during training," Ethan explains. "We'll spread out to all the cabins once the campers get here."

"Right." I nod. So that's why so many beds are made.

Ethan grabs a phone charger from his bunk, but Mackenzie hurries over and taps his arm, despite the fact that he's already looking at her. "Yeah?" he asks.

"Sorry, I forget," Mackenzie says and signs. "What's your sign name?"

"I have two," Ethan says and signs. "My usual one is like an *E*"—he demonstrates, shaking the letter in an animated twisty motion near his head—"because of my hair and how excited I can be. But for camp, we like to pick summer words for everyone, since not all campers arrive with a sign name."

"That's why I forgot. You have two," Mackenzie says and signs. "What's your camp one?"

"Socks," Ethan says and signs. "Because"—Ethan sticks out his foot to show off his bright-yellow socks.

"I still need a sign name. For camp or just in general." Mackenzie pauses, clearly hoping Ethan might get the hint. But when no one answers, she turns to me and says, "It has to be given to you by a Deaf person."

"I know," I say and sign, trying to keep my tone neutral.

"Lilah already has hers," Ethan says.

"Right . . ." I smile, remembering. "Weren't you the one who gave it to me?"

"How could I forget?" he says. "*Bug.*"

The memories come flooding back. "*Bug,*" I sign, holding my thumb to my nose, and crunching down my index and middle fingers twice. I love it. There's no mistaking this sign, unlike when I'm listening and I mistake someone mumbling "like, uh" and assume it's my name.

"Why that sign, Lilah?" Mackenzie asks.

"Her very first summer at camp, she had so many ladybugs land on her. A sign of good luck." He smiles. "'Ladybug' got shortened to 'Bug,' and it stuck." He checks his watch. "Okay, we'll let you get unpacked. Meet Mackenzie and me outside, and we'll walk over for dinner."

I unzip my backpack and toss any nonessentials up into my bunk so it's lighter to carry around all summer. An old faded-purple JanSport, soon to be filled with first aid items and a waterproof Otterbox for hearing aids, is now a proud symbol of my new junior counselor status. I tuck my water bottle, decorated with stickers, into the side pocket.

I scan the room, hoping to find a place for my duffel. But there's not much space to leave my stuff on the floor, especially since I tossed my empty mesh laundry basket into the only free corner. I hoist the bag up to the foot of my bunk, wavering when it's stuck over my head because I'm not tall enough to push it the rest of the way. This was not the smartest decision.

The floorboards move beneath me, and I feel my bag sliding off the bed. I'm about to drop it when an extra pair of arms comes to my rescue, pushing it onto the top bunk. I turn around, expecting to see Ethan or Mackenzie, but it's someone else.

A guy about my age is standing there in a blue baseball cap and a Cubs T-shirt that fits him perfectly. He looks like he belongs in the team's dugout, although his hat has a cursive *L* on the front that I don't recognize. A small tuft of hair curls at his forehead. He has a warm-brown complexion and kind, dark eyes that are set on me. He's standing with his hands loosely clasped together, ready to sign, with a woven bracelet around his wrist, perhaps from last summer.

My heart is racing, and I'm not sure if it's from lifting the bag or from realizing who helped me. "Thanks," I say breathlessly.

"*You're welcome,*" he signs. He points past me and signs something else.

I freeze. I want to answer him in sign, but I'm unsure exactly what he's asking. He gives a small shrug, likely knowing that I didn't understand, and walks around me to grab his backpack from his bunk . . . which is directly below *mine*. Of all the beds I could have chosen! At least he won't be able to hear me if I snore in my sleep.

"*Are you new this year?*" This time he mouths the words a little bit, which I know is purely for my benefit.

"Um, no." I beg my brain to remember any of the ASL I practiced. "Long time ago, I was here," I say and sign. "As a camper."

"*Wait . . .* " He tilts his head to the side. His wonderfully expressive eyebrows do a lot of communicating for him as he raises them and leans forward. "*I think I remember you. Bug, right?*"

"Whoa," I say and sign. "Yes! You were a camper here, too?" I am certain I would remember him.

"*Yeah, and then* ———," he signs. I don't follow most of his response, but he raises his hand from his chest to his head, signing that he's grown taller. "*I look different, maybe.*"

"Oh right, good," I say and sign, nodding while my brain still races to try to process more of what he signed.

"*Good?*" His eyebrows are raised and there's a mischievous glint in his eyes.

"Good, as in, I think I remember you now, too," I say and sign quickly, cursing my limited vocabulary and feeling the blush rise on my cheeks. I stare down at his worn running sneakers that are caked in dry mud and laced with bright-green cords.

"*I'm I———,*" he signs.

"Sorry," I say, hoping that my frustration at my lacking ASL doesn't come across as overly apologetic. "*Again, please.*"

He smiles and patiently spells out his name again. "*I-s-a-a-c.*"

"*L-i-l-*" But my hand is shaking, and I mess up, jumbling my letters. I close my hand into a fist, take a brief pause, and start again. "*L-i-l-a-h.*"

"*Camp sign name Spider,*" Isaac adds, signing with one wrist crossed over the other to resemble the eight-legged creature. "*Like—*" He makes a web-slinging gesture, a clear reference to Spider-Man.

"You and your friends always won all the games!" I say, forgetting to sign, but he reads my lips and nods enthusiastically. I do recall a small group of boys about my age who were always off playing sports. I shake my head, smiling. "*B-a-t man, too?*"

He nods and points toward me excitedly. "*Yes!*" He shows me the sign. "*Bat. He's a counselor here, too.*"

"*Awesome.*" I'm still smiling ridiculously. "I thought no one here would remember me," I say.

He watches my lips, grinning. "*Nah.*"

We just kind of look at each other for a moment, reconciling the little kids we used to be with the person in front of us now. He's still standing beside me, near enough for me to pick up the citrus of his freshly washed tee, which already has a hint of musty outdoor aroma, soon to include traces of campfire smoke, sunscreen, and cut grass. His scent puts me at ease. I guess being this close to people comes naturally at camp. Strangers at the beginning of the season can be very best friends by the end. While this interaction wasn't as smooth as I would have liked it to be—my signing impressed no one—it's just a matter of time before I can hopefully converse with him better. I've got all summer.

"*Let's go eat?*" He nods toward the cabin door.

"Yeah, Ethan said it was almost dinnertime," I say, grabbing my backpack. Crap, I forgot to sign my response again. I can't keep doing this. I'll just have to push through, even if I don't know the word for something yet.

Isaac and I head out of the cabin, where Ethan and Mackenzie are waiting, and we all start walking to the dining hall. Isaac turns around and walks backward to face us as he signs, "*What's for dinner?*"

"*I have no idea. Maybe pizza?*" Ethan signs.

Rather than going along the perimeter path, we cut through the large grass field for a direct route toward the dining hall. We move together in a semicircle so everyone is visible for the conversation, a necessity for both signing and lipreading. It's little things like this that bring back memories of my time as a camper at Gray Wolf. I'm thrilled with how much of the signing I'm able to follow, even if it's only been simple communication so far. Maybe all my practicing made a difference.

"*Yeah, hopefully pizza,*" Mackenzie signs.

"*Same,*" I join in, ready to prove my language skills. I throw in another sign I'm able to conjure from memory. "*I'm really hungry right now.*"

This doesn't spark the chorus of "same" reactions I'd expected. Isaac throws his head back, squeezing his eyes shut while his mouth hangs open in silent laughter.

Ethan sports an amused grin. "Are you sure that's what you meant to say?" he says and signs.

Mackenzie winces. "Awkward." She leans into the sign, wobbling her body side to side while she raises and lowers three extended fingers on both hands.

I turn back to Ethan, desperate for an explanation, but instead, Isaac waves at me, still wiping tears of laughter from his eyes with his other hand. Deaf waving isn't like a casual hello. Rather, it's like reaching out to slap a table to get someone's attention: You bend your wrist forward to hit the air horizontally as many times as it takes to get the person to look at you.

I want to cover my bright-red face, but I have to leave my mouth visible. "What? No one else is hungry?" I ask, with my hands resting on the straps of my backpack, suddenly apprehensive about signing.

Isaac holds up one finger on his left hand, drawing his right hand to his chest where he signs the word "hungry," slowly running the C shape down from the base of his throat. He holds his left hand forward with one finger out to emphasize the single movement.

I shrug, not sure what he's getting at, because that looks similar to what I just signed, so he takes a different approach. He signs the word the way I did, moving his hand up and down his chest more than once. He shakes his head no, raising his eyebrows.

"Oh, so I signed it wrong?" I ask.

"It's okay," Mackenzie says and signs. "I've made that mistake before."

Great. Once more, I look imploringly toward Ethan.

"If you sign 'hungry' like that," Ethan explains, "it means 'horny.'"

"What?" I hope I misheard. Did I really sign to everyone that I was horny right now?

Isaac steps closer to me and takes hold of the back of my hand. *No*, it's not a romantic gesture, although his action still sends a shiver down my back. Deaf interactions can be touchy. Lots of reaching out to get each other's attention and to emphasize certain things being said. As we're walking, he moves my hand from my throat to my chest once, nodding yes. He lets go and repeats the sign against his chest multiple times, vehemently shaking his head no.

"I . . . see where I went wrong." My embarrassment turns to anger when I realize Mackenzie has interpreted what I just said in sign for Isaac. It shouldn't have to be like this. "*Sorry.*"

Mackenzie falls into step with me. "It's all right," she says and signs. "Everyone makes mistakes when they're learning."

"I'm tired of learning. I just want to be fluent," I say, holding my hands tight against my chest. "I should know it already."

We're getting closer to the dining hall. I slow down and check my phone, not wanting to walk beside Mackenzie. Isaac and Ethan converse, and Isaac reaches into his backpack and pulls out a Fruit Roll-Up, scrunching most of it into his mouth so he can still sign with Ethan while he's eating. He's about to shove the wrapper into his pocket when he glances back at me.

"*Still hungry?*" He lifts his eyebrows. That's all it takes for the blood to rush right back to my face. I shake my head. Isaac tilts his head and widens his eyes into an apologetic puppy dog stare. "*Sorry, that wasn't funny.*"

"*It's fine.*" I tap my thumb against my chest, confident I know this sign.

He leans forward with eyes wide. "*Friends?*"

"Yeah," I say, nodding. "*Friends.*"

I speed up to keep pace with the group but hide on the opposite side of Ethan. My brain is spinning—that's enough conversation for now.

CHAPTER FIVE

This evening there's only one long table set up in the center of the dining hall. We're a small staff of ten, so each of us grabs a folding chair from the stacks along the wall and we squeeze together. There's no food at the buffet station. The camp chef will be here in a few days. Instead, there's a platter of grocery store sandwiches and bags of chips on the counter near a Gatorade jug full of water.

"Welcome to training week, counselors!" A man sprints to the front of the hall, clapping. Ethan follows, standing by his side to interpret. "For those of you I haven't met yet, my name is Gary. This is my second year here at Gray Wolf."

Gary looks . . . like a Gary. He's a high school science teacher with short, graying hair. He's wearing a tie-dye T-shirt and khakis, a uniform of sorts. For the next ten minutes, Gary outlines what we can expect during training, as well as once the campers arrive. I may or may not tune out at the end, eager to get on to the eating portion.

"To recap, training will cover safety, familiarizing ourselves with the grounds, and refreshers on games and activities."

Gary stands in stark contrast next to Ethan, who is interpreting with less enthusiasm than he would if the campers were here, but with plenty of facial expressions still. They're so different. Old and young. Hearing and Deaf. Reserved and energetic. Gary is lean and sports a scraggly beard, while Ethan is stocky and has tied his hair into a topknot.

"And the storm cellar is here in the dining hall basement," Gary says, wrapping up his spiel. "I do have one last point to make, now that the usual summer procedures are out of the way. As you may or may not know, I'm usually the guy camps bring in when things aren't looking too hot in one way or another." He must be greeted by a lot of concerned faces, because he immediately clarifies. "What we have here is a simple budget issue."

That makes sense. Gray Wolf was never a state-of-the-art campground, but it does look worse for wear than I thought it would. And I'm not sure how anyone is supposed to know about this place with such an outdated website. But where does the money come from? Any kid with a qualifying hearing or vision loss can attend, and it's all free, which is why my parents were able to send me here when I was little.

"Essentially," Gary says, "the original source of financing has been depleted over the years, faster than additional funds have been procured. We'll need some new revenue to keep things going."

To keep things going? I'm finally back at Gray Wolf, but is it possible this could be the last summer? Talk about terrible timing. This is the most deaf-friendly job I'll probably ever have. And there are so many more kids who should experience this place.

"Obviously, we don't want to have to charge our campers," Ethan interjects.

"Exactly," Gary says. "Things aren't that dire yet. The board and I are discussing solutions. One of which is to woo some new donors."

Isaac waves and asks a question, which Ethan relays to Gary. "So what exactly does this mean for us this summer? Is anything changing right away?"

Gary knows to face Isaac as he responds, and Isaac glances back and forth between him and Ethan's interpreting. "This year should look similar to last summer. But as you know, we've been cutting a lot of the typical activities, such as the occasional off-site trips."

Around the table, we all solemnly nod in understanding. I guess that means I'm not getting the chance to go horseback riding anytime soon.

Gary tries to lift the mood. "We'll be raising money so that camp can not only continue to exist but once again thrive!"

He wants to be reassuring, but I'm stuck on "keep things going" and "not only continue," which suggest things are, in fact, pretty bad.

"I'll be giving a few tours over the summer to these potential donors, but nothing that should interrupt the usual routine. Oh, we may have a luncheon at some point. But for the most part, you can just pretend they aren't here." He nods and checks his clipboard. "Yep, I think we can go ahead and eat dinner." He looks back up at us. "Any questions?"

Our group is still digesting the news and too hungry to come up with any thoughts.

"Okay, Ethan will pass around your group assignments. Read through the children's profiles to identify any dietary requirements and other needs. You have my cell, and Ethan's, and each other's. I'm used to good old-fashioned walkie-talkies, but for obvious reasons, phones are a better fit here for a variety of accommodated communication. Text or call me with any emergencies. Oh, and you have our lovely nurse's number as well."

"Yes. Hello, everyone!" the elderly, bubbly camp nurse says and signs. She's sitting at the head of the table beside where Gary is standing. "I recognize many smiling faces. I'm excited to get to know you better when we have our first aid and CPR training."

I'm surprised there's finally a nurse with a working knowledge of ASL. Honestly, it should be a requirement for the job, but she is the first one as far as I know.

"Let's eat!" Ethan says and signs. "After dinner, you're free for the rest of the night."

Mackenzie throws both hands into the air to start a round of sign language applause. "My, I just love this," she says, and wiggles her fingers in the air in silent, overly enthusiastic celebration.

Ethan hands me a deck with the profiles of my campers. Since I'm a junior counselor, I've been paired with someone over eighteen—and of course, that happens to be the new staff member, Mackenzie . . . Yay, me.

~~~

While we eat dinner, the two counselors sitting beside me introduce themselves as Bobby and Simone respectively.

Bobby is a former camper with low vision. He's got a splotch of sunscreen near one of his eyebrows. Still, his attempt to coat his pale complexion was unsuccessful. None of us spent that much time outdoors today, but the sunburn on Bobby's face grows redder by the minute. His cane is folded up in the pouch of his backpack, presumably because he primarily uses it after dark. But from what I've already observed at dinner, despite hovering at least a foot taller than Simone, he likes to default to grabbing onto her arm when he needs a guide.

Bobby is the epitome of clashing colors in a purple shirt and orange shorts, but Simone has the athleisure look down, sporting the latest Old Navy line from head to toe. She's Black and studying to work with blind and low-vision kids. She and Mackenzie are the only two counselors this summer without a hearing or vision loss.

"So I don't know how I feel about having randoms wandering around camp," Bobby says, taking a bite of his sandwich and letting most of the lettuce fall out onto his plate.

"Is this something we should tell parents up front?" Simone asks.

"I'm sure Gary's on top of that. Gotta keep the children safe. What do you think, Lilah? As the resident child here," Bobby jokes.

"Come on, I'm seventeen." But I don't take it too seriously. I've been amused by the banter between Simone and Bobby and am glad to be easily roped into the conversation.
~~~

"But not eighteen yet, so where's the lie?" Bobby says. "You didn't answer my question."

"I don't know . . . I mean, if people want to see what they'd be donating their money to, that should be fine, I guess." But then I imagine a squad of four old dudes roaming around on a little golf cart like they're on a paid safari, clicking away to take zoomed-in photos on their phones. "Okay, it has the potential to be weird."

Simone agrees. "Yeah," she tells Bobby. "It really depends."

"Couldn't there be another way to bring in the money?" I ask. "Online or something? I mean, seeing how out of date the website is, that'd be a technological challenge."

"Yeah, this place is ———," Simone says.

"What was that?" I ask.

"This place is getting desperate for money," she repeats, a bit louder. "Wages could use a lift. I almost had to take a different job this summer."

"But she wouldn't dare," Bobby says, nudging Simone's arm. He turns toward me. "This financial stuff is probably part of why Ethan didn't get the promotion." He pauses, nodding to where the others are sitting. "There aren't any ears named Gary nearby, right? I'll fill you in on our off-season drama since last summer."

I look around. Our camp director and nurse have already cleared their places and are chatting near the door. "You're good. What happened?"

"I don't know if you were old enough to really know this the last time you were here, but we didn't have an assistant director before. They made the position just for Ethan, rather than letting him be the director, 'cause they'd rather keep Gary around."

"Couldn't they have been co-directors?" I ask.

"My thought exactly . . ." Simone chimes in.

"Okay, but Lilah. Do you remember beeper baseball?" Bobby asks, diving into a tangent.

"Ouch," I say. "How could I forget." It's a game obviously meant for the blind, but those of us who aren't cover our eyes to play. Whoever is in the catcher position watches the pitch and uses a long stick to poke deaf batters to let them know when the ball is thrown. This camp is all about accessibility, which may sometimes be taken to slightly unreasonable levels in the name of a fun challenge.

"I'm gonna destroy everyone in a game tomorrow." Bobby grins. "I brought plenty of bandanas."

"I think it's a little skewed in your favor, with a bunch of blindfolded Deafies in the outfield, but we'll let you have this victory," I say.

"Better keep the ice packs ready—" Bobby is interrupted.

Simone grabs his arm. "Nah, you gotta change that."

"But it's my faaaaaaaaavorite," he drags out the word. What are they talking about? "Can't right now anyway." He holds up his fingers, slimy from the mayo in his sandwich.

I strain my ears over the clatter and echoes of the dining hall and realize Bobby is playing music.

Simone rolls her eyes and reaches into his pocket, retrieving the phone and changing the song. There are clearly zero personal space boundaries between these two, but I can't figure out if I'm getting relationship vibes or not. As if by instinct, I glance down the table, and my gaze lands on Isaac. This whole meal he's been in rapid-fire, one-handed sign conversation with two other counselors. I must be watching too obviously, because he turns my way and locks eyes with me. He smiles, and I quickly look away.

"You mind turning it up while you're at it?" I ask Simone.

"I got you," she says, adjusting the volume to the perfect point where I'll be able to hear more of the music without it overpowering her and Bobby's voices. As she leans back into her seat, the chair nearly topples over with the weight of her bag hanging over the back.

"Whoa! What do you have in there?" I ask.

I don't know why she'd want to carry around such a load all day. All we're required to have is a flashlight, a first aid kit, and a waterproof Otterbox case to hold hearing aids and other devices during swim time.

She grabs the bag and shoves it under the table. "A few books. I'm close to done with one, but I've got two more to have a choice on which to pick next."

"Oh, are they Braille?" I ask.

"Yep, for reading practice," she confirms. "They're massive."

"And *dirty*," Bobby adds.

"Shut up, Robert," Simone says, but her mouth curls into a small grin. "There's nothing wrong with reading romance, especially during the summer. They're fun."

"Hey, dinner wasn't bad, right?" I say, eager to change the topic. "I remember eating a lot of cold nachos."

"Yeah, that's why we make trips to the store," Simone says. "Or Mackie's or Freddy's."

"Do counselors leave, like, every night?" There's so much about this part of camp—the after-hours—that I want to explore.

"Gosh no." Simone takes a sip from her water bottle, leaving me in suspense. "It's literally, like, twenty-five minutes to get to any of those places."

"We only have from nine thirty until midnight," Bobby says. "If we're not on duty."

"That makes sense," I say.

"And it's not like we make enough to be spending money all the time anyway," Bobby says.

Yeah . . . if I want to come back and work again as a senior counselor next summer—that is, if there's a Gray Wolf to come back to—I'll definitely need to be earning a bit more so I don't go to college with an empty bank account.

~~~

"Hey, girl," Mackenzie says and signs, standing close to me as I refill my water bottle. She lets down the sleeves of her T-shirt, which she'd rolled up for dinner. Everyone else is getting ready to leave the dining hall. "What are you doing tonight?"

"I'm not sure yet." I don't know what to do at camp without a schedule structured down to the minute and an early bedtime. "What about you?"

"I'm going to go catch the rest of golden hour." She points outside. "Since we have free time during training week, I figured I'd make a bunch of extra videos to post in case the next two months get hectic."

"Videos?"

"For my YouTube channel I told you about! Gotta keep the sponsors, you know?" She nods for me to move aside so she can
~~~

fill her bottle. "Do you want to guest in one? We could do a fun summer song. I can teach you all the words."

"*No, that's fine,*" I sign, and casually walk away.

Just how much does she make with that crap? It sucks that someone like Mackenzie can make money while Deaf creators often struggle to get views. I can't think of a single reason why I would ever want to appear on Mackenzie's channel. I don't want people to assume my less-than-perfect signing skills mean I'm just another hearing person trying to use ASL for clout.

"Hey, junior counselor!" Ethan waves for my attention. I'm relieved, hoping I'm about to be included on some plans for tonight, but then I notice the bucket of soapy water beside him. "I got a first job for you to do," he says. "*Time to put you to work.*"

"Guess that's what I'm here for," I say, mimicking the sign he did. "*Work. Work. Work.*"

Ethan slides his hand down his face as I walk up to him and grab the bucket. "Lilah . . ."

I raise my hands, exasperated. "What now?"

"This is 'work.'" He demonstrates the sign. The right fist taps over the left, forming a small X shape. "This"—he repeats the sign the way I'd done it, a bigger, more vertical X with the wrists clashing together—"is 'make out.'"

Great. I made another embarrassing mistake. Ethan taps his foot and continues to do the sign, moving around in a ridiculous fashion loosely based on TikTok moves. I don't know if I'm ready for this much summer camp counselor enthusiasm.

But Isaac is.

He comes out of nowhere to join Ethan. So do the friends Isaac was eating dinner with, even though they have no idea why Ethan started dancing in the first place. There's so much energy, emotion, and personality that goes into ASL, and it clearly translates to their approach to this job. The way they move around, eager to take up space. It's not just vocabulary and grammar that I need to learn, but also how to set my expressions and movements free.

I laugh to hide my awkwardness, and hurry to clear any remaining trash on the table so I don't get roped into dancing. I've already embarrassed myself in front of Isaac today. He doesn't need to witness my incoordination, too.

Stepping aside, I'm about to plunge my hand into the bucket to fish for the cleaning rag, when someone taps my shoulder.

It's Isaac. He takes off his baseball cap and runs a hand through his loose curls, then gives a cute little wave hello and points toward the door. Some of the others are heading out, probably back to the cabins, except Isaac's two friends who are waiting by the entrance for him. Isaac signs something to me, but it's too fast.

"*Sorry, slow, please,*" I sign.

He nods and signs again, slower. He's switched around the order of what he's trying to convey as well. But still, I only get one word.

"Lake?" I ask, repeating the sign. But I still can't piece together the rest, which he assumes from my concentrated stare.

He switches over to fingerspelling. "*B-r—e.*"

Crap. I know each letter as I see it, but I'm so focused on identifying each one that once he reaches the end, I can't remember what I just saw so that I can string it all together into a word. So instead, I smile, nod, and step away.

But Isaac is persistent. He waves at me, shaking his head with narrowed eyes. I immediately regret what I just did. He's calling me out on it, and rightfully so. I can't believe I tried the "smile and nod" move here, of all places. I'm used to doing this to hearing people—shutting down conversations I can't follow—but I'm positive that hearing people must do this to Isaac all the time when they can't figure out what he's trying to communicate, like I just did.

"Sorry," I say and sign. "I'm tired. A lot of signing today. I'm still learning."

He shakes his head reassuringly. "*It's fine.*" He spells the word again, but now I'm frustrated and upset at myself because Isaac has to work this hard to try to talk to me. He's so cute and sweet, but I can only talk to him with, like, a kindergarten-level comprehension.

"Ahh," I say, theatrically shaking my head and staring at the ceiling. If it was anyone else, I wouldn't be flustered. But I so badly want to communicate with Isaac better than I am right now. "*I'm sorry. I will practice all night. I'm awful.*"

But Isaac's laughing. Not at me, but with me. He holds up a hand. Not in a stern way, because his fingers are relaxed and slightly curved. He's simply motioning for me to wait.

He waves his arms, trying to get his friends' attention, but they're facing the other way. So Isaac lifts his foot high and stomps the floor, which gets them to look up. Isaac beckons them to walk over.

The white girl has one light-blue cochlear implant that sits behind her ear and is affixed to the side of her sleek blond ponytail. The Black guy, wearing a White Sox hat, nods hello. He most likely has a similar hearing loss to Isaac, since he's voice-off and not using any devices.

"*This is L-i-l-a-h,*" Isaac signs to his friends. "*Bug.*"

He signs something else too fast to follow, and fortunately the girl steps in to interpret. "I'm Natasha," she says with a strong deaf accent. "And this is Jaden."

"*Flower and Bat,*" Isaac chimes in with their camp sign names. He quickly tells Natasha something to relay to me. "We have a 'first day of training week' tradition," she says, "where we hang out at the lake at night."

"That's fun," I say.

Isaac and Jaden nod eagerly. Jaden signs something that I kind of catch, but Natasha is already interpreting for me anyway. "Not until it gets dark out. Are you coming?"

"Okay, maybe," I say and sign. I'm sure it'll be a good time, but what's so exciting about it?

"*It's great,*" Isaac signs. "*There's a fun surprise, I promise.*"

Natasha starts to repeat, but I'm eager to reply and show Isaac I knew what he was signing. "*Really, a surprise?*" I smile. "*Okay-okay.*"

"*We'll just ——— for now,*" Isaac signs.

"Chill," Natasha says, observantly picking up on what I understood and what I need clarification on. But her voice is flat, like she really doesn't care to be interpreting right now. Some Deaf people choose to "turn off their voice" and primarily sign, even if they still speak occasionally. If this is Natasha's preference, it is a little unfair that she's acting as our go-between right now because she has the implant. I wish we could all just be signing.

The three of them start to walk to the door, signing together about something and not looping me in. I doubt Natasha is excluding me on purpose, but it's hard not to feel left out.

"I need to finish cleaning first. I'll catch up," I shout after Natasha, my hands hanging helplessly at my sides.

"Cool," she says, indifferent.

When Isaac turns to see why I'm not following them, she signs to him. Part of me hopes he'll offer to stay behind with me. Yet how would that go without an interpreter nearby? Isaac waves back but walks on with his friends.

I'd just slow down their conversation anyway. I can tell that Isaac switches over to a more English-based sentence construction when communicating with me, which is easier to follow since I'm still unfamiliar with ASL grammar. But when Isaac, Natasha, and Jaden all use true ASL, I'm lost—picking up words here and there, but not truly comprehending yet. I want to get to their level as fast as I can.

I hurry to wipe the table, my head down and arm stretching as far as I can to reach the opposite side. I don't hear the side door open, but I catch a glimpse of its movement out of the corner of my eye. Some guy who looks to be a few years older than me walks in and starts rummaging through the leftover sandwiches. He wasn't at our staff meeting earlier. Gary or Ethan would've mentioned if someone was arriving late.

"What are you doing?" I ask.

"Sorry to frighten you," he calls out. There's something funny about his voice.

"Are you working here this summer?" I ask. He's clearly not one of the counselors.

"Yeah, just popping in to grab some supper."

He's average height with blue eyes. His swept-back blond hair is damp, and so are the sandals he's wearing, which leave a trail across the hardwood floor. But what my glance can't avoid is that he's not wearing a shirt underneath his unzipped jacket. There's a gold chain dangling at his chest, beneath two tattoos.

"Um." I shake my head and look back at his face. "But you're not a counselor?"

"No, I work down on ———." He points to the window behind him and continues preparing his plate. I can't remember the layout of the campgrounds well enough to have any idea where he gestured toward, and I couldn't hear the word he said.

"What?" I ask, tilting my head.

"What?" he repeats, looking mildly offended, but I can't tell why. "What's it to you?"

"Well, I didn't hear you . . ." I say, startled by his slight change in demeanor. "You know, 'cause we're at a Deaf camp."

"Oh, sorry, I didn't think you were. I've never met a deaf person before." He leans against the counter and takes a bite of his sandwich. "You should say 'pardon,' by the way."

"Pardon?"

"Precisely. Instead of 'what.' It's less aggressive, but then again, you *are* American."

"Right . . ." I smile, amused by his playful banter despite the cultural misunderstanding. But I can't hear him well enough to discern his accent. "And clearly you are *not*? What brings you here?"

"The Camp American program. I'm from England. The plan's to work at Gray Wolf and then travel around the States once the job is done."

"Interesting." I didn't know that program was a thing. It honestly feels like something out of a movie—bringing a cute British guy to the Midwest. "So what exactly is your job?"

"Lifeguard." He puts his food down on the table I just cleaned, then pulls two chairs over from the stack along the wall.

Is one of those for me? I wouldn't mind hanging out and getting to know the lifeguard, but I should go find the counselors. "I wish I could stay, but I've got to get back," I say, gesturing to the spare chair.

"It's actually for my partner." He looks toward the side door as a second lifeguard walks in, stuffing a notebook into his back pocket and eyeing the food. "Ben! Hey, mate, took you forever. I already grabbed the best-looking pieces."

My face flushes red. I'm embarrassed that I assumed the chair was for me. "Right, there's two of you!" I say, picking up my backpack and taking a step back.

"Sorry, I can grab a seat for you if you want," the lifeguard says to me, glancing back at Ben.

"No, really, that's okay," I say, heading out. "I'll see you around."

And I will—at the lake, or the pool, or maybe even after-hours. I don't even know his name, but I can definitely tell this would be Kelsey's choice for a summer romance.

He calls after me, so I turn around. "Did you say something to me?"

"Yeah." He gives a patient smile. "I wanted to say I'm ________."

"What was that?" I lean forward, then smirk. "Pardon me?"

He chuckles and—oh gosh, was that a wink? "No worries," he says louder. "I'll turn up the volume. Just saying that I'm Oliver."

"Thank you." I blush again, grabbing my backpack straps with both hands. "I'm Lilah."

"Glad to meet you, Lilah."

There are communication barriers for me with both ASL and English. At least I'm more familiar with navigating the spoken ones. "And hey," I say. "If you're looking for something to do, we're all gonna be at the lake later." I nod to Ben as he takes a seat. "Both of you, of course."

"You are?" Oliver, looking a little alarmed, glances over to Ben to see if he knew about the plan. Oh, I guess lifeguards have to be at the lake whenever anyone is there. Ben just shrugs, and Oliver turns back to me. "All right. We'll see you there, Lilah."

"Right, bye!" I wave and dash out of the dining hall, amused at how easily disconcerted a British accent could make me. Seriously, a hot British lifeguard? Kelsey and Riley will be so jealous. I can't wait to text them later. There's so much about returning to Gray Wolf that I wasn't expecting.

CHAPTER SIX

Back at the cabin, Bobby, Simone, and Mackenzie are lounging around, checking their phones after a long day. I'd assumed Isaac and his friends would be here, but I guess I never asked to clarify where they'd be hanging out before lake time. So I flop onto my bed and do some scrolling through social media.

Sure enough, as soon as it gets dark, Simone and Bobby get up. She walks over to my bunk and asks, "Want a ride? We're gonna commandeer the golf cart."

"Definitely." There's only one cart, and Gary's usually the one who drives it. I climb down from my bunk, staring at Isaac's things. Because Isaac's going to be sleeping a few feet away from me tonight. How'd I almost forget about that?

"I'll give you a hint about this camp tradition," Simone tells Mackenzie and me. "Put on your swimsuits."

I was already planning on changing, since Isaac had given me a heads-up about the lake, but Mackenzie looks shocked.

"What is it?" she asks.

"Hurry up and get ready. Don't worry, I won't look," Bobby jokes, unfolding his cane and navigating out the door.

Mackenzie and I change quickly and meet them outside the cabin a few minutes later.

"Night swimming?" Mackenzie asks. "Is it safe?"

"It's fine, we do it every year," Bobby says. "Worry more about me driving us there."

Simone and I laugh but share an incredulous glance as Mackenzie hurries to the wheel. Bobby and Simone jump on the back, so I take the passenger seat.

Our cart whizzes full speed, bumping along the gravel path and dodging holes that appear in the small headlight radius, all the way to the lake on the outskirts of the campgrounds.

"Don't go down to the beach," Simone instructs, leaning forward over the back to point ahead. "Pull over on there."

"About time!" Ethan shouts. He's waiting in the middle of the tall bridge that connects the other half of the campgrounds from across the lake with Isaac, Natasha, and Jaden.

It's growing dark, but there's no need to be quiet. These are our campgrounds, and we can be as loud as we want. There's a misconception that a gathering of deaf people is silent, but that couldn't be further from the truth. At camp, we crank the volume on everything to the max.

"Are you ready?" Ethan asks, still shouting. "We're jumping off this bridge!"

"That's the surprise?" I climb out of the golf cart, letting out a nervous laugh as I step forward to look over the rail. It's not as high as I imagined, but it's still a long way down.

Mackenzie remains in the driver's seat. "Nope. I'm not doing this."

"That's all right. You can guard the electronics." Ethan secures his hearing aids in his backpack.

"You jumping with us, Lilah?" Simone asks.

"Um." Everyone else, besides Mackenzie, is already waiting in their swimsuits. Simone reaches out and squeezes my hand. Isaac nods and smiles. "Okay-okay," I say and sign.

I undress down to my one-piece and kick my shoes off. Then I pull out my hearing aids. The night is darker without them. Quieter, obviously. The noise around me has been reduced to a hum. Murky, too, like I'm already underwater. It's not just the volume that's dropped, but the clarity of sound, too. Usually this makes me self-conscious. Isolated. Literally down a sense, I grasp at straws to fill in the blanks, especially around other people.

But not right now. I don't feel limited; I feel bold. It's not often that my ears get the chance to breathe. I can no longer hear the creepy creaking of the old bridge or the whooshing of the night wind. I've also tuned out the voice inside my head telling me to be scared. I lean into this fearlessness and step toward the bridge. The wooden slats are rough and cold beneath my bare feet.

Ethan is the first to climb and sit on the top beam. The bridge must've made noise when he did because Bobby shouts, "Everyone wait for me! Someone guide me over."

Since I'm nearest, I get Bobby and ask, "Aren't you basically completely blind in the dark?"

"Basically completely!" He reaches out. "Your arm, pretty please."

I stick out my elbow. Bobby grabs hold. I've never guided anyone before, but I'm copying how Simone assisted him earlier today. I walk several paces and transfer Bobby over to her.

Mackenzie calls out something, still not budging from the golf cart. "You seriously ———."

"What?" Simone shrugs. I read something on her lips about her job being to "lead the blind."

"To their death?" Mackenzie shrieks.

Meanwhile, Ethan jumps. I hear traces of his delighted shouts on the way down but no splash. I rush forward to inspect the water below, where the rings ripple out like sound waves.

His head pops back above the surface. Whew. "*What are you waiting for?*" he signs, kicking his feet frantically beneath him so he can hold both hands out of the water.

Behind me, the golf cart shakes the bridge. Mackenzie is flooring it around the path and down to the beach, taking away our main source of light. All we have left is the full moon.

"*Fun surprise?*" Isaac slides down the rail to be right next to me. I nod but my body shakes. He raises his eyebrows questioningly. "*Nervous? Or cold?*"

"Both," I say and sign as well as my quaking hands allow.

We both look down at the water. He inches closer and wraps an arm around me—a moonlit embrace. If I thought I was flustered around him earlier, that's nothing compared with right now. He might not have heard the gasp I let out when his skin made contact with mine, but he surely felt my chest rise and fall.

"*We can wait and watch them first,*" he signs with his free hand, gesturing toward his friends. Natasha and Jaden wave for him to join them, signing something rapid-fire, and I wait for

Isaac's warmth to pull away, but he doesn't move. "*Go ahead. I'll help her.*"

As in, *me*.

Natasha and Jaden hold hands and leap together, screaming into the night.

Bobby is now standing on the second rail of the bridge, attempting to swing his leg over the top. "You ready, Simone?" She paces back and forth. I can't tell if she's more nervous for him or herself. "Okay, I'm gonna drop!" He hugs the top of the rail, with the majority of his weight on the other side, ready to plunge toward the water. "Rescue me, Simone!" His voice trails off as he plummets into the lake.

Simone slowly climbs over the rail. "He's the one on a swim team," she says, gesturing with one hand for clarity, loud and clear, then pinches her nose and jumps. She immediately finds and loops her arms around Bobby, who, in a matter of seconds, swims to the giant inflatable trampoline tethered in the deep, where the others are gathered.

"*Ready?*" Isaac asks. His deep-brown eyes are wide and curious. I can feel his breath on my cheek as he gives my shoulder a reassuring squeeze. A smile creeps onto my face. I can do this. Maybe he'll even hold my hand.

I give a small nod, reaching back to my ears, needing to confirm that I did, in fact, take out my hearing aids. I obviously can tell the difference, but it's a nervous tic of mine whenever I'm about to dive into a pool or step into the shower. Or jump off a bridge.

Isaac effortlessly climbs onto the top rail and holds out a hand, offering to help me up. And then, he doesn't let go. Expertly reading the emotions on my face, he raises his thick eyebrows, asking if I'm good to go. I squeeze his hand, mouthing the word "yes."

He counts, "*Three, two, one,*" and we launch ourselves into the night.

As soon as we're airborne, my adrenaline overtakes my fear. But it's all too brief, and then I crash through the surface of the lake with a splat. Fishy water rushes up my nose. We'd drifted apart, but Isaac finds me. I float to the top, sputtering as I emerge. My hair is a sopping, tangled mess.

Isaac treads beside me as I blink out the stinging water, so I turn away, but he swims around to face me. "*You okay?*"

"*I'm fine,*" I answer slowly, careful not to splash myself in the face as I sign. I hold my breath and dip my head back under, gathering my hair sleek behind me and out of my face.

"*Happy you jumped?*" Isaac raises his thick eyebrows.

"*Yes,*" I sign, smiling deliriously, the adrenaline still coursing through my veins. "*I was scared, but you really helped. I don't want to,* um . . ." I search for the sign. "*Miss, m-i-s-s?*" He nods. I love that he doesn't mind filling in the blanks for me. "*I don't want to miss something just because I'm scared.*"

"*I understand. Happy to help.*" He wraps an arm around my waist to keep me above water.

"*Thank you,*" I sign, painfully aware of how much that sign resembles blowing a kiss. And how we're so close together that if I were a confident flirt, I could lean forward and actually kiss his cheek.

But I don't manage that. We just swim side by side toward the others.

It's exhausting, trekking all the way to the trampoline that's floating between an inflatable iceberg and flat lily pad platforms. Isaac and I climb the ladder and join the others. I lie back, letting the water coming up from beneath the bouncer mesh slosh over me. The stars are bright in the sky this far away from the city. I stare up, admiring them, ready to fall asleep right here in this spot. This is going to be an incredible summer.

~~~

We've been hanging out on the trampoline for a while when Simone casually sits up and notices something in the distance. She looks out to the beach, then says something to Bobby.

"What?" I ask, following her gaze. Someone is yelling, and it isn't Mackenzie, though she's still waiting there on the golf cart. "What's happening?"

Simone raises her voice. "They want us off the lake," she relays. "It must be the lifeguards."

Whoops. I did invite Oliver and Ben to join us. I'd assumed we'd be hanging around the beach or something, not partaking in an activity that's against the rules. I squint through the darkness and see the two of them stripping off their jackets, each grabbing a red buoy and wading into the water.

The other counselors have all sat up, too.

"*Who is it?*" Jaden asks.

Isaac and Natasha shake their heads, but Ethan fills them in. "The lifeguards," he says and signs.

"The British are coming!" Bobby shouts. He's the only one still lying on his back on the trampoline.

I read Simone's lips as she whispers, "They're cute this year..."

The lifeguards reach us. Ben climbs the ladder and stands on the top rung, towering over our group. "Well ———," he
~~~

shouts. He has a strong accent, clipping off the ends of words and making it very difficult for me to understand him. "——— trouble if we ——— hours."

"What if you joined us?" Simone asks. Bobby shakes his head.

"Sorry!" Oliver shouts from the water. He says something else, quietly, that makes Simone giggle.

"Okay." Bobby sits up so quickly that the whole trampoline sways on the water. "You know what, why don't you give us a minute, and we'll make our way back to the beach." He shouts even louder, his tone stern. "We're being kicked out, everyone!"

Ben shakes his head, confused by Bobby's outburst. "Cheers." He jumps back into the water to rejoin Oliver. The two float on their buoys but don't move any farther.

"What do they want?" Natasha says and signs, looking straight at me since Ethan's already jumped down into the water.

"*Lifeguards say time to go . . .* " I sign slowly, unsure how to phrase "kicking us out." "*Now is not—*"

But as I'm contemplating what words I have in my arsenal to formulate a better explanation, Natasha interrupts me. "Just speak, I'll read your lips."

Ouch, I was trying here. "We're being kicked out by the lifeguards," I say, my hands clasped in my lap. I try to catch Isaac's eyes, but he and Jaden are already on their feet. They bounce off the trampoline, launching themselves into the water.

Simone offers Bobby help getting down, but he ignores her and crawls straight to the edge, right over my legs. "Sorry!" he shouts. "I'd be able to find my way if Simone hadn't abandoned me for her new boyfriends."

"Come on," Simone says, rolling her eyes. "*Shh*, they'll hear you."

Bobby dives into the lake, waiting for Simone to jump in after him. He's one to joke about everything, but is he genuinely jealous? I think I heard "new boyfriends." So does that mean he's Simone's boyfriend? Or was?

"Where are you?" he asks. "Why is no one else splashing into the water?"

"———— help?" Oliver says. The lifeguards kick their way over to Bobby.

"Nope, I can swim," he says. "Better than you. The only thing is I don't know which way the beach is."

"I'm on my way," Simone says. There's a hint of exasperation in her voice.

When we all make it to the shore, Mackenzie is waiting for us. She's scowling, gripping the wheel of the golf cart tightly, probably feeling left out.

Simone guides Bobby up the beach, but he detaches from her arm as soon as he can follow Mackenzie's voice to the golf cart, where he hops on for a ride back. Simone follows and sits beside him. They seem to be having a serious conversation.

The rest of us grab our bags. Natasha and Jaden jostle for the last seat in the cart, but Jaden beats her to it. "*Later,*" he signs to her with his tongue sticking out as the four of them speed away back to the cabins.

I wipe the wet sand off my feet, putting my shoes on to walk back up the path toward the cabins with the others. Wrapped in my big beach towel, I carry my backpack off one shoulder. My ears are still too wet to put my hearing aids back in. I look around for Isaac, but Oliver approaches me.

"Hey, really sorry about ————," he says. I can't catch the rest of what he's saying. So I turn to face him. What I don't notice is the large tree root in front of me, so I trip, arms flailing—but Oliver catches me before I fall. Still, this is not as embarrassing as walking into a street sign while trying to look at and talk to someone, which has happened to me more than I'd care to admit. But this is definitely up there.

"Thanks . . ." After an awkward pause, I steady myself and we walk again. "Sorry, I'm not staring at your lips in, like, a weird way. I'm trying to read them so I can figure out what you're saying since I can't hear you at all right now . . ."

"I see," he says, and once again says more that I can't understand, even though he seems to be slowing down and speaking louder. His hand is outstretched at the ready in case I trip again.

"Sorry," I say, gesturing toward my mouth. "With the accent and everything, the lips aren't much help. It'd be great to talk later, though, when I can hear you."

He nods understandingly and pats my shoulder. "It's okay," he says, then jokingly puckers his lips, waves goodbye, and lets me rejoin the counselors. He starts heading back to the beach to rejoin Ben.

I stop momentarily to let the staff catch up with me. I can just make out Isaac walking my way and glancing at Oliver as he jogs past him. Then Isaac steps next to Natasha, extends his towel, and wraps it around the two of them while her teeth chatter from the cold.

Um, okay. Are they a thing? She leans over to rest her head on Isaac's shoulder.

Isaac glances over at me, probably wondering why I'm staring, so I rush beside Ethan, not wanting to stand there awkwardly.

Ethan's got his phone flashlight on, but instead of directing it straight to the path in front of us, he shines it up so we can see each other's faces.

"What time do we have to wake up tomorrow?" I ask, raising my arms to tie up my damp hair.

"Wake up?" Ethan repeats. I nod. "Probably seven?" he says and signs. "So set your alarm for that."

"Alarm clock?" I confirm, and it's his turn to nod. "Yikes, I didn't bring mine."

My phone's alarm isn't loud enough, and its vibrations aren't strong enough to reliably alert me, so I usually depend on my parents dragging me out of bed each morning, which really won't be sustainable when I leave for college in a year. This didn't even cross my mind when I packed for the summer. When I was a camper, the counselors woke me up every morning—so now what?

"You didn't bring one?" Ethan asks. We're both making sure the other understands what we're saying, since neither of us is wearing our hearing aids, but he seems to be rubbing my mistake in my face just a bit. "Someone can make sure you're up. I've got my earthquake alarm, and so do many of the other counselors."

Ugh, this makes me feel like a little kid, needing to depend on other people in the morning. And with my luck, it'll probably be Mackenzie standing over me every morning, especially since I'm assigned to her group. She already acts like she knows so much more than me.

I can't think of anything that frustrates me more right now—until I glance to the side and see Isaac and Natasha walking together, huddled under the same towel.

CHAPTER SEVEN

Mackenzie's hand reaches up and grabs my ankle. I shake my foot and grumble, "I'm up." But I peer through the slats of the bunk bed, and as soon as she's walked away, I fall back asleep with my arm dangling over the edge.

Something touches my fingers. I peer down to find Isaac looking up at me from the bottom bunk. He taps my hand again before framing his face to sign, "*Wake up.*"

He's already dressed for the day, freshly showered and everything, just lounging in bed now, waiting for the rest of us to get ready to embrace the day. I roll back over, quickly brushing my hair and wiping the crust out of my eyes. Didn't Isaac go to bed just as late as I did? Is he one of those intense athletes who wakes up early to run every morning no matter what?

Isaac reaches his arm up along the wall, signing with one hand, "*Ready? Yes? No?*"

I stretch my arm down past the mattress. "*No,*" I sign, snapping my fingers closed. But he takes hold of my hand, gently pushing my fingers to my palm to form "*yes.*" When he lets go, I sign, "*h-a h-a*" before withdrawing my hand from his reach.

This seems extra touchy. Almost flirty, right? It can't be my imagination. I glance around the cabin toward Natasha, who isn't paying attention at all. She's busy jumping on Jaden to wake him up. I hope the walk back from the lake last night was just Isaac and Natasha being good friends. I'm not jealous of Natasha—I don't think? It's just that she has such a cool signing style, and she's the counselor I'm most intimidated around since she seems so clearly annoyed when I slow down a conversation.

Someone stomps the floor and makes a loud "hoot" for attention while flicking the lights on and off. Ethan is slouching at the door frame next to a wide-awake Gary. I crawl over to retrieve my hearing aids from my backpack at the foot of the bed.

"Looks like you all had a late night," Gary says and Ethan interprets. "Rise and shine, counselors. CPR and first aid today. Fortunately for you, our nurse is running a bit behind to lead training."

After twenty minutes of everyone getting ready, we gather inside the dining hall, where all the furniture has been pushed against the wall. On the floor are a few different stations with first aid and CPR practice gear. The lifeguards quickly stop in to grab breakfast from the cereal bar, and I wave hello.

Ethan calls out, waving his arms. "Everyone, pair up!"

Simone and Bobby are already together. So are Natasha and Jaden . . . which means Isaac still needs a partner. I turn and make eye contact with him, and he gives me a sweet smile, but then Mackenzie taps his shoulder, asking him to work with her. He turns away to join her, leaving me all alone.

"How do you sign B-a-n-d-A-i-d?" Mackenzie says and signs to Isaac.

He demonstrates the word for "bandage," which Mackenzie repeats, moving her hand in the wrong direction. It's a small relief to me that Isaac demonstrates the sign himself, rather than taking hold of her hand to guide the correction, the way he did with me. Maybe the way he helped me last night means . . . he likes me? I'm not completely imagining everything that happened last night at the lake, right? I'm really overanalyzing this now.

"Um, so . . ." I say, walking up to the front where Ethan and Gary are standing with the camp nurse. "I guess I'm the odd one out."

"Nope," Ethan says, stepping toward me. "You're the lucky one who gets to be my partner!"

And it turns out, I *am* the luckiest, because Ethan knows his stuff. While everyone else is struggling with the first aid kit, Ethan has fitted my arm into the perfect sling. It's almost enough to help me ignore the fact that Mackenzie gets to spend all day sitting close to Isaac and wrapping him in bandages.

"This is, like, professional," I say, admiring his snug technique.

He beams. "I'm an educator. I've done so many of these." He holds up two old reusable training bandages. "Want a wrist one, too?"

I hold out my hand eagerly. "Should I be nervous? Did anything bad happen last summer?"

"Oh, I just meant how many training sessions I've done. I hope to God I never have to use all these skills in real life. Honestly, at camp it's usually just splinters and scratches. Nothing that tweezers and a Band-Aid can't fix, but it's nice to be prepared." The wrapping is cool across my palm and a nice break from all the work my wrist has been doing since my signing has ramped up. "Oh, and one little kid lost a tooth. Like, *lost it* lost it. Probably swallowed it."

"Ew."

"Yeah, and it was hard to convince them that the tooth fairy didn't make camp visits but would have a surprise for them when they got back home."

I've been so worried about being able to communicate with campers or having them like me that I forgot about things like injuries and homesickness. It's not just language skills I need to work on but being a reassuring and authoritative figure for the little kids.

"Oh, I'm sorry," Mackenzie shouts and signs to Isaac upon realizing that he can't communicate with both of his hands wrapped and bandaged. He shrugs and lies down on the ground, crossing his arms across his chest like a mummy, and closing his eyes to take a nap for the remainder of practice time.

~~~

"Still got that imprint of third base across your face, Lilah?" Bobby teases as we settle into the dining hall for dinner before we watch the last remaining first aid training videos of the day.

"You can stop reminding her," Simone says.
~~~

We got an afternoon break to play beeper baseball. I definitely cheated and pulled my blindfold up to see the ball and get a hit, but my vision was still obstructed. The way to score is to make contact with a tall inflatable bag at either third or first base. I scored a face-first collision run, but at what cost? Any harder, and I might have actually needed first aid from Ethan.

"It does sting still," I admit. I unwrap my sandwich and take a huge bite. "Hmm . . ." I say, thinking out loud.

"What?" Bobby's always eager for a scoop.

"I was wondering if I should ask you something." Simone, Bobby, and I are the only ones sitting at the table yet. Everyone else is still grabbing food, refilling their water from the orange Gatorade jug, or making a trip to the bathroom. "You like gossip, right?"

"It's my middle name," he says, mouth full of Italian bread. "Well?" he asks impatiently.

I try to think of the most casual way to ask this question, even though it's been in the back of my mind all day. "Is Natasha . . ." I whisper.

"Not dating Isaac," he says, a little too loud for my liking.

"What? That's not—"

"Sure it is. Even when I can't see, I see all. Remember that." He pauses for dramatic effect. Simone nods for emphasis. "Pretty sure she's into Jaden. He had a girlfriend last summer, but they broke up. Now Natasha will be starting at his college this fall, so . . ."

"How do you know all this?" I ask. "You couldn't have overheard anything, because they mostly sign."

"A little birdie told me."

Simone rolls her eyes. "It's Ethan. He always blurts things out loud during intense ASL conversations."

"Plus, Natasha was only a junior counselor last summer, and Jaden was already eighteen and a senior counselor," Bobby continues. "So that might be a thing, but who cares? Break the rules."

"The rules?" I ask. It didn't dawn on me that there'd be any, like, no dating between junior and senior staff. I am still technically stuck in that in-between area. Always caught in the middle. Or is it that going out is discouraged in general while we're working here? There's no way they can possibly uphold that.

"Sorry, Lilah. That also means you can't date me, either," Bobby says.

"Shh," I say. "That's not—"

Simone narrates her reaction this time for Bobby's sake. "I'm rolling my eyes. Just so you're not missing out on my reaction here."

"There can't be a rule against dating," I say. "'Cause, like, you two are . . ."

The silence could be cut with a knife. Both are suddenly very interested in their dinners.

"Oh?" I scramble to rectify this.

"We were last summer," Simone answers. "But I wasn't sure if I'd be back."

"So not this summer?" I ask.

"That remains to be seen," Bobby says.

There's clearly history here that I'm not aware of, so I better extract myself from this conversation quickly. Luckily, Simone beats me to it and changes the topic.

"Let's not talk about us." She leans in closer and lowers her voice. I'm glad she keeps her mouth visible, rather than leaning into my ear. "This conversation is clearly about Isaac."

"Shh," I say again, flustered. "Is it that obvious?"

"Why did it take you so long to get to the trampoline last night?" Bobby asks, dragging his words out slowly. "You *were* the last ones."

"Careful, Bobby, she's practically melting into her chair." Simone takes a drink of water. I do the same, hoping measured sips will slow the blood flow to my cheeks. "There does reach a point in the summer where people like to pair off."

"My money's on you two," Bobby says, slapping the table for good measure, drawing several eyes toward us.

"Once again, I'm begging you to stop," I say, now that others, namely Isaac, are watching us curiously.

"Hey, I just wanna talk about love," Bobby says, but fortunately he doesn't add anything else incriminating, until he says, "Don't forget to invite me to your wedding."

"Okay, now you're really getting ahead of yourself," I say.

"When counselors hook up, it's either for, like, seven weeks or seventy years." He casually takes another bite of his sandwich. "Simone, when is it that Amy and Brandon are getting married?"

"They're together?" I actually remember them. Amy was so enthusiastic, and Brandon was . . . a little creepy, admittedly.

"September," Simone says, ignoring my question.

"Hey, plus-one, wanna carpool?" Bobby asks Simone.

"I did get my own invitation," she says.

"I mean, hopefully I don't have to find a new date before the wedding . . ."

"All right, fine," I say. "Enjoy your wedding drama. Now really, can we talk about anything else, please," I add, after once again accidentally making eye contact with Isaac. I'm relieved when he smiles back, so I try for some small talk.

"*Long day,*" I sign across the table. "*Finally dinnertime.*"

"*Finally.*" His mouth makes the "pah!" shape as his eyes twinkle. "*I'm very hungry.*" He does the sign slowly, and I know he's 100 percent teasing me. Must've left a good first impression there.

I'm positive Simone and Bobby were exaggerating Gray Wolf's rules on relationships. If anything, it might be discouraged, rather than flat-out banned. Like, it's probably about keeping it after hours rather than putting it on display in front of the kids. *That* I can understand, but it also means the amount of time I'll have to interact with Isaac is about to be sharply cut down when campers arrive.

CHAPTER EIGHT

Training week is going by fast, and I'm physically, and mentally, exhausted. There was a lot more sitting around learning safety protocols than I'd expected. But also plenty of breaks for going over the games and outdoor activities, during which I often tried to coincidentally end up by Isaac's side. Before I know it, it's Saturday and almost time for the final training week staff meeting. Campers arrive tomorrow.

We're still waiting for everyone to make it to the dining hall. I got here early because I had to stop by the lot and check on my car, but where is everyone else? Director Gary is sitting alone at a table in the corner, making notes on a mess of papers in front of him. He waves for me to come talk to him.

"Grading papers?" I ask, standing there hesitantly. Why did he call me over?

He chuckles at my boring joke and nods to the empty chair across from him. "Join me here for a second."

I take a seat, but he doesn't say anything. Instead, he flips one of the pages and frowns.

"What are you working on?" I ask. "I'm not in any sort of trouble, am I?"

I search my brain for why I could be here. Did he suddenly realize that I'm not qualified for this role? Did I somehow fail first aid training? I swear I was paying attention. Well, for most of it. Some of those videos were really long. Or did Simone and Bobby tattle on me for having a crush on a counselor, and Gary wants to stifle that before it becomes a potentially rule-breaking situation? Okay, that might be illogical.

"What? Oh, no. Nothing like that," Gary says. "The opposite, in fact." He scratches something out on the paper and writes what appears to be my name next to the word "Friday." "I'm putting together the on-duty assignments. It's complicated this year because, as assistant director, Ethan will be on call at night, rather than assigned to a specific shift. There's already got to be some alternating and doubling, so basically we're short a counselor for one of the weeknights."

"I see . . ." But I don't really know where he's going with this.

Gary looks up at me. "It's unconventional, and we've already got you taking on a lot of responsibility as a junior counselor, but would you be fine with covering one of the weekly shifts?"

"Oh, sure." I shrug. "What exactly would I have to do?"

"While campers are here, we have two people on duty from lights-out until counselor midnight curfew. During these hours, the rest are off the clock. You'd hang out at the small firepit or in the staff cabin, so long as you make regular checks for any wanderers or bathroom-goers—that sort of thing."

"That makes sense."

"But it's only a watch, so if something major comes up, you get ahold of Ethan or me."

"Sounds good." I nod, pleased to already be given extra responsibility.

"Thanks, kid. I've got you on Fridays. And you'll be partnered with . . ." He searches through his schedule again right as Isaac walks through the swinging doors of the cafeteria. "Ah, sure, Isaac. Yeah, that'll work. You'll be partnered with him. Could you let him know?"

"Oh, sure!" I jump up from the chair, already dreading the fact that I'm going to need to fingerspell for this conversation. "Hey, Isaac," I say and sign. "I have to tell you—" Crap, I can't think of the next sign. I know this one already, I'm sure of it. Ugh. "Something," I say.

He nods, taking off his baseball cap and stuffing it in his backpack as he sits at the table, pulling out the chair beside him for me. As in, I'll probably sit next to him for all of dinner now? Whew, deep breath. I hide my face as I kick my bag underneath the table, then smooth my ponytail and turn to face him. My leg accidentally grazes his knee, but he doesn't move away.

"Gary," I start, pointing back to the director, "told me to tell you," I say and sign. "Friday nights. On d-u-t-y work . . ." I catch my wrists before bending them too far like "make-out" again. "With me."

He's got his elbow on the table, finger pressed against his cheek as he leans back, watching me with amusement.

"*You understand what I said?*" I mouth the words, my lips fighting back laughter at the way Isaac is watching me right now, but I'm signing with more confidence.

"*What you signed,*" he corrects, still smiling. "*Yes. Friday nights we'll work on duty.*"

"*Duty,*" I repeat the sign, committing it to memory. "Okay, cool."

So every Friday night it'll be Isaac and me, alone at the small campfire in the cabin circle, huddling together by the warmth of the flames and the light of the moon? I mean, how often do campers really leave in the middle of the night? I certainly never did. I just need to brush up on some conversational topics here so we're not just sitting there awkwardly, like we somehow already are right now . . .

"So, um," I say, hands out in front of me, helplessly.

"*Our first dinner with the ———,*" Isaac offers, signing slowly.

"The cook?" I say and sign, repeating his motions, and he nods. "*I hope it's good!*" Come on, Lilah. *Think.* You have to be capable of talking about something more interesting than this. "*So are you ready for campers tomorrow?*"

He bobs his head yes. "*Will be fun.*"

And just like that, his friends arrive. Natasha and Jaden sit across the table, and Isaac converses at true speed. I excuse myself to refill my water, then return to find that Mackenzie has taken the seat on the other side of mine.

"Perfect, Lilah," she says and signs. "We can practice our one-handed signing together while we eat!"

"*Yeah, awesome,*" I sign back, unenthused, still holding my bottle in my left hand.

I spend the whole dinner sitting next to Isaac but feeling so far away.

~~~

In the clatter of everyone washing dishes and stacking chairs along the wall, I don't realize someone is calling my name until a hand gently taps my shoulder.

"Hey, Lilah." Oliver's standing there, dressed casually in fitted sweatpants and a plain white T-shirt, with a knapsack hanging over one shoulder. "I hate to be a bother, but do you have a car here?"

"Oh, yeah. I do, actually. What's up?"

The counselors are all leaving the dining hall to head back to the cabins for the rest of our final night off before campers arrive. I was kind of hoping there'd be another Gray Wolf staff tradition like the lake, but it doesn't seem like it.

As Simone walks up from behind Oliver, she mouths to me, "Ooh, get it!"

Oliver glances over his shoulder, then back at me for an explanation, but I just laugh it off. "Anyway, you were saying?"

"Right." He clasps his hands together. "Ben and I are running low on our travel-size toiletries and other things that made more sense to purchase here. Any chance you could give us a lift to a shop tonight?"

"Sure . . . How about now? Before it gets dark." *My first off-site trip!*

"Yes, thank you so much." Oliver turns and calls out to Ben, who is at the dishwashing station, dumping his meat loaf into the nearby trash. "Ready now?"

"Wonderful! Let's go," Ben says. As soon as the three of us are outside the dining hall, he adds, "And can we please find something else to eat? That was horrendous."
~~~

They walk with me back to the cabins so I can get my car keys and glasses from my suitcase. Isaac is sitting in his bunk checking his phone, which is plugged into the wall.

"*Where are you going?*" he asks when he notices the car keys.

"*Store. Want to come?*"

"*Sure,*" he signs, following me outside the cabin where his friends are sitting around the campfire with no flame burning yet. "*I can ask Natasha and Jaden, too?*"

"Ah, I can only fit five in my car," I say, holding up my hand to indicate the count.

Isaac isn't looking at me when I say this, but he sees Oliver and Ben waiting outside the cabin for me. He slowly shakes his head. "*That's fine. Another night.*"

"Oh," I say, watching him walk away. "Okay."

Oliver leans forward and waves for my attention. "Shall we go?"

"Yes, let me check directions before I lose this sliver of service. I think there's a Super Mart kinda far away, but there's a pharmacy and a Mackie's a few minutes closer."

"Perfect," Oliver says, taking a quick peek over my shoulder at the map on my phone. "We'll follow your lead."

I'm suddenly relieved that my parents made me clean this old car before driving it to camp. It's not super reliable anymore. I usually only use it to get to and from school, so I can't be the one doing all the trips this summer, but I'm sure a few outings won't hurt.

I put on my glasses, since I've been going most of my time here at camp without my usual contact lenses. I let Ben plug in his phone to the stereo so he can play his music, mainly to avoid being judged on my random music choices. They chatter most of the way to the store, and I do my best to read their lips out of the corner of my eye or through the rearview mirror, but for the most part I sit quietly and let them chat.

It doesn't take too long for Oliver and Ben to find what they need in the pharmacy, but when I drive us across the street to the Mackie's parking lot, neither of them wants to get out of the car.

"Let's just go through there," Oliver says from the passenger seat, pointing to the drive-through.

"Well . . ." I say, clasping my hands together, noticing a sudden urge to sign. "I can't really hear with those."

"That's all right, I've got you," he insists.

I carefully drive around the U-bend to the drive-through speakers. As I park, the jumble of noise to my left starts, which Oliver understands perfectly. He leans over the middle compartment to respond, but he's too far from the microphone for the employee to hear him.

"Sorry, let me just ———." Oliver scooches even closer, hand on my arm, as I turn my head to the side to get out of his way. After placing his order, he asks Ben and me what we want. There's sometimes a relief to just letting someone else handle social interactions for me.

"The chicken nuggets," I whisper to him.

He relays, a jumble of noise says something back, and he turns to me again. This follow-up question is exactly why I let him speak for me. "Sauce?" he asks me.

"Sweet and sour." My face is way too close to his, so I press farther back into my seat.

As we drive around to the window, he relaxes back into his spot. "Is Mackie's better over here?"

"Probably worse, if I had to guess," I say.

I wonder what the other counselors are doing. It would be a perfect night for s'mores around the fire or something. But the lifeguards and I eat our fast food on the long drive back to Gray Wolf so it doesn't get cold.

"So, do you like working here?" Oliver asks after we park back at the campgrounds. As we walk through the trees, Ben is still finishing the rest of his milkshake but bobbing his head along encouragingly to Oliver's question.

I nod. "Can't beat being outside all summer. Did you ever go to camp as a kid?"

"Not really. This kind of thing isn't the same in the UK, know what I mean? Not enough sunshine," Oliver jokes.

"Really?" I ask. "I suppose you just spend all your time running around castles instead."

He might genuinely laugh at this—or at me—but it's a nice, quiet laugh. I have to pay close attention to his mouth because his accent is tricky, particularly in this dim light. He smiles, running a hand back through his hair. "Well, there is actually a small castle in my hometown . . ."

"Seriously?" I can't imagine living next to anything besides cornfields.

"Don't be too impressed," Ben chimes in. "There are at least a couple thousand in the country."

"Have you ever been?" Oliver asks.

I tilt my head, unsure of the question. "Been where? To England?" I ask, and he nods. "No, I haven't. But it'd be nice to travel, maybe study abroad one day." How accessible is foreign travel? I'll probably have to just figure it out as I go.

"Definitely. Let's exchange info. You can let Ben and me know if you ever make it, and we'll show you around."

I smile and hand Oliver my phone. "Helpful for this summer, too. I may need a lifeguard the next time we break into the lake after hours.

He grins. "Of course, safety first."

I'm surprisingly comfortable around him—dare I say, maybe even a little bit flirty. At school, I'm just that quiet, awkward girl that people may or may not know wears hearing aids. But here, the elephant in the room has been addressed from day one. I can present myself however I want.

CHAPTER NINE

"Lilah, please help Mackenzie with the lice check," director Gary instructs from behind the welcome table, scribbling something on his clipboard. It's finally Sunday, and after moving our belongings to the new cabin assignments this morning, we're now sweating under the afternoon sun and waiting for the kids to show up.

"What?" I ask, disgusted.

"Ah, yeah." Gary sticks his pen behind his ear and points to me. "I can tell you heard that by the look on your face." He points to the open rear doors of the camp van, which he's loaded with the set-up supplies. "Grab another chair. It'll go faster with two people."

I scrunch my face even more but oblige, fetching a wobbly, old folding chair. It won't unfold, no matter how many times I kick and step on the bottom rung. Isaac is standing at the welcome table, helping Natasha and Jaden organize the kids' Gray Wolf T-shirts, but he walks over to help me.

"*Can I try?*" Isaac asks me.

"Please," I say and sign.

In two kicks, the chair is set up next to Mackenzie's. Isaac looks at the station, then back at me, with a sympathetic look. "*L-i-c-e.*"

"Bleh," I say, making a face again.

"*I hope you find nothing, zero, no l-i-c-e,*" Isaac signs with added emphasis.

"*Same.*" I reach back to fashion a tight high ponytail, sliding one of the purple hair ties off my wrist to secure it.

"*No shirt?*" he asks me.

Isaac's in khaki shorts and his gray counselor polo that has a little wolf on the front and the word STAFF, in big and bold type, across the back. As junior staff, I should also be in matching attire, but Ethan apologized for the shortage earlier and stuck me with the camper version—a gray tee with the logo large on the front. Counselors usually only wear this uniform on pickup and drop-off days so that parents can easily identify staff. But I'm still feeling left out.

I sigh, shaking my head.

"*I have an idea. One second.*" He walks back over to the welcome table to grab his backpack, retrieving a big roll of gray duct tape. "*Turn around.*"

He bites the strip with his teeth and rips it into smaller pieces. I pull my hair to the side and let him attach it onto the back of my shirt. He gently rubs his hand across my back to make sure it's secure. Once he's done, he pulls out his phone and takes a picture to show me. He's fashioned the word STAFF.

"*That's perfect,*" I sign, staring at the photo, then carefully reach around to feel the back of my shirt. "*Thanks.*"

"*No problem.*"

"Lilah!" Mackenzie shouts, waving for my attention. "I need to teach you what we're looking for," she says and signs.

"*Good luck.*" Isaac cringes and walks away.

Mackenzie has barely finished explaining how to comb through hair and search the scalp when several cars drive up, unloading eager children with sleeping bags. A pair of brothers stops by the head-check. I slide on a pair of plastic gloves as one of them sits in front of me. The boys have buzz cuts, so I'm fairly confident the one that I'm examining is clear, but Mackenzie looks over my shoulder to confirm. If she's doing quality control, why am I even here? I'm more than happy to let her do it all.

Another young boy is very chatty during the whole process, peppering Mackenzie with questions. "Where are your hearing aids?"

"Oh, I don't need them," she says. "But yours are really cool."

"But you're not blind, either," the kid says. "Why are you here?"

I suppress a chuckle at this kid's bluntness.

"I'm a sign language interpreter," Mackenzie says, getting ahead of herself by several years.

"Why do you wanna be that?" he asks.

"My best friend is a CODA," Mackenzie says and signs with her free hand. "Child of a Deaf Adult. She isn't deaf, but her parents are, so she knows ASL. I didn't know what I wanted to study in college until I met her."

The kid seems satisfied with this answer because he turns to question me. "Are you new? I don't remember you."

"I—" But another rush of campers is arriving, and there's a line forming in front of us. "Sorry, bud, it's time to find your counselor now."

Mackenzie signs to everyone who comes to our station, which I'm grateful for because it means I only have to add, "*Hi, my name is L-i-l-a-h. Sign name Bug.*" But some campers are more persistent than others in trying to sign more to me, assuming that will help get their message across. I hate having to rely on Mackenzie when I fall short, but I'm glad to be able to sign my responses on my own.

Whenever one of the girls arriving at our station is part of Mackenzie's group, she lets me know, since I'll be working with them, too. "This should be another one."

"*My name ———,*" the girl signs as she sits down at my chair, but instead of fingerspelling her name, she goes straight for the sign name.

"*Like h-o-n—*" Mackenzie starts, but the girl cuts her off and repeats the sign. "Right, her name is Honey," Mackenzie says and signs. "So that's her sign name, too."

"That's very cute," I say while gently moving her braids aside to search her head. She seems to be about nine or ten, on the older end of our group, which comprises ages seven through ten.

Ethan and Gary are taking turns escorting campers to the cabins. They'll get settled in and play something while they wait for others to arrive, such as Duck, Duck, Goose, which for our purposes is more like a game of Pat, Pat, Shove. In this version, kids don't have to try to listen or read the lips of the person walking around the circle.

"Finished!" I say and sign, moving in front of Honey.

"*Thank you!*" She stands but doesn't walk away yet. Honey signs something to me, but I stare blankly. She repeats herself, tapping her foot for good measure. I saw the word "counselor."

"Yeah, Mackenzie is your counselor," I say and sign, taking my best guess.

"No," Mackenzie says, stepping in. "She's asking about you."

"Oh, right." I nod. "*J-r counselor. I'll be helping your group.*"

"*Cool.*" Honey smiles and runs off.

Finally, after a long, hot afternoon, the arrival of campers has slowed to a stop. The parking lot is back to empty, with the exception of a few staff member vehicles and Gray Wolf's giant van.

Ethan gets up from the welcome table and comes over with Gary's clipboard. "Just one left. The last of your group. She's notoriously late every year. We'll give it another ten, and if she's not here yet, Gary can check her in later."

We wait. Mackenzie is about to plop down in one of the folding chairs when a large pickup truck comes squealing into the lot. Ethan looks at his watch. "With one minute to spare." Instead of greeting the truck, he goes back to the table and sits down beside Gary.

A man in camo pants and a sleeveless top steps down from the driver's seat while a young girl jumps from the passenger side, clutching a duffel bag in her arms. The father, I presume, pulls a giant adult-size sleeping bag from the truck bed. Mackenzie walks to greet them, but they only lift their heads in acknowledgment and head for the table.

"Hi, Blake!" Ethan says and signs, calling out to the camper.

But Blake's dad waves him off. "That's all right, we'll deal with this one here." He points to Gary. "She doesn't need that sign language. She's got the hearing aids for that."

Blake nods in agreement with her dad. Ethan purses his lips but lets Gary handle the paperwork. Choosing to sign or not can be personal preference, but this dad should really let his kid decide for herself. My parents didn't pursue ASL, but at least they were never against my learning it.

"Over here," Mackenzie calls for Blake to stop by the head-check.

"Ah, better not have lice. You're not my responsibility for the rest of the summer, you hear?" he says, then looks up at Mackenzie.

That's certainly one way to think about it . . . I *don't* like this guy.

Blake sits down and pulls her blond hair back, revealing dark-green hearing aids—a camouflage casing. A little embarrassed by her dad, she gives an apologetic shrug.

"Any other permission forms I need to sign?" Blake's dad asks at the check-in table. "For horseback riding trips and whatnot?"

Gary clears his throat. "We actually aren't doing any off-site activities this summer."

"Well, that's a rip-off." The dad grumbles but doesn't complain further. Good, because he's not actually paying anything in the first place. Even if he's just sending Blake to camp for the free childcare, I'm glad she gets to experience Deaf culture. When I was a kid, my counselors were Deaf role models. It's on me to be that person for Blake now.

After the all clear at head-check, Blake waves goodbye to her dad and follows Mackenzie and me to join our group.

Our cabin is a cozy wooden rectangle with wall-to-wall bunk beds, just enough to sleep six campers, Mackenzie, and me. Simone and Natasha's teens and tweens are sharing the slightly larger building next door.

Several girls in our group are enthusiastically reuniting, thrilled to be back. A couple of others seem like nervous newcomers, carefully going over their bed setups one more time. I can already tell this is the cleanest this cabin is going to look for the whole summer.

I'm leaning on my bunk, sneaking a quick look at my cell phone, when someone shouts.

"What are you saying?" Blake screams. "Just talk!"

Blake and Honey are standing face-to-face in front of the corner beds. Mackenzie tries to distract the other girls, but they're all watching the argument.

Honey's hands are flying. Her teeth clenched. I didn't think I'd see this sweet girl so angry, let alone with the amount of fury in her eyes as she stares down Blake. On the other hand, Blake looks indignant. She sits down on the bunk, still clutching her giant sleeping bag. Her duffel is at her feet, beside Honey's bags.

Honey leans forward, still signing; then Blake slaps Honey's hands away from her.

"Blake, you do not hit!" Mackenzie jumps forward to restrain Honey from lunging toward Blake.

"I didn't," Blake said. "I had to get her out of my face."

"No," Mackenzie continues. "You do not touch someone else like that. Ever. Or we will call your parents and you'll go back home."

"It's not my fault," Blake says, her hands balled into fists at her side. "I don't know what she's saying."

Mackenzie takes a deep breath. "Lilah, do you mind?" She nods toward Blake, while she bends down to sign with Honey.

Right, I need to help defuse this situation somehow. Am I supposed to reprimand Blake? I crouch down beside her. "What's going on?"

"She was in my face, being super annoying," Blake whines, "and wouldn't leave me alone."

"She was saying"—Mackenzie turns back to us—"that you are sitting on her bed."

"No, I'm not. I picked this bed," Blake says.

"Her stuff was already there," Mackenzie says and signs, pointing to the bags. "But the top bunk is free, so you can have it."

"No, it's not fair. I don't want that one." Blake crosses her arms. "You just like her better because she's Deaf."

Mackenzie sighs. "She was there first. We're all going to get along and have a good time, okay?"

"The top bunk is cool," I offer, hoping to help somehow. "That one over there is mine. See it? We'll be next to each other."

Blake scrunches up her face, not wanting to lose the fight but interested in the new bed. "Fine." She stands and throws her sleeping bag toward me. It's heavy, but I hurry to push it up to the mattress before she changes her mind. "Only because you talk to me normally."

"I—" But I can't think of how to constructively correct her statement, though I need to because we have an audience of young campers standing at the opposite corner. "I'm still learning, too," I say and sign. "We can practice together."

"Whatever." Blake crosses her arms again. "My counselor last year never forced me to learn. I wish she was back."

Ouch. Being a good role model for Blake is going to be more challenging than I thought. "And you don't have to if you don't want to," I say and sign, ignoring Blake's eye roll when I start moving my hands. "But it's great knowing more and more sign, so maybe you'll enjoy it, too."

Mackenzie meets my gaze and winces. She holds up her watch and conjures a cheery voice. "Looks like it's time for icebreakers!"

CHAPTER TEN

All through the next day, we do our best to keep Blake and Honey separate. Unfortunately, this means that Blake just clings to me. I'd rather be interacting with the other campers and improving my ASL, but Blake's got it lodged in her head that she's too good for it and refuses to even attempt to sign back.

She's not even the only one in our group who doesn't know sign language. But when Mackenzie led a mini ASL 101 class during breakfast, with the assistance of Honey and two other campers, Blake was the only one who didn't sign along.

We've made it to dinnertime, and I'm hopeful for more group bonding during our evening activity at the lake. Blake's tugging on my sleeve, trying to get my attention again, but I'm distracted by the beeps coming from my right ear. Low battery.

I take out both hearing aids and set them on the table, reaching down into my backpack for spare batteries. They're stored in a little pinwheel shape on a rectangular strip. I pull the flap on the opposite side of the cardboard, spinning the wheel so two new ones fall into my palm. After these, there's only two left in the pack. I make a mental note to restock from the stash in my suitcase. The batteries may last about a week, so I change both at the same time; otherwise my life would be constantly interrupted. I peel the orange sticker off the back of each new one and open the compartments on my hearing aids to make the switch.

"Where are you going?" Blake panics as I stand to throw away the dead batteries.

"I'll be right back." I look over my shoulder while walking away, noticing how frightened and alone she seems sitting with the group. Maybe she should have thought about that before she alienated her entire cabin on the first day.

Mackenzie and I gather the campers, and we walk with the other groups down to the lake for evening games and a formal introduction to the lifeguards. Ben and Oliver work at the pool, too. But we'll spend the most time with them at the lake since there's more to do here, with large inflatable toys to climb on and jump from into the water, canoes to take out past the swimming area, and a small beachfront to play in the sand.

Ethan has everyone take a seat at the big firepit that's right outside the fence guarding the lake entrance. This area is clearly meant to hold much larger gatherings than our camp of a little more than thirty. Was Gray Wolf ever large enough to fill all this seating? It would be great to have events here year-round—has Gary thought about renting out the campgrounds during the off-season?

Simone's group is the three oldest girls, who are blind and low vision. She guides them, one on each arm and one holding on to her backpack, to sit at the top of the circle near Ethan and the lifeguards. The girls all have their own ways of navigating, but right now they're having a bit of fun clutching their counselor. As they pass, Simone tells me with a sly grin, "They want to sit close to the accents . . ."

But Phoebe, the camper holding Simone's bag and wearing sunglasses past dark, scoffs. "We can hear them perfectly well from farther away. It's not like we need a closer vantage point."

I chuckle. The way the sun is setting, I have to strain my eyes through the glare over the water to see Ethan, Oliver, and Ben. The lifeguards are in standard red swim trunks paired with gray crewneck sweatshirts. Almost every day we'll take the campers to either the pool or the lake, if not both, but I wonder what the Brits are supposed to be doing in their free time.

When everyone finds a seat, Ethan hoots and throws his hands up. "Attention," he says and signs. "I know we're excited, but we need to focus before we can start tonight's beach games. Even though we're not swimming, we'll be at the lake a lot, so it's important to know the rules." He steps to the side and gestures for the lifeguards to speak.

"Right," Ben says, but he turns and looks at Ethan. "If I just, then you'll ———."

Ethan nods, already interpreting what Ben is saying.

"Carry on," Oliver chimes in.

"I'm Ben," he continues. "And this impatient fellow is Oliver. We'll be your, um, lifeguards this summer. The rules are— I'm sorry, should I slow down?" He turns back to Ethan. "I mean, can they hear me or do you need ———?"

Ethan nods for Ben to keep speaking, giving a cheerful smile to hide any irritation in his eyes. Interpreting done well doesn't need to be slowed down. Oliver looks my way and offers an apologetic smile. I bite my lip to keep a neutral face. After Simone's comment the other night, I can't stop thinking about how Oliver is cute, if in a "not exactly my type" kind of way.

Oliver takes over for a stumbling Ben. "It's pretty simple. No running on the beach, unless we're specifically playing beach games, like tonight. Don't go into the water unless we lifeguards are present." He's got plenty of admirers already. The two giggly girls with Simone take turns whispering into each other's ears. Oliver isn't oblivious to this, and smiles my way again, continuing his litany of rules. "If you're going past the roped-off area of the lake, you must be wearing a life jacket. In fact, if you're not a strong swimmer, you should wear a life jacket at all times, anywhere on the beach."

After going over the rules, Ethan reminds the lifeguards of a few basic signs he taught them during training week, namely "no and "stop." Finally, we're released, and the campers descend upon the beach.

Isaac flags down Ethan, who asks the lifeguards something. Then Oliver jogs back to the shed attached to their cabin and returns pushing a beach wheelchair. He holds it steady while Isaac helps one of his campers transfer from their usual seat to the bigger-wheeled, more sand-friendly chair. Isaac nods a quick thank-you to Oliver, then hurries off.

On the beach, Ethan divides us all into teams, and the games begin.

The rope scratches against my palms. Couldn't we wear gloves or something during tug-of-war? The relay races we started with were more my speed.

Ethan tried to form six evenly matched teams, but of course Blake decided she had to be on my team, so one of the older boys took her place. I don't want to say we're the weakest team, but most of us are tiny humans. And the other team, which Isaac is on, is easily going to drag us across the finish line.

"Is anyone else even pulling?" Bobby shouts from a few feet behind me. He's standing in the loop at the end of the rope, trying to step backward, but he's sliding in the sand.

"Ah!" I shriek when Bobby accidentally pulls on my hair.

"I don't want to lose!" Blake shouts, stomping her feet.

"Then pull," I shout back.

The beach is chilly. Most of the campers put on jackets, but I thought my long-sleeved shirt would suffice. Paired with shorts, it's not the warmest style, but it's my favorite summer camp look. At least it's protecting my arms from rope burns.

My team inches forward. With each pull, my hands end up painfully sliding back. There's maybe only a foot left until our tape marker crosses the middle line, deciding our losing fate. Ethan is standing by, waiting to declare the winner.

But the rope slacks, and I stumble backward. Somehow my team gains a few steps.

"Whoa, who hulked out?" Bobby shouts. "We're back in this thing!"

Isaac has released his grip on the rope and is now running to our side. He squeezes between me and Bobby and starts pulling for my team.

"What are you doing?" I shout, turning my head back to look at Isaac.

He just smiles and nods for me to face ahead.

"Let's go, team!" Bobby barks out, shaking the rope for emphasis.

We're holding on and making gains, but my hands are on fire. I can't take it anymore. I have to let go, throwing my arms up in the cool air.

Our opponents go in for a big pull right at that moment. My team flies forward across the line, and Isaac's face makes direct contact with my elbow. We collide and fall to the ground.

There's sand all over me. Clumps of damp sand everywhere. It's in my shorts, up my hair, and on my face. I spit out a few grains at the crease of my lips.

The other team is celebrating its victory, and everyone moves aside to make room for the next match. Isaac gingerly inspects his forehead, which is bright red. He stands, extending one hand to help me up while the other holds the side of his face.

"I'm so sorry," I say and sign before reaching up to accept his hand, but I recoil as the scratched skin on my palms stings on contact.

Oliver climbs down from his chair. "Oi, do you need some ice?"

"*I-c-e?*" I sign to Isaac, wincing as I form the letters with my burning hands.

Isaac nods and follows Oliver inside the lifeguard station. I want to go with him, but Blake grabs my arm and Natasha beats me to it.

"Come over here with me," Blake begs, pulling me to the fence where the rest of our team has already found a seat.

"Um, in a minute. Let me go check on Isaac." If the pain in my elbow is any indication, Isaac's head must really hurt.

They return quickly enough, with Isaac holding a ziplock bag full of ice to his forehead while Natasha walks circles around him, attaching the bag to Isaac with several feet of plastic wrap.

Oliver walks straight up to me, carrying something in one of his hands. "Here, hold this," he says, reaching out and placing a few small ice cubes in my palms.

"Ahh, that's so cold." A shiver goes down my back.

Oliver taps my shoulder and says something I don't catch.

"Sorry, what was that?" I ask. "Pardon?" I add, with a cheeky smile.

"That was quite the collision," he repeats, grinning. "I take it you're okay?"

"Yes, thank you." I hold up my cupped hands in gratitude.

"All right, back to it." He returns to climb up to his lifeguard post. Ben's already taken his place, so the two sit closely side by side in the large chair.

I walk Blake over to the other campers. "Wait here, I promise I'll be right back."

She digs her feet into the sand and sighs. Part of me empathizes with Blake. But I like to think I was always much more open to the Camp Gray Wolf experience than Blake has been so far—hopefully after a few days of settling in she'll tone it down.

I toss the cold ice cubes back and forth between my hands and walk back across the beach to Isaac. He is leaning up against the fence, shoving away Natasha, who is still giddy with her plastic wrap. He reaches up and rips the end of the strand from the container.

"*You look like—*" She sticks both arms out and walks like Frankenstein's monster. Isaac rolls his eyes.

Natasha supposedly has a thing for Jaden, but it pains me to admit that she and Isaac would make a cute couple. They probably just have a comfortable sibling dynamic, but what if Natasha's really in a love triangle with Isaac and Jaden? Just because she's interested in Jaden doesn't mean that Isaac couldn't also have a crush on her. I mean, isn't that who Isaac would want to be with? Someone who doesn't have any communication barriers?

I'm intruding, but I need to apologize. Isaac was just trying to help my team, and now he's got ice attached to his face. Natasha ignores the fact that I'm standing next to her and secures the loose end of the wrap.

Isaac peers out at me, shoving the bag up so it's not falling in front of his eyes, and smirks. "*Coming back for more?*" He mimics throwing back his elbow.

I bite my lip and shrug, dropping the ice and drying my hands on my shorts before signing, "*I'm sorry.*"

I should have thought through my apology to come up with more signs to put together. I could sign the word "okay" and raise my eyebrows in question, but that doesn't feel sincere enough. I don't want to only speak and make him carry the burden of lipreading—that's kind of the worst.

Don't get me wrong, lipreading is helpful. In fact, I generally need to see someone's mouth to "hear" them. But it's far from reliable. Not the magical process you see on TV.

When I speech-read, I use the mouth shapes I see to supplement the slivers of words that I hear. Combining them, I get something resembling the sentence that was spoken, but there are often gaps, leaving me to do guesswork and make assumptions to fill in the missing pieces. Sometimes clarification on a single word is enough for me to solve the entire puzzle. But I'm basically playing the part of Sherlock Holmes . . . all day, every day. It's exhausting. And *not* how I want to communicate with Isaac.

"*Are you okay?*" I sign.

Isaac immediately sticks a thumb to his chest. "*It's fine. I'm good.*" But in his current wrapped state, he looks the opposite of fine. "*Really,*" he adds, then gestures to Natasha. "*She's just ________.*"

I recognize the sign but can't place it. "*Again, please.*"

He signs the letters slowly. "*J-o-k-i-n-g. Joking.*"

I nod, getting it on the first spelling, but he looks skeptical, unsure if he can trust that I actually did.

Natasha stares at me. Isaac signs something fast with the word "worried," but that can't be right. He nudges her to interpret what he signed for me.

"How do you not understand? He's signing so English," Natasha mutters, maybe assuming I wouldn't catch it, but it makes me feel even more intimidated around her. She sighs and translates for me. "He says it was an accident. And not to worry about all this, because I can be a little extra with stuff like this." She heads back to her campers.

"*Can you help me?*" Isaac asks, undoing the plastic. "*I don't need this. It's freezing.*"

"*Sure.*" I reach up to unravel it, having to step closer to Isaac. I lean against the fence beside him.

Isaac is sitting on the middle rung, his eyes perfectly aligned with mine. I reach forward to undo the wrap around his head; we are inches apart. I'm doing everything I can to look anywhere but directly at him. I blush as Isaac stares at me. He notices my hands and reaches out to inspect them, mouthing the word "ouch."

"*Are you sure you're okay?*" I ask.

"*Perfect now.*" He smiles, wiping the condensation from his skin. "*You should have been my first aid partner.*"

I laugh, my response coming to me in sign easily this time, with my confidence growing. "*But Mackenzie knows everything.*"

"*True.*" Isaac lets out a quiet chuckle, raising his eyes to the sky.

Mackenzie made sure everyone knew she'd been certified in first aid/CPR before. And then there's me . . . just trying my best and already the cause of 100 percent of the injuries that have occurred this summer.

"*But we would've had more fun,*" Isaac signs.

Part of me wants to ask why we didn't team up, then. The way I remember it, we locked eyes, and he could have just walked right over to me. But I'm not going to ruin this moment by bringing that up.

"*Well, next time,*" I sign.

"*Next time?*" He raises his eyebrows. "*More training?*"

I laugh. "*Right, wait one year and we can be partners.*"

Isaac presses his lips together to suppress a smile. "*I guess I'll wait.*" He nods toward the campers, who are shuffling about, since the next game of tug-of-war just ended. Time to get back to work.

I step away from the fence as he tosses the wrapping in the nearby trash. Isaac catches up to me. He uses one hand to hold the ice pack to his head, but as we walk past the lifeguard stand, he casually slings the other around my shoulders.

CHAPTER ELEVEN

Who knew counselors were this exhausted all the time? It's been a week with the campers, and having to remain high-energy through everything takes effort. Keeping the peace between Honey and Blake is a lot.

My first on-duty night was largely uneventful. I'd been a little nervous, anticipating spending an entire evening alone with Isaac and trying to stock up on conversation topics I could sign about—but the entire staff ended up gathering around the campfire that night until curfew anyway.

If I'm not hanging out with the counselors, I usually either go down to the lake to see Oliver and Ben or relax somewhere alone, scrolling through my phone to catch up on what's happening in the outside world.

Somehow, despite the long, busy days, the staff stays up late every evening. Which is great . . . until Mackenzie has to shake me awake the next morning at seven.

I'm fighting through yawns all breakfast, hoping the girls want a chill Sunday morning at the lake. But *nope*. They all just agreed they want to try the canoes. Of course.

We throw our cover-ups on the beach chairs. After I get the Otterbox out of my backpack, Blake yanks out her hearing aids and tosses them in. One of the other girls, Savannah, is standing near me, so I ask her if she wants to be in my canoe.

"I do!" Blake shouts, infinitely louder now.

"I figured," I say. "And you?"

Savannah nods. She's one of our younger ones, and a bit shy, but has been slowly venturing out of her comfort zone.

"Can I hold your cochlear?" I extend the Otterbox. She's deaf in only one ear. She shakes her head and doesn't pull off the processor. "Are you sure?"

"It's waterproof. I swim with it all the time."

I guess there's no harm in letting her keep it. I've seen cochlear receivers fall off and float in the pool all the time, with campers having to constantly put them back on. So I add my own hearing aids to the box and clasp it shut, securing it in my backpack.

"Make sure you get their hearing aids," Mackenzie says and signs to me.

"I know." Even though we're practically acting like co-counselors, Mackenzie has a tendency to micromanage. It's as though she needs to prove she's a better counselor than me and remind me that I'm here to assist her. But let's be honest, I'm practically just Blake's babysitter at this point.

Mackenzie and I lead the girls over to where the canoes are stacked against a tree at the edge of the water. I hand out life jackets to everyone. Since Ben is up in the lifeguard chair, it's Oliver who comes to take down the boats for us.

Standing by the storage shed, I get a glimpse into the connected cabin where the lifeguards bunk. I'd assumed it was just a hangout spot for them to cool off in the shade while they weren't working, not where they sleep. But there are bunk beds and a kitchen table and a very nice and complete setup. It must be strange for the two of them to be down here at the lake, so far away from everyone else.

Oliver slides the canoes into the water. "Counselors in the middle first."

I climb in slowly, tiptoeing a few inches into the water before placing a foot square into the center of the boat. Oliver offers his hand to help me complete this balancing act. Mackenzie is overeager and doesn't wait, hopping too fast and losing her balance as it wobbles.

"Easy there." Oliver reaches over to hold her canoe steady, as well. He doesn't let go and nods for the campers to join with their paddles, Blake and Savannah taking the benches in front of me.

I assume I'm going to be doing more than my fair share of the paddling, but Blake surprises me. As soon as Oliver pushes us out, she starts tearing through the water. We're soon in the middle of the lake, with Mackenzie far behind us.

We stop paddling and sit still on the water, letting the ripples fade away. The morning air is fresh and crisp; the sun beats down on us.

Back at the enclosed swimming area, Bobby and his boys are sitting on the edge of the pier, fishing. My guess is Max will join their group when he gets here. Simone and her girls are building a giant sandcastle. Natasha, Jaden, and their campers are in a war, trying to bounce the opposing group off the giant trampoline. Meanwhile, Isaac and his young kids are climbing the giant inflatable iceberg. He leaps off the top, cannonballing into the water.

Blake's growing impatient. "Let's go out there." She points to the far end of the lake.

"I don't think we're supposed to go that way," I say.

"So what." Blake starts paddling again.

"It's hot," I say. "We can go back to the beach and swim."

"No," both girls protest. Blake grins, eager to have an ally in Savannah.

At the beach, Oliver raises both arms above his head, getting the attention of a few people. He points to Isaac and signs, "*No.*" Through a chain of waves, Oliver gets Isaac's attention and repeats his no, making sure it's clear that the cannonball launch from that height is prohibited. Isaac shrugs half apologetically and returns to helping his campers climb up the iceberg.

I reach over the edge of the canoe to cup a handful of water and splash it up onto my arms. I run my wet fingers through my burning hot hair. "Much better."

"I can't reach ———." Blake climbs onto her seat and stretches her arm to touch the surface of the lake. Savannah does the same.

Oops. I should have realized the campers would copy me. Unfortunately, they both choose to lean over the left side.

"Wait—" I shout, but it's too late. Mackenzie's canoe is just catching up to us when we topple into the lake.

Water shoots up my nose—an uncomfortable sensation getting a little too familiar with how much time we spend at the lake. My life jacket bops me back to the surface, as do the girls'. But our canoe is still floating upside down.

"Whoa, that was fun!" Blake shouts. She adds something else about swimming out here, but I'm too busy trying to flip the canoe back over to respond.

Mackenzie shouts something. "What happened here?" she continues, signing.

Isn't it obvious?

"Uh, we flipped," I say.

Mackenzie frowns. "You're not supposed to do that."

I do my best not to roll my eyes. "It wasn't intentional."

Mackenzie kneels and reaches out to push the hull, helping me flip this thing upright. Oliver is paddling his way out to us on his lifeguard board.

Blake keeps swimming farther away, so Oliver goes after her. I try to climb back in, since it'll be easiest to get myself in first and then help the girls up. Maybe. I'm not really sure of anything, except that I'm definitely bruising my stomach flopping back into this canoe.

Oliver guides the campers back. I pull Blake in, but Savannah is frantically searching the water. "I don't see it!" she shouts.

"See what?" Mackenzie asks. Oliver looks around, following Savannah's gaze.

Savannah starts to panic. "I don't see it!"

"Your cochlear?" Mackenzie looks at the camper, then directly back at me. "I told you ———."

"She didn't want to leave it," I say nervously. Why did the magnet detach so easily? Isn't it supposed to be on the surface somewhere near us? "It floats. Campers wear them in the pool all the time."

"That's the *pool*," Mackenzie says and signs, emphasizing the word. "A clear body of water where we could grab it from the bottom if it sinks." She groans. "What color was it, Savannah? Here, get back in the canoe. We'll keep looking. I said, what color is it?"

"Black." Savannah reaches her arms up to me, and I help her up.

With the dark-green lake water and plenty of leaves on the surface, it's going to be a difficult search.

"What are ———," Oliver asks me, but I'm unable to read the end of his question. Mackenzie decides to answer anyway.

"Her cochlear implant receiver. Like a hearing aid, but it's a magnetic attachment, and she wears it like this." Mackenzie points along the side of her head.

Oliver paddles off, searching a wide perimeter. He reaches down and fishes out what ends up being a twig, before coming back to us empty-handed.

"It's not caught in the canoe, right?" Mackenzie asks me.

I take a peek under the seats, but there's nothing there. "Shit," I mutter. Mackenzie glares at me, but none of the campers heard me swear or paid any mind. I'm grinding my teeth, hating that Mackenzie is going to see this all as a sign of her superior counselor status.

Eventually, we have to give up and return to the beach. Mackenzie finds Ethan, and the two of them go back out on the lake with the camper to search again until lake time is over.

On the walk to lunch afterward, Ethan falls into step next to me.

"No luck?" I ask.

He shakes his head.

I sigh. "I'm sorry. It's my fault. I should have made her take it out."

"Hey, don't worry," he says and signs. "You'll only have to pay a couple thousand."

"What?" I do *not* have that kind of money. My parents are going to be so mad.

"*I'm joking. I'm joking.*" He swings his backpack around and pulls a blank form out of a folder. "It's probably all under warranty, but Gary will have to call Savannah's parents and let them know. You just need to fill out this accident report."

"That doesn't sound great." I stare at the form. There are a lot of questions on it.

"We go through plenty of them. Any lost items, or even something as simple as a Band-Aid for a scratch, we have to fill out a report for."

"I really should have made sure she took it off first."

"Campers lose things." Ethan shrugs. "We try not to have them lose the expensive things, but there's always a lesson to be learned."

"Ouch."

Ethan laughs. "Sorry, that was a bit lecture-y."

"Yeah, got plenty of that from Mackenzie already."

"You're doing fine, I promise. Just get the paperwork done at lunch."

~

It's pool time this afternoon, and I've still got my swimsuit on underneath my clothes because there was no point in changing after the lake.

Honey bounces up and down at the shallow end to keep her head above the water. I take a seat on the stairs nearby, not wanting to get my hair wet again if I can manage that.

"*Like,*" Honey signs to me. "*I know* ———."

I shake my head. "*Again, please.*"

Honey rolls her eyes and gives me one word at a time. "*Like.*"

"You like swimming?" I say and sign.

She waves her hands to indicate that I'm on the entirely wrong path here. She tilts her head. "*No, pay attention.*"

I know that phrase well because Ethan uses it every day during announcements. After this morning's cochlear incident, I'm a little unsure about myself, but I know Honey would make a fantastic counselor one day.

I glance around, wondering if someone could interpret for me, but the only person I see is Natasha. She seems to grimace at me before looking away, likely assuming exactly what I was going to ask of her. So I turn back to Honey and slide both hands forward alongside my face, giving an agreeable expression and signing, "*Okay, I pay attention.*"

"*I . . .* " Honey signs slowly. "*Know . . . someone . . . like . . . you.*"

"Someone like me?" I say and sign. "Like, a friend who looks like me?"

"*No.*" She snaps her fingers. Then she gives a large, silly grin. "*A boy. A boy likes you.*"

"Uh, no," I say. "*You're too funny.*"

"*Not funny! Fine, I won't tell you who.*" She holds a finger to her lips, but points across the pool to where Isaac is floating on brightly colored noodles with his campers. Honey giggles and paddles away from me.

Okay, my interest is piqued. But even if Isaac actually does like me, how would Honey know?

Once she's farther away, Blake practically materializes beside me. "Throw me!" She points toward Isaac, who is now tossing his campers up out of the water to plunge back down with a big splash.

"Oh, I don't know if I can do that," I say. "But you can hold on to my shoulders and I'll swim around?"

"Fine."

As we wade through the water, another one of our campers grabs onto my arm. And another onto my other arm. On a normal day, I might not entertain this, since it's taking all my energy to drag these girls around the pool, but they're having the time of their lives, and I need to prove to myself that I can be a good counselor. Staying upright is difficult at the deep end, where I have to be on my tiptoes, but I'm a few steps away from more solid footing in the shallow part when someone grabs me tight around the stomach and pulls us all underwater.

I pry the little kid's arms off and jump back to the surface, helping the girls to the side of the pool, where we all try to catch our breath. The young boy, Cole, swims after us. "I wanna play, too!" he shouts.

"No," I say sternly, still coughing up water. "You can't jump on me like that." I turn to my campers. "Girls, are you okay?" They all nod.

Cole doesn't move away, though. He reaches out to grab my shoulders while kicking his legs to splash up a ton of water. "My turn!"

"No, no, no," I say and sign, turning away to cover my face. I will draw the line at behavior that endangers anyone. No good counselor would tolerate that anyway.

I look up across the water to see Oliver, who's approaching the edge of the pool beside us and blowing his whistle. He reaches down and lifts the boy off my shoulder.

"Can he hear me enough?" Oliver asks me. I shrug and nod.

"It's not safe to jump on people," Oliver tells Cole, talking loud and clear. "Remember our rules?"

"Sure."

"Good," Oliver says, standing back up. "Now apologize."

"What?" Cole asks.

"Say sorry," Oliver says and signs, putting his extremely limited ASL to use.

"*Sorry,*" the boy signs, and swims off.

The girls have already grabbed hold of a few noodles and are floating away, but I take a moment to catch my breath at the edge of the pool. It's good for Blake to have some bonding time with just her fellow campers.

Oliver's still standing beside me.

"Hey, stranger, didn't I just see you at the lake?" I smile, shaking my head. "It's been a day."

"I'll bet." His voice is quieter now that he's not talking to the camper, but I've caught most of what he's saying on his lips. "Do ——— to drink?"

"A drink?" He nods. My mouth is dry. "Good idea."

I'm about to scooch down the wall toward the ladder, but Oliver takes a few quick steps over to the lifeguard chair and returns with his water bottle. He untwists the cap and hands it to me.

"Thank you." I gulp down almost half of it.

He sits on the edge and puts his feet in the water, letting out a sigh of relief. "It's scorching."

"Come on in, you'll feel refreshed! Splash around and get your hair wet."

Ben is walking around the perimeter of the pool. I catch him glaring at us, and Oliver does, too. "I'm supposed to be in the chair, but a quick dip won't hurt."

He slides in, running his fingers through his hair as he shoots back to the surface.

"Better?" I ask.

"Much."

"Thanks for not splashing me when you jumped in. After today, I think I'm half lake water and half chlorine."

"Oh, you wanted me to splash you?" Oliver sends a few droplets my way.

I smile. "Um, didn't you mention something about how you're supposed to be in the chair?"

"If you insist . . ." He sends a few more drops my way before planting his hands at the edge of the pool, easily hoisting himself back out of the water, impressively smooth. He climbs back into his seat.

"Well, if you're going to be good at your job, guess I should go be better at mine," I say to him before swimming back to my campers.

I pass Isaac, who I realize has been watching us, treading water in the deep end with his group. I give a sheepish smile, but he ducks under. His forehead still has slight noticeable bruising from last week's tug-of-war collision. Perhaps that's why he's so hot and cold around me.

"Look!" Blake shouts over to me, so I join the girls. "I can do a flip."

"Ooh, let me see," I say.

She demonstrates, holding her nose the entire way. "You try!"

"I'm not sure . . ." I didn't even want to get my hair wet, let alone do underwater flips.

"Please," the girls chant.

I make sure the area is clear, take a deep breath, and submerge myself. But as I'm halfway through my flip, someone grabs my back.

There's that kid again, this time holding on to my swimsuit straps. I fight my way to the surface.

"Stop. What are you doing?" I call out. I try to shrug off his hands. But Cole latches on tight, nails digging into my skin.

As I push him away, there's a tight snap against my neck. My swimsuit straps are ripped from the seams. I grit my teeth, barely managing to keep my composure. My face must be pure rage.

Isaac swiftly swims across the length of the pool over to me. He scoops Cole up out of the water and away from me, making him climb up the stairs and take a seat near the changing rooms.

Honey kicks her way over, laughing.

"*What's funny?*" I sign one-handed, making sure to keep my suit secure with the other. "*This is not funny.*"

"*I told you, boy likes you,*" she signs. There's my answer. Honey was telling me *that* little twerp has a crush on me? That isn't funny at all and doesn't excuse his behavior.

"Where are you going?" Blake asks as I move over to the edge.

"I'm getting out now. Ask Mackenzie to come play." Mackenzie is sitting under the shade on her phone. About time for her to snap back into her perfect counselor mode.

I carefully climb the stairs, where Isaac greets me with his towel. He holds it out, wrapping it around me, enclosing me for a moment in a hug. He starts to pull back, but I'm not ready to move quite yet and rest my head against his chest, realizing too late that maybe this wasn't meant to be a prolonged embrace. But Isaac immediately squeezes his arms around me tighter. I take a deep breath and let him hold me steady, my knees buckling. Water drips from my hair to the floor, and soon we're both standing in a puddle. I sigh, then lean back and look up at him.

The concern in his eyes is adorable. "Okay?" he mouths.

I nod and lean back. "*Long day. Thank you.*" I shrug, gesturing to the towel, though I'm really thanking him for the hug.

Isaac glances back at the pool and sees his campers erupting into chaos. I try to hand back his towel, but he motions for me to hold on to it. He reluctantly steps away and dives back into the pool.

Simone walks over to inspect my swimsuit. "Yikes, girl. I can try sewing this back up for you."

"You think?" We walk over and take the spot where Mackenzie had been sitting in the shade. I shrug the towel down my back an inch so Simone can glance at the swimsuit.

"Never mind," Simone says. "When you take this off, it'll all unravel."

"Great." I take a deep breath.

"Do you have a spare suit? We can ——— store tomorrow."

"Yeah, we're gonna need to. This is my only one."

"No problem," Simone says, noticing that I'm still looking in Isaac's direction while wrapping myself tight in his towel. "Okay, lovebird. I guess I'm going to owe Bobby money, aren't I?"

"Did you two seriously bet on this?" I laugh. "Maybe focus on your own relationship."

"Aaah, don't tell me that," Simone says, flustered, but her eyes immediately dart to Bobby.

"Come on, it's clear that he, like, loves you."

"I know," she whispers. "That's the scary part. But then what? ——— long distance and shit? I don't know. I'm only nineteen. What if I just met him too early?"

"Whoa, okay, maybe you're getting ahead of yourself here." This is the first moment where it's super clear that she's equally into him. I do not feel qualified to give any relationship advice.

"Exactly. ——— lose him as a friend, you know?"

"But you could just see where it goes," I say.

Simone throws her towel at me. "How about you *go* get dressed?"

"Fine . . ."

When I return from the changing room with my hearing aids back in, Gary is pulling up to the pool in his golf cart. He walks inside the gated perimeter, leaving two unfamiliar passengers behind.

"How is everything?" he asks.

"We had a little bit of a situation," I say, pointing to Cole, who is still in the time-out chair, then raising my torn swimsuit. "He got . . . very clingy."

"Ah, sometimes kids get attached. It's easy to get overly excited at camp. They may mean well, but they don't understand how to respect boundaries or space. Especially here, you know." Gary reaches out and pokes my arm. I shrug and nod. "Don't get me wrong, I'm not excusing this. In fact, I'm sorry you had to deal with that behavior."

"Yeah, this job can sometimes be harder than I thought," I say. I didn't mean to admit that out loud, but the words pour out of my mouth.

"With any work, there are always good and bad days." Gary nods reassuringly. "But if anything ever makes you uncomfortable, please come to Ethan or me. That's what we're here for. Got it?"

"Yeah." I appreciate Gary's response. It's nice to know that counselors aren't expected to tolerate this.

But now there's something else that doesn't sit well with me. Standing outside the tall chain-link fence surrounding the pool, staring into the swimming area, are two old dudes wearing golf attire. One points toward a few campers who noticed him and gives them a cheerful wave.

"Uh, who are they?" I point to the men, not even bothering to be discreet.

"I'm in the middle of a tour for potential donors," Gary explains. "Showing them the property, but I wanted to stop here and check in for a minute. So"—he claps his hands once and steps away, but then calls back—"Lilah, you're taking on responsibility as a junior counselor this summer, but camp is still supposed to be fun. Don't forget that."

"Right, thanks."

He smiles. "It's through the ups and downs that you bond with your fellow counselors."

My eyes dart toward Isaac. That hug—it really happened, right?

It's just been such a long day. I sit back down beside Simone. "You see them, too?"

"Yeah," she says. "Maybe show them the pool when we're not here. Kinda weird having old dudes stare at us in our bathing suits."

"I mean, it doesn't even have to be gross. I just don't like having people around watching us."

Isaac climbs out of the pool and walks over to me. I offer him back his towel, and my heart skips a beat as he dries his face and sits beside me on the same lawn chair. "*It's weird having people watch us.*"

"*That's what I was saying,*" I sign back. "He thinks the same," I tell Simone.

"We still have that luncheon coming up soon," she says.

"This feels old-school. Couldn't there be a different way to raise money?" I say, then signing for Isaac, "*Maybe a different way to raise money?*"

"*Yeah, so we don't have to ——— on people coming here.*" He sees my head tilt and spells out, "*D-e-p-e-n-d, depend.*"

"*Right.*" I smile, grateful that he could tell exactly which word I needed clarification for. "*Thank you.*"

CHAPTER TWELVE

I sat out of swimming all day today, since I'm still without proper attire after yesterday's pool debacle. In the staff cabins after hours, I search for someone to go to the store with.

"Hey, Simone, do you still want to go to the store tonight?"

"Right, Lilah needs a new swimsuit," Simone says, nudging Bobby, who's sitting beside her. "Let's go."

"Um, we're on duty tonight," Bobby says.

"It's *not* Monday again already." She checks her phone. "Wait, how is that possible?"

"It pains me that you dread our time together that much," Bobby jokes, but he genuinely smiles when Simone reaches out for his hand. "Is there someone else you can go with, Lilah?"

Natasha and Jaden are standing by the door, and Isaac walks over to me. "*Did you need to go shopping? Come with us?*"

"Yes, please," I say and sign before turning back to Simone and Bobby. "Don't worry, I'm tagging along with the others. Enjoy your evening. Remember to watch the campers."

On the way to the parking lot, we run into Ethan, who needs to pick up some supplies for tomorrow's activities. So all five of us pile into Natasha's little car. Jaden claims the passenger seat. Isaac hops into the back, and Ethan tells me to take the middle, motioning for me to slide all the way over until I'm practically in Isaac's lap.

Natasha turns to sign. "*Food first?*"

Everyone agrees, and she hits the ignition, music immediately blaring from the speakers. The car shakes the entire way to the Mackie's across the street from the Super Mart.

Jaden opens the Notes app on his phone and types in his order, passing it around for the rest of us to enter ours. We pull up to the drive-through. Instead of stopping at the speakers, Natasha heads straight for the window. When she parks, she adds her order to the note as well.

We're waiting, but no one is there. Natasha waves until an employee finally comes, but they don't open the window.

"*We're Deaf,*" Natasha signs, pointing to her ear and cochlear implant. She holds out the phone with the orders on it.

But the worker ignores her and points back to the speakers. I can read part of what he's saying—"don't order here."

Natasha points to her ear again and holds out the phone. He just shakes his head. Ethan types "We're Deaf, here's our order" on a large-text app on his phone and gives it to Natasha. But after Natasha shows the message, the employee just walks away.

"*W-t-f,*" Natasha signs. "*He left?*"

A car arrives behind us, flashing its headlights. The employee comes back, this time with their manager, who opens the window.

"*We're Deaf, here's what we want,*" Natasha signs one-handed, holding out the orders on her phone.

The manager mumbles something back. Natasha makes the gesture asking him to write it down. The manager squints to look at all of us in the car and shakes his head.

Ethan catches what the man says next, and signs up to Natasha, "*He thinks we're faking . . .* "

"*We're far from the city right now,*" Jaden signs. "*Maybe not a lot of deaf people ———.*"

The car behind us honks. The manager shouts and gestures for us to move our car. Natasha is braver than me—she holds out her phone again. With her strong Deaf accent she says, "This is what we want."

Isaac is tensing up beside me. I lean into him; my hand drifts to rest near his knee. He inches his own closer until our pinkies are side by side.

The manager is still yelling and refusing us.

"*Could try a-p-p?*" I sign one-handed to Ethan, guessing we might try to just enter the order ourselves. I mean, I don't have it downloaded and the service around here might be too spotty to do so, but maybe someone else has it already.

"*No, let's go,*" he says.

Natasha nods, flips off the manager, and drives away. When we're back on the road, she screams out her frustration.

"Seriously, why'd they do that?" I frown.

"I swear, that could've been the easiest order of the night for them," Ethan says and signs. "It was all written down right there. Takes two seconds. Then we're gone. But they'd rather pull that shit."

Following some more venting, the rest of our evening errand trip is swift and joyless.

I notice eyes on us as we sign throughout the store, but I'm learning to ignore other people. Ethan stocks up on the arts-and-crafts supplies for tomorrow, then Isaac, Jaden, and Natasha grab a bunch of snacks to get us through the night. I find a perfectly average cheap swimsuit. We fly through the self-checkout line and head back to our safe haven in the woods.

~

The next morning, the grass is still damp from dew, but we gather the campers in a circle on the ground to play a game before our scheduled Tuesday afternoon hike. The person standing in the middle has to pick someone who is seated and say, "Honey, if you love me, please smile," and then that person has to get through a response of "Honey, I love you, but I just can't smile" without actually smiling in the slightest, to avoid going in the center.

I'm a champ at this game. So far when we've played to fill time between other activities, no one has managed to get me to the middle of the circle. Ethan announced that right now we only have time for one more round, so I'm in the clear. That is until, for the first time, Isaac is the one who steps toward me.

He fakes going to the camper to my right but pivots and stops in front of me, batting his eyes and holding up four fingers on each hand to sign the word for "eyelashes," channeling the theatrical nature of the game. The campers are dying with laughter. I clench my jaw tight, but my lips quiver and threaten to betray me.

"*No, no, no,*" he signs, stretching out his arm, pretending to caress the side of my face. "*Wait for me . . .* " I take a deep breath. He inches closer. "*To sign . . .* "

I know exactly what's coming, as well as the response it will elicit from me. Looking up at the sky, I feel a blush rise in my cheeks, very aware of how many people are watching.

Isaac waves for my attention before continuing. "*Honey, if you love me . . .*"

Of all the ways to sign "love," he used the *I-L-Y* sign. I mean, it's all part of the game, right? He's still pointing to himself as I shake my head, facing him directly and forgetting that he's not done with his request.

"*Please . . . smile?*" He tilts his head and gives a wide grin of his own, which is contagious. Very much so.

It's taking *everything* I've got to keep my expression neutral. Now comes the hardest part.

"*I love you, honey,*" I sign super fast, biting my lip and watching his head lean forward, eyes wide in anticipation. No big deal—I'm just dropping the *L*-word, casually, to a guy I'm super into in front of an entire crowd of people. He rests his chin on his knuckles and bats his eyelashes again. "*But I—*" Then Isaac switches it up, dropping his smile into a dramatic frown and clutching his hands to his heart. Peering at me with those big brown eyes.

And I forget to clench my mouth tight, letting slip the edge of a grin.

Game over.

"*I got you!*" he signs, jumping up in celebration. "*Finally! A victory!*"

As the kids and staff break the circle and get ready for the hike, Isaac helps me up. He's still laughing, and I playfully swat him away.

"*Why are you laughing?*" I sign, standing up on my toes to get in his face, the game-ending smirk having not yet left mine. But this makes him laugh even harder, a mostly silent, wheezing, full-chest, adorable kind of chuckle. "Are you seriously giggling right now?"

He watches my lips, reading them carefully, and purses his lips together, nodding.

I stand back flat on the ground and sign this next part quickly before I lose my confidence. "*Okay, that's cute.*"

Then I hurry away, leaving Isaac there, smiling.

CHAPTER THIRTEEN

The weather for the next few days is spotty. Storm clouds drift in on Wednesday, but we still get to be outdoors most of the day. The light drizzle turns into a proper downpour on Thursday, though. We're stuck with indoor activities or hiding out in the warmth of the dining hall for extended meals. After hours, most of the counselors gather in the staff cabin. I grab a jacket from my bunk and step outside to join them, pulling up the hood to cover my hearing aids from the drizzle that remains. Ethan and Isaac are at the firepit, fighting the light raindrops to get a small flame going.

Ethan catches me looking their way and waves me over. He and Isaac haven't managed to start the fire yet, but they've gathered a decent amount of damp kindling. Ethan's got a raincoat on, while Isaac is sitting on the bench, legs scrunched up, in an oversize bright-green poncho.

"Not going well?" I call out, bunching up the ends of my jacket sleeves in my hands as I walk over.

"Nothing's dry enough," Ethan says and signs. "I'll be right back." He jogs off down the path in the direction of the craft barn and dance barn.

"Why are you here? It's raining," I say and sign to Isaac.

"*Rain is almost finished.*" He shrugs. "*Want to* ———," he asks, along with a familiar Y-shape sign, but at the moment I can't remember it.

"*Again?*"

"*S-t-a-y?*" he fingerspells.

"*Right, stay.*" I smile. "*Maybe . . .* "

To sweeten the deal, Isaac stands, reaches into his backpack, and pulls out his beach towel, resting it across the drenched bench for me. He also rips a few blank pieces of paper from a beat-up sketchbook and crumples them in his hand, stepping back into the circle to toss them under the big logs. He picks up a lighter that's been sitting by my foot, dries it off with the edge of the towel, then squats by the fire like a little green frog.

Flames consume the kindling, and soon, a proper fire is burning. Isaac jumps up, holding both arms out to the pit, showing off his creation. He bends down again to carefully fan the flames, throwing a few more pieces of crumpled paper inside.

"*Nice work,*" I sign. I can't stop staring, totally amused, so I gesture toward his outfit. "*Where'd you get this?*"

"*I don't know, it's so old.*"

He sits beside me, and I lean away, thinking the water droplets I felt were from his poncho, but it turns out the rain is picking back up. Isaac quickly undoes a few of the plastic buttons on the side of his poncho. He throws the dismantled green sheet over both our heads and backs, so we both huddle together.

"*I thought the rain was almost finished . . .* " I sign, but I don't really mind, because we're pretty cozy at the moment.

"*Whoops, hopefully soon,*" he signs one-handed. He looks back at the fire. "*Still going!*"

"*For now.*" I glance around, realizing Isaac and I have been alone for a while. "*Where's Ethan?*"

"*I don't know.*" But Isaac doesn't look around. Instead, he crosses his legs and spins his body on the bench to sit and face me. But he doesn't say anything. Does he want to tell me something?

I wait as long as I can comfortably bear him looking at me, until I sign with a smile, "*What's up?*"

He shrugs. "*Long rainy day.*"

I nod in agreement.

"*So many bracelets!*" He holds up an entire arm's worth of about twenty dangling bracelets, which were not-quite-skillfully threaded by his campers. I take a moment to brag and show off my equally large collection.

"*My camper Honey made, like, eight of these,*" I sign.

He points to the one made of colorful duct tape and raises his eyebrows in question.

"Oh," I say. "*I made that one. Looks okay?*"

"*Nice.*" He smiles, running his fingers over the smooth weaving. "*You'll have to make me one.*"

I press my lips together, trying to not look too eager. "*Sure, I will.*"

He peers out from under our cover to look back at the sky. "*I want it to finish!*" He looks back at me, his eyes wide with sincerity. "*If we have to play more indoor games tomorrow . . .*" He shakes his head. "*No, thank you. But,*" he starts with a sparkle in his eyes, "*I'll beat you every time in Honey, If You Love Me now.*"

"*No, no, no,*" I sign, tapping my fingers together close to his face. "*When we play again, I'll win.*"

"*Really? Are you sure?*" He squares his shoulders toward me again and leans forward. I can see his breath in the cold air. "*Honey . . . if you—*"

"*Noooo . . .* " I do the motion once but hold the O-shape on my mouth. Then, I start chuckling.

"*See, I win again.*"

"I wasn't playing," I say and sign, making no effort to stop my laughter.

Ethan is still nowhere to be seen. Maybe he wasn't planning to come back. Somehow, the fire is still burning—a small light in the darkness of overcast clouds. It gives the illusion that we're nestled in a small space rather than in a wide patch of field. It's just me and Isaac. And we'll be on duty again tomorrow night. Perhaps we'll be alone then, too.

"*What's up?*" It's Isaac's turn to sign. We're back to this. I laugh and face the fire, but he waves at me. "*What?*"

"*What what?*"

"*No, that's my question.*" He smiles.

"*I'm asking, too.*"

He tilts his head, dropping an arm and letting his hand graze my knee. The fire pops, sending a few sparks toward us. He looks to make sure none landed on me before meeting my eyes once again.

"*You know, right,*" I sign, adding the part that I'm nervous to share with a mumble, "that I like you."

Isaac watches my lips closely, and his eyes go wide.

He *has* to know already. Oh gosh, my heart is beating so fast now. Did I just make a huge mistake?

"*Can you say that again?*" His hands are shaking a little. He seems to be holding his breath.

"*Never mind! Look, your fire's still going.*" I turn away, briefly hide my face.

But he reaches out and nudges for me to face him. "*But I know what?*"

"Um." He's going to make me say it again. And I do actually know all the signs to put together this sentence.

Is it too soon to tell Isaac how I feel? Is it too soon to even be having these feelings? I just don't know. Time is warped at summer camp. Have we been here only a few days or a few weeks, really? It also feels like it's been ages. The boundaries and barriers of everyday life don't exist. And, heck, I even bunked in the bed above him the first week, so that brought us instantly close.

But all this won't last forever. There's a limited number of camp weeks. Then it's over.

With this timeline, maybe it isn't far-fetched for me to admit my feelings so plainly. I could wait around and hope for something to happen. Or I could say something. He probably feels the same way I do.

The game. The hug at the pool. Reaching for my hand at the drive-through. Sitting so close to each other right now.

"*What?*" he asks again, leaning even closer.

My hand is shaking as I draw it to my chest. "*I think I . . .* " He's hanging on to every word. "*I think I like you.*"

That's when Isaac smiles. And my heart is ready to burst.

But then he furrows his eyebrows, and his hands start flying, signing so fast I'm completely lost.

"Ah, sorry, what?" I say. "*Slow, please, sorry, again.*"

"*We not* ———."

"We not?" I immediately slide out from under the poncho and stand in the rain.

He jumps up and shakes his head, wanting to further clarify.

"*D-o-n-t,*" he spells.

"Don't?"

He nods. Crap, where is this going? Why did I say anything? I'm ready to run away, but he waves for me to stay.

"*We don't really know,*" he signs, gesturing from me to himself.

I can't believe this is happening. I totally read this all wrong, and he must not feel as I thought. I'm so embarrassed I can't even look at him.

"We don't really know each other?" I ask. Isaac reads my lips and nods.

I must've caught him off guard, but why is he being so confusing? I turn to walk away, but he reaches forward and taps my arm. "*Y-e-t.*"

"So, you don't . . . like me?" I say. The words must come at a whisper, but it doesn't matter. My arms feel too heavy to match with sign.

"*I didn't say that.*" He seems startled, confused, out of his element.

"It's fine," I say and sign, jabbing my thumb to my chest. "*Forget I said—*" I can't call to mind the word for "anything." I take a few steps backward.

He waves for my attention, signing something with the word "slow," but my brain is already spiraling. "*Wait,*" he signs, with a panicked, apologetic look on his face.

I need to get out of here. What was I thinking? I spin around, effectively ending the conversation, and speed away.

He's right. We don't know each other yet, really. But before this, we were bonding, which is impressive since we can barely communicate as it is. What did I expect would happen by confessing my feelings? The more I think about it, what if he's just trying to let me down gently? Seriously, there's no way he likes me back.

I ignore what looks like a party in the staff cabin and go straight to bed. I carefully shine my flashlight to avoid waking the campers as I climb into my top bunk, collapsing face-first onto my pillow, wishing I could fall asleep. But I keep replaying the whole conversation with Isaac in my mind. Over and over. I go over the memory, overanalyzing and changing his response every time, ranging from "we don't really know each other" to "I don't like you."

And, of course, we have another on-duty shift together tomorrow night.

How am I going to face him after this?

~

"Nope," I say, seeking out Simone at breakfast in the crowded dining hall the next morning. I ran straight to her after making accidental eye contact with Isaac. He gave me such a sympathetic smile. It was painful.

"What's wrong?" she asks, loading her plate with pancakes.

Bobby walks by, and I nudge him. "You were wrong."

"Someone's cranky this morning," Bobby says. They both can tell I'm upset and wait for me to elaborate.

"Isaac doesn't . . ." I say, letting them infer what I'm talking about. "And it was embarrassing and terrible, and I'm not gonna talk about it."

"Let's get you some extra pancakes," Simone says, wrapping an arm around me.

Bobby quietly asks, "But what happened?"

"He said we don't know each other well enough." I add the one word that I've been clinging to hopefully. "Yet."

Bobby wipes a hand down his face. "That sweet, sweet boy. Doesn't he know that's the whole point? To get to know each other?"

"I guess not," I say, loading my plate full of syrup to drown my sorrows.

Back at my table, Blake takes advantage of my apathy this morning by topping her pancakes sky-high with chocolate chips. Honey waves at her to save some for the rest of them, but Blake ignores her.

Someone taps my shoulder, and I have to brace myself in case it's Isaac.

But it's Oliver.

"Hey, friend, any chance you want to hang out later? I've got some things to catch you up on." He looks like he's been dying to talk about something.

"Oh, really?" I'm intrigued and happy for any distractions.

He smiles wide but notices my bad mood. "And about whatever's clearly bothering you right now, too."

"Yes, please. Oh, wait . . . no. I, unfortunately, am on duty tonight."

"That's rough," Oliver says.

"Very rough. But actually, apparently our entire staff gets tomorrow off for a Saturday night break, since our director and nurse will watch the campers. They said some restaurant—Freddy's, I think? You should join us, and we can catch up."

"Perfect, I'll see you tomorrow." Oliver smiles. "Well, and at the lake in, like, an hour. And probably at the pool . . . and any water-based activity."

CHAPTER FOURTEEN

After breakfast, we spend a couple hours at the lake. While campers swim and hang out at the beach, we observe from a distance as potential donors arrive for Gary's luncheon and gather at the picnic tables under the big pavilion. The campers are just as watchful of these strangers as they are of us. Gary is busy running around and setting up tin trays of food while one of the guests stands at the grills. There are probably about fifteen people visiting. Where did Gary find them all? How much money do we need each of them to give? It seems like many of them are here with family members. It doesn't feel great to need their charity, but at the same time, it's necessary to make sure Gray Wolf is affordable and accessible to as many campers as possible.

When it's time, we gather our things and march the short distance over to where the visitors have congregated. Mackenzie pulls her crumpled gray staff polo from her backpack, and I do the same with my camper T-shirt, which still has the tape lettering Isaac did across the back. But I try to put Isaac, and however he feels about me, out of my mind in order to get through this lunch.

At the pavilion, our cabin chooses a table at the back, and we all stick together. Gary tries to discreetly gesture that we should leave space at each table for our guests, but all the other groups clump together as well, not wanting to sit interspersed with the donors. I don't blame us. Our visitors all seem to be hearing, and none have shown any proficiency in sign language, though I do recognize a light skin-tone hearing aid on one of the older men.

Mackenzie tries to coax some of us to come chat with the potential donors, but none of the girls follow, so she goes on her own and appears to be having a grand time. Other than Mackenzie and Gary, the rest of us aren't particularly in a social mood, but Assistant Director Ethan is doing his best to be professional.

When the food is ready, Ethan calls for our attention, drawing all eyes to himself. "We're so grateful to have our special guests here today," he says and signs. "And even more grateful that they helped us prepare lunch. I know we're all starving, so we'll let the kids go ahead and line up for food while Gary lets you know a little more about Camp Gray Wolf."

Gary takes a spot next to Ethan and gives a brief introductory speech while we file to get food. But on the walk back, Gary is positioning all the campers and staff on only one side of the picnic tables so our guests can sit across from us.

Sure enough, I'm only a few bites into my burger when a couple walks up to me.

"Is this spot taken?" a cheery old man with a gray receding hairline asks. A woman who I suspect is his wife hovers closely beside him. They seem like nice grandparents, the kind who spend most of their retirement volunteering.

"Please join us," Mackenzie calls from the other end of the table when our campers, being too shy, don't answer or hear the man in the first place.

"Don't mind if we do." The man leans forward to put his plate down, carefully lowering himself onto the bench. "I'm ________," he says. "And this pretty young lady with me is my wife, ________."

"Nice to meet you, Bill and Susan," Mackenzie says and signs. It's helpful that she's one of those people who repeats names after meeting someone.

Everyone else takes their seats. Most of the potential donors seem unsure who they could easily converse with, and campers who are normally very vocal are keeping to themselves. I want to do the same, but I also know what's at stake with this luncheon and force myself to do my best to engage in the conversation, mostly nodding along while Mackenzie talks.

"Yes, I'm studying to be an interpreter. This camp is amazing practice. It's almost a rare thing to be able to immerse myself in American Sign Language this way. It's such a wonderful experience." She makes it sound like this entire summer is homework and we're experiment subjects, rather than just disabled kids enjoying time outdoors.

Susan is directly across from me, trying to get my attention while I drink from my water bottle.

"What?" I ask.

"Is your shirt in the wash?" she repeats.

"My shirt?"

"The polo," she clarifies.

"Oh, we didn't have enough." I turn my shoulder, demonstrating the duct tape that practically screams "donate some money so I get a polo next year." "And I'm only a junior counselor this summer, so this works."

"Interesting. Does that mean you're new this year?" Bill asks.

"Well, I was a camper. But now I'm seventeen—well, eighteen this fall, and yeah." *Really coherent here, Lilah.* "So I'm a junior counselor."

"Very impressive," Susan says, looking truly proud for some reason. "Then will you be a senior counselor next summer?"

"I'd like to be."

Bill takes a bite of his hot dog. He says something before he's finished chewing, so he holds his napkin over his mouth while he talks. I shake and tilt my head to the side. He wipes his beard, places the cloth down, and repeats himself. "How'd you like being a camper?"

"Great. It's an important place to meet other people like me." I hope my response doesn't sound too rehearsed, but that's what they want to hear, right?

"Of course," Susan says. She takes a sip of soda, formulating her next thought. "So you're hearing impaired?"

"Hard of hearing," I correct her, though I also dislike this preferred terminology. It feels so medical and outdated, more suited for the elderly than for someone as young as I am. There's also a misconception among hearing people that these terms mean my hearing loss isn't significant and that simply shouting could do the trick, which is far from accurate. Therefore, I primarily use "hard of hearing" only when I'm worried about not being "deaf enough" to use "Deaf." Because my hearing falls short of a profound ninety decibels, some might argue that the severe loss isn't diagnostically deaf, making me feel like I have to watch my step with my own identity.

Bill elbows his wife. "Saying 'impaired' isn't P.C. these days."

"I'm so sorry," Susan says. "Do you wear hearing aids?"

My hair is frizzy from the lake, down and spilling over my shoulders. I push it back after setting my fork down on my plate, turning my head to show both my hearing aids.

"Look, they're purple," Susan says. "How fun, hiding behind all that gorgeous hair. I never would've guessed since you're so pretty."

"How long have you had them?" Bill asks.

"Um, since I was a baby."

"You like them?" he asks. "They work well? One of my buddies needs to get a pair, but he keeps dragging his feet on going to the doctor."

"Audiologist," I mumble.

"What was that?" Bill asks.

"Audiologist," I repeat.

"Right, that's the one." He chuckles. "Maybe I need my hearing checked, too. As I always tell my grandson, he shouldn't listen to music that loud on those big headphones of his or he'll regret it later in life." Bill takes another large bite to finish off his hot dog.

Bill doesn't realize he just said that he doesn't want his grandson to become someone like me.

"Do you use other resources?" Susan asks. "Do you lip-read?"

Uh, yeah, I've already been lip-reading this entire time, but I know exactly what is coming next.

Without making any sound, Susan over-contorts her mouth and slowly asks, *Can . . . you . . . read . . . my . . . lips?*

I give a polite nod and take another bite of my food, large enough that I won't be expected to speak. Can Mackenzie jump back in already? Unfortunately, she's already been roped into conversation with other donors who need her to interpret so they can talk to Honey.

"So, seventeen," Bill says. "That must make you almost done with high school. Thinking of going to college?"

"I'm going into my senior year. Still figuring out places to apply to, but I've got a couple schools on my list." Never mind the fact that, with my current grades, some of those places might be a stretch.

"Good, very good," he says. "Go to college."

"Yes," Susan chimes in. "You're so well-spoken. I'm sure you'll do very well."

"Well-spoken?" I repeat. I hate what she's implying. Susan gets fidgety, trying to come up with a response.

"Yes, well, I mean, look at you!" she says cheerfully. "One might not even know you were deaf at all. You certainly don't sound it. College won't be hard for you."

This woman knows nothing about me yet feels perfectly fine making and voicing this assumption. She thinks I'm intelligent because I talk clearly?

"I have school accommodations that I'll continue to use in college." I stand with my plate. "Um, Ethan waved to me. I have to go help with something," I lie, needing to blow off some steam.

"Yes, no problem," Bill says. "Great to meet you. I'm sorry, I don't believe we caught your name."

"Lilah."

"So great to meet you, Lilah," Susan says. "We keep all those who suffer from disabilities in our prayers."

Now I'm walking away, fuming. I've gotten "well-spoken" many times throughout my life. It's meant as a compliment, but what they mean is that because I'm "well-spoken," I don't sound deaf, and therefore I don't sound dumb. It's not long ago that "deaf and dumb" was the actual label. The incorrect assumption that those who use a visual form of communication aren't as intelligent. A driving force behind oralism and audism. It's absurd and plain wrong.

Plus, I'm not always "well-spoken." I mumble without realizing it . . . a lot. Hearies expected me to do the years of speech therapy it took to get to where I am today. They don't know how much it takes to seem like a "normal" hearing person. My brain has to work overtime and process so much just to have a "normal" conversation. Yet I do all this, and they rarely provide accommodations, even when such measures could often benefit everyone.

The fact of the matter is, I have a significant hearing loss. One that impacts my life, no matter how well adjusted I've worked to be. It's not on par with someone who has lost a few decibels to loud music. By telling me I seem "normal," they're not only shrugging off my disability but telling me I don't fit their lowered expectations of people with disabilities. I find no pride in that.

I hurry over to Ethan and lean on his left shoulder. "Hey, wanna come here for a second?"

Ethan appears relieved to be rescued. As he stands, he sees the look on my face, which apparently needs no explanation. He takes a deep breath. "*Good food, right?*"

"*Good food,*" I sign.

We walk over to the counter, where Ethan helps himself to another french fry. Now that we're farther away, I'm ready to complain. "This lunch is going to be the only one this summer, right?"

Ethan sighs again, but shakes his head and holds up a hand, indicating that I should stop. "I know. Trust me, I know," he says. "And hopefully it is the last event, but we'll have to see how it goes."

"I feel like I have to put on a show. Perform my disability for charity."

"*Did you like coming here as a camper?*" he asks.

"*Yeah . . .* "

"*Do you want to keep this place going for all the other kids?*"

"*Yes, I do.*"

He takes a deep breath, lowering his voice and turning out to look at the lake. I follow to read his lips. "Then let's think twice before we insult the people who could sign the checks and make this place possible."

~~~

At the end of the day back at the cabins, I'm still dreading my Friday evening shift with Isaac. I've been in a funk all day, worried about the future of Gray Wolf and nervous about my situation with Isaac. Why did I have to tell him I like him? If I hadn't, tonight would've been a great time to hang out and relax and forget how stressful lunch was. But instead . . . I have no idea what to expect.
~~~

Plus, the girls were arguing all day. Blake has toned it down, but not enough. Every time it seems the tension has dissipated, something sparks it anew. And even though I'm communicating solidly with our signing campers, Mackenzie keeps unnecessarily stepping over me to interpret.

"I'll let you know when I need your help," I tell her, having already signed back to Honey that she can use her flashlight to read in bed for a few minutes. Cabin bedtime is a lot of work each day, without Mackenzie constantly on my case.

"Well, I have to make sure," Mackenzie says.

I shake my head but glance down at my watch. It's already 9:20 p.m., and my shift starts in ten minutes. "Ugh, do I have time to shower?" I ask myself out loud, feeling grimy and exhausted but in no mood to rush.

"I don't know. You have to make sure you're on duty right on time," Mackenzie chimes in.

Ignoring her, I rush to grab my bath towel, fresh clothes, and toiletries from my bunk. It's not the end of the world if I'm a few minutes late to the firepit or staff cabin, since most of the other off-duty counselors are still around right now. They can help if campers need anything urgent. In my flip-flops, I walk as fast as I safely can over the uneven dirt to the bathhouse.

The lights are dim and flickering. It makes me miss my camper days when a counselor would be sitting in the entryway on the plastic chair waiting for everyone to be done. It's eerie being here alone. But even this is less terrifying than the idea of sitting at the firepit with Isaac again.

I hang my towel and pull back the plastic curtain to one of the shower stalls. I keep my flip-flops on while I undress so I don't step on this nasty floor. Maybe if the campgrounds had nicer showers, we'd be less inclined to call a dip in the lake or the pool a good-enough wash. After putting my clothes and towel on the hook and hanging my toiletry bucket over the rail, I turn on the water. I'm moving as fast as I can, but time is slipping away. My watch already says 9:28 p.m. There are two minutes until the start of my shift.

I step into the stream of water, but the pressure is so terrible I can hear it spurting out in bursts. I push my hair back so I can get the front wet.

Wait. *I can hear it spurting in bursts.* Why can I hear it? I move my hands from the front of my head down to my ears . . . and find that I still have my hearing aids in.

"Shit." I step away from the water, coming dangerously close to the gross wall. "Shit," I say again. How did I forget to take them out?

I stop the shower. I didn't bring my Dry & Store. It's a little gray dehumidifier box that needs to be plugged into the wall, which I thought would be too much work. Maybe Ethan has his?

I'm still dripping as I throw on the clothes I'd been wearing before, rather than my pajamas. I dry my hearing aids with my towel, leaving my things behind as I race back to the cabins.

The small campfire is already burning bright. As I rush past, Isaac waves at me. He's already changed into flannel checkered pajama pants with a gray Yosemite hoodie.

"*Hey, I want to talk to you,*" he signs, but I keep walking. "*You okay?*" he asks.

"I—" I cup my hearing aids in one hand and show him. "*Where's Ethan?*"

Isaac is confused but points to the staff cabin. I hurry away and find Ethan crashed on a pile of spare mattresses in the corner of the room.

"What's up?" he asks, immediately sitting up. "Is everyone okay?"

I hold out my hearing aids. "Do you have your Dry & Store?"

He does. Ethan takes the devices so they can dry in his cabin for the night and be back to working condition by morning.

I rush back to the bathhouse, take the fastest shower of my entire life, drop my things off in my cabin, and finally, more than fifteen minutes late, make my way to the campfire for my shift.

Isaac has pulled the bench close to the flames and is poking the logs with a long stick. He doesn't look up when I take a seat across from him. I shouldn't have panicked so much over my hearing aids earlier. They've gotten wet before and turned out fine. I'd give anything to go back and respond differently when Isaac told me he wanted to chat. Maybe I was just trying to avoid him again in case I didn't like what he had to share. But it could have been something good. Or something completely meaningless about our shift.

We sit ten feet apart across the firepit, ignoring each other's presence, until he finally looks up. "*Okay?*"

I nod.

"*Your hearing aids?*"

"*They'll be fine now.*"

He looks away. What did he want to talk to me about? There's no way I'm asking him, so I guess I'll never know.

It dawns on me how much effort Isaac's been putting into communicating with me this summer, from day one. It must not have been easy for him. But now my ASL skills are better, and somehow, Isaac and I are here, not communicating.

This is awkward as hell, but maybe I'll find some way to break the ice.

I wave toward him again. "*Nice fire. Did you—*" He signs again to cut me off before I can ask if he built it himself.

"*Sorry. I'm tired.*" He leans back against the picnic table, then pulls a Nintendo Switch out of his backpack and a Fruit Roll-Up from his stash.

"Oh, okay," I say to myself, burying my face in my phone.

But when Jaden shows up a few minutes later, Isaac suddenly decides he's in a chatty mood after all—just not with me. I marvel as his hands fly at true speed.

I stand to leave, wanting to spend the rest of my shift somewhere else, but Jaden waves for my attention. "*Hey, you can stay with us. You and I haven't chatted much.*"

I can't tell from the embarrassment on Isaac's face whether he's told his friends about last night yet or if this interruption is a coincidence.

"*If she wants to go ———,*" Isaac signs.

"*That's okay,*" I sign to Jaden. "*Thanks, but maybe later.*"

Most everyone else is chilling in the staff cabin for the evening, except Mackenzie, who probably went to bed early. Ethan and Gary are at a square folding table in the corner going over some paperwork. On the two extra chairs next to them are stacks of pizza.

"Ooh, nice. Much better in here," I say, helping myself to a spare slice and sitting on the floor beside Simone.

She asks something, but I motion that I don't have my hearing aids in, so she repeats louder, "Awkward?"

"Yeah," I say. She knows exactly who I'm hiding from.

Bobby's lying in one of the spare bunks. "All right, let's get a game going or something."

"Sure, what do we got?" I take a bite of my pizza.

But Natasha, sitting against the opposite wall, waves toward me. "*Is Isaac out there?*"

I nod.

"*Why are you in here?*" She narrows her eyebrows in question.

Okay, Isaac . . . just how much did you tell your friends? And I thought this couldn't get any worse. I guess news spreads quickly among a small summer camp staff.

"*He doesn't want me there.*" I turn back to Simone, not wanting to answer any more pestering questions, but the next thing I know, Natasha is standing in front of me, offering her hand to help me up.

"*Come on, let's bring out the pizza,*" Natasha signs, looking in the direction of the campfire.

"*Really?*" I ask. "*It's awkward.*"

"*You're fine; come on.*" She picks up the pepperoni box. "Take cheese," she says and signs. "Isaac doesn't like pepperoni."

I drag my feet but follow her out of the cabin. But on the way to the firepit, I see a camper walking away from their cabin. It's too late for them to be out and about.

"I need to check if that girl's okay," I tell Natasha, gesturing in that direction. "But I promise I'll meet you in a few. Really, I promise."

Natasha looks doubtful but signs, "*Sure, that's fine.*"

I hurry away for my on-duty responsibilities. Natasha can join her friends in the meantime, and they can all hang out without me slowing things down or making it awkward.

The girl is Phoebe, one of Simone's blind campers—the one who's a year younger than me. She's walking swiftly, cane outstretched. Her hair is still in a smooth middle-part low ponytail, but she's abandoned her no-nonsense sunglasses.

"Are you all good? I'm coming up to you now." I give her a heads-up but don't hear what she starts to say, so I call out, "Sorry, I don't have my hearing aids in right now. One second." I get to her side where I'll be able to lip-read what she's saying. "Hey, it's Lilah. Sorry, I should be able to hear you somewhat now. What's up?"

"Uh, okay." She hesitates, but when she speaks again, it's practically a whisper. She's barely moving her lips.

"I'm sorry, can you speak up a little?"

"I'm just going to the bathroom," she shouts, her patience wearing thin.

"Yes, of course! My bad. I should have guessed. Do you need any help? I know the path dips a bit up ahead."

"Nah, I'm good. It's in the same place it's been for the last ten years I've been here, so . . ."

"Of course. You're Phoebe, right?"

"Yeah," she answers loudly. "And I did call out to see if anyone was around, but then I figured I'd just go to the dang bathroom. You know, wander in that direction and eventually someone would find my body."

"That's dark." My eyes go wide, but I'm amused.

"I know." She chuckles nervously to make sure I understand it's a joke.

"Well, I don't want to keep you. If you do need anything, feel free to shout as loud as you want. I promise, there are a few people who will hear you and wake up."

Phoebe sniffs the air. "Is that pizza?"

I look down at the box I'm holding. "Um, yes. But aren't you on the way to the bathroom?"

"Yeah, yeah. I also don't want to go to sleep. Nine o'clock is too early of a bedtime."

"Maybe we'll get you permission to stay up late one night."

"Lilah, you're basically my age. Stop sounding like an awkward adult."

"Ha. Sorry, most of the campers I talk to are the little girls." I look at the distance toward the bathhouse. "Do you need any help the rest of the way?"

"Nah, I'm good," Phoebe says, but she doesn't move yet. "So hey, do you like being a junior counselor? I want to be one next year."

"Oh yeah? You'd love it."

"How do you know? You don't know me," she teases.

"And you don't know me. Maybe I'll murder you in your sleep." Shit, I might've matched her dark humor with a little too much severity. I can't read her face right now; she's so serious. Just because I can speak to her like a peer doesn't mean we're familiar enough to goof like this.

I'm about to apologize for the joke when Phoebe bursts out laughing.

"Guess I wouldn't see it coming. Or I'll get you first, since you wouldn't hear it coming."

"Ah, touché." I like this girl. Maybe we would be friends if I hadn't missed the last few years of camp. "All right, I'll catch you later."

The campfire is about a third of a soccer field away where Natasha is pushing Isaac to stand, nodding in my direction.

He realizes I'm there with a camper and jogs over. I walk toward him as Phoebe goes on her way without me.

"*Is she okay?*" he asks me.

I glance back, watching her walk into the bathhouse, and nod. "*Yeah, just a bathroom trip.*"

He nods back to the campfire. "*We've got pizza.*"

"*I know,*" I sign, holding up my own box.

"*Right.*" He runs a hand through his dark hair and avoids looking straight at me when he signs, "*My friends want you to come sit with us.*"

"Do you"—I say and sign one-handed—"want me to?"

No hearing boy would stare at your lips this much unless they were about to kiss you. But Isaac is just watching what I'm saying.

"*Yes.*" He nods nervously. "*Yes, I want you to sit with us.*"

I smile. That's a good sign.

"*Okay, I'll be there soon.*"

~~~

Phoebe makes it back to her cabin. None of the other campers emerge tonight, but fortunately, I don't even need excuses to get away from the campfire, because I'm holding my own.

Natasha and Jaden carry the bulk of the conversation, but I follow along all right, still worried about slowing things down by chiming in. But whenever I get lost, Isaac seems to intuitively know. He lifts a single finger to the side of his head, flicking it up once while raising his eyebrows in question. "*Understand?*"

If I nod, he smiles and jumps right back into the conversation without missing a beat.
~~~

If I furrow my brow and shake my head, he backtracks and figures out what I missed. "———, *water m-e-l-o-n, you know, red, green fruit? Watermelon. Jaden and I played baseball with a big, round one. I threw it high, and Jaden hit it.*" Isaac turns his shoulders, role shifting to demonstrate Jaden's actions, holding his hands overhead and mimicking a sword. "*Whoosh, sliced right through.*" With increasingly animated movements, incorporating more and more ASL grammar, Isaac demonstrates the watermelon exploding, over both him and Jaden, chunks sticking to their hair and juice running down their faces.

"*Really?*" I laugh. "*Are you serious?*"

"*True business, that really happened.*"

I stare across the fire, watching his eyes crinkle as he grins. It almost feels like the beginning of summer again, before I went and made everything awkward between us.

CHAPTER FIFTEEN

The campers are excited for tonight's dance—the first one of the summer—and the counselors are eager for a staff outing that will follow. Gary and the nurse will stay on-site while the rest of the staff gets Saturday night off. It'll be our first long break after two weeks with the campers. All conversations during the day revolve around plans for the evening.

Before lunch, our cabin tries to decide what song to perform for the talent show, which is happening before the dance. And by "decide," I mean bicker. Although we're all wearing matching friendship bracelets, we haven't achieved group unity yet. The girls are zoning in on one pop hit, but Blake has yet to relent.

"I don't want to sign anyway," she complains.

"If you don't want to, then why does it matter what they pick?" I ask.

"Fine." She crosses her arms and lies back on the grass while the rest of the girls practice together in a circle. But I notice Blake is singing along to the loud music, just refusing to move her hands.

I nudge her. "Hey, try it with me. I still have to learn a lot of the words, too."

"I don't want to."

"Okay, well, what else are you going to do?"

"What do you mean?" She sits up.

"Well, we're all going to be signing this song. So, are you going to dance? Sing out loud? Or fall asleep on the stage?"

Blake makes a face. "Why would I do that?"

"You're falling asleep now, aren't you?" I smile, trying to coax her into lightening up. "Come on, try signing with me. We can make mistakes together!"

"Fine, only because you're being so annoying about it." Blake follows along with the other girls but quickly grows frustrated and stops.

"*Maybe she's not smart,*" Honey signs, giggling with another camper.

"Hey!" Mackenzie says and signs, waving toward Honey. "*Don't say mean things.*"

"What'd she say?" Blake asks.

I shake my head, nonchalant. "Nothing, really."

"*I want to play my favorite game now,*" Honey signs. She turns to the side to mimic a second player. "*Honey, if you love me,*" she signs back in the direction where she'd been standing, then turns back around to embody herself again. "*I love you all.*" She blows kisses to the other girls.

"We can do that game if we have time before lunch after finishing this song," Mackenzie says and signs.

"It's okay," I tell Blake, who looks lost. "If you really don't want to, you don't have to."

All of this is really her choice to make, but she has a new resolve, perhaps feeling left out. Honey has been a popular leader in the group, and Blake might be growing tired of going against the grain. "No, I'm going to do this."

We slow down and start back at the top, and Blake makes a sincere attempt. So this time, when Blake messes up a sign, Honey leans forward and repeats it, slowly. Blake rolls her eyes but follows along, and Honey confirms that Blake has done it correctly. They're . . . not fighting? Where did this progress come from? I don't know, but I'll take it. That's the most these two have worked together all summer.

~

I'm picking off the burnt edges of my grilled cheese, not feeling lunch, when Ethan taps me on the shoulder. "Grab your stuff and pretend to go to the bathroom—but meet me outside."

What in the world?

Ethan is whispering to Simone now, too. I take a final bite, grab my backpack, and leave my food behind. If I had randomly left the table earlier in the summer, Blake would have immediately noticed my absence. But today, she actually took a seat between two of her fellow campers rather than by my side.

I walk past the single-stall dining hall bathroom and head out the side door. I sneak around to the front, ducking low to avoid the windows. Isaac and Bobby are waiting a short distance from the entrance. Simone and Ethan are close behind me.

No one seems too concerned, so I figure this isn't an emergency. "What's up?" I say and sign.

"All right, that's everyone," Ethan says and signs. "I've come up with a new game: Counselor Search. Basically, a large-scale hide-and-seek."

"Hide-and-seek?" I ask. That brings back memories of sitting in a closet or hiding behind a curtain at my grandmother's house.

"Trust me, the kids are gonna love it," Ethan continues. "You four go anywhere on the campgrounds. After lunch, I'll send the campers to try to find you. They'll search together in groups with the remaining counselors. So keep your phones on you, in case the game ends and you're still hiding." He looks down at his watch. "You've got about ten minutes to get settled, so . . . good luck!" Ethan shoos us away, signaling that we're supposed to hurry to a hiding place now.

Bobby follows the path and ducks into the nearby dance barn. Simone runs for the pool. Isaac yanks off his baseball cap, holding it to his chest and sprinting in the direction of the cabins. So I guess I'll go toward the lake?

But where am I going to hide? Maybe behind a canoe? But that's past the sectioned-off part of the lake, and I don't see Oliver or Ben anywhere, so the campers wouldn't be allowed to search down here anyway. There isn't much else, except for the picnic tables, which don't offer enough cover.

I head back over the bridge, pausing to catch my breath. These places are too spread out. The campers are probably starting the game any minute now.

At the base of the bridge is a giant, hollow tree trunk, whose opening faces away from the path. What kind of bugs and critters have made this space their home? I'd likely be able to peek out to see if anyone is heading this way and remain hidden enough to evade notice when the campers reach the lake. So I detour a few feet off the path and around to the other side of the tree trunk. But when I stick my head in, someone stares back at me.

"Aaah!" I scream, and Isaac lets out a surprised gasp.

"*Shh.*" He jumps up and grabs my shoulders.

My heart is still threatening to explode, so I put a hand to my chest and take several slow breaths. "*You scared me!*"

"*You scared me!*" he signs, checking his watch and crouching back into the tree trunk.

I have no idea where else to hide. But when I step away, Isaac leans forward, beckoning me to join him.

"This might be a tight squeeze," I say to myself.

Isaac crouches and sits against the trunk, knees pulled to his chest. I follow suit and clutch my backpack in my lap, to make sure the straps aren't visible and giving away our hiding place. There's just enough room for us to sit side by side, but even then, he has to hunch forward. I wish I'd worn leggings instead of shorts today, knowing that I'm dooming myself to a million bug bites.

"*Fun new game,*" Isaac signs, barely able to turn and face me since our shoulders are wedged together.

I nod, unsure how much chatting we'll do. Last night around the campfire was actually decent, so we've made progress.

Sitting here together in the tree, Isaac reaches for his pocket, putting his hat back on and scrolling through his phone. I guess we're not talking now. I try to think of anything other than *does he like me or does he not?*

Then my backpack buzzes. I'm careful to avoid elbowing Isaac as I reach to unzip my bag and get my phone.

Sure enough, I have a text—my very first one ever—from Isaac.

Isaac: So . . . Why'd you try to steal my spot?

His eyebrows are narrowed in an amused way. I tilt my head, but he points to my phone.

Lilah: I clearly did not know you were here because you scared the crap out of me!

Isaac: You're not supposed to scream during hide-and-seek. I think that gives away the hiding spot . . .

Lilah: Good thing probably no one heard me :)
My heart is still racing so fast from all that running.

Isaac: Whoops sorry

He nudges my shoulder as an apology, which certainly doesn't help the situation. The campers better find us before I die in this tree.

This feels like the point where our conversations up until now have tended to fizzle out. I'm nervous and unsure of what to say next. Even though we barely know each other, I feel like I've known him forever.

I haven't responded to Isaac's last text, so he drops his phone on his lap. I'm going to make more of an effort here.

Lilah: So . . . dogs or cats?

Isaac grabs his phone so fast. I turn to hide my obvious smile.

Isaac: Hmm

Lilah: Obviously dogs

Isaac: Wrong, the answer is cats

He includes a GIF of a cat waving hello with its paw.

Isaac: Favorite candy? Can't beat M&M'S

Lilah: Except with strawberry cheesecake jelly beans

Isaac: Cheesecake jelly beans?

Lilah: Don't knock it till you try it

Isaac: All right, favorite vacation?

Lilah: Hmm I like road trips

Isaac: Me too! Especially hiking at national parks

Lilah: Hence that Yosemite hoodie you have

He nods several times and turns to me. "*My favorite one.*"

Lilah: Okay, favorite color?

Isaac: Green. And yours is purple.

He looks up and points to my hearing aids, purple hair tie, and several of the bracelets on my wrist.

My hand shakes as I sign, "*See, you do know me . . .* "

I quickly second-guess myself. Why did I reference that night? But . . . is that a faint blush rising on his cheeks? He looks away from my eyes and buries his face in his phone to type something else. I'm somewhat relieved when it's just another question.

Isaac: Now the most important: Cubs or Sox?

Lilah: Go Cubs go

Isaac: Whew, we couldn't share this tree otherwise

Lilah: But that's not a Cubs hat?

I point to the baseball cap he's wearing, which despite being the same blue color, has a cursive *L* on the front, rather than a *C*. I've been curious about it all summer.

Isaac: My Dominican team, los Tigres del Licey. I go to games when I visit my grandparents.

Lilah: Very cool. You know Spanish?

Isaac: Trilingual, what up

So he lip-reads not only one spoken language but two. Meanwhile, I opted out of foreign-language classes because the listening components proved impossible. I'm impressed and must be staring at him in amazement because he nods to ask "What?"

Lilah: Dang you're so smart. Yet we're here texting because I'm not good enough at sign yet.

Isaac: You're picking it up fast! Sometimes it helps to have a break

Lilah: Yeah but I feel like I should already be fluent and it really bothers me that I'm not

Isaac: Even in the beginning you were already signing with me. So many people I know at school don't even bother to try, they just talk to me by writing.

Lilah: Which is what we're doing right now . . .

Isaac drops his phone to his lap again and grins. "*Okay, let's sign. What's up?*"

"Eek," I say, dropping my phone as well. Okay, but what to sign? "*We are in a tree.*"

"*Big tree,*" he signs, blowing out his cheeks to denote size. "*We are ——— in a big tree.*"

I shake my head. Wait, didn't Ethan just use that one? If I had to guess . . . "*H-i-d—*"

He nods immediately before I can even finish the word. "*H-i-d-i-n-g, hiding.*"

"*We are hiding in a big tree,*" I sign. He's signing English for my benefit, but I appreciate him shifting methods with ease. "*Lots of bugs.*"

"*Perfect for you, Bug.*" He smiles, using my sign name.

"*Not perfect if they bite me.*"

"*Need bug spray?*"

"*No, no.*" I mimic spraying a canister, then hold my hands out to gesture the puffs of aerosol going into our faces in this small space. I briefly close my eyes and stick out my tongue dramatically while signing "*Dead.*"

Isaac laughs—a wonderful, quiet laugh, where his mouth transforms into a smile as his chest rises and falls. "*Okay, no bug spray. Are you ready for the break tonight?*"

"*Yeah, the restaurant.*" I make the sign, but I'm unsure if I got it right, so I spell out "*R-e-s-t-a-u-r-a-n-t.*"

He furrows his eyebrows and shakes his head.

"*Wrong sign?*" I ask, confused.

Isaac waves his hand to clarify. "*That's the right sign, restaurant. But F-r-e-d-d-y-s is not really a restaurant.*" He chuckles.

"Oh," I say. "*What is it?*"

Isaac starts to sign an explanation when two girls run off the path and stop directly in front of our tree.

It's Blake and Honey. They're shoving each other, but then Honey points at us.

"I found them!" Blake shouts at the top of her lungs.

Honey reads her lips and shoves Blake again. "*No, I found them.*"

"Hey, everyone, I found Lilah and Isaac!" Blake shouts again. "Points for our cabin!"

"*We get points for our cabin!*" Honey signs. The two enthusiastically run back together to the rest of the group.

Isaac crawls out of the tree and offers his hand to help me up. I brush off the dirt and notice several red welts on my legs. The bugs got me good.

Isaac notices. "*New reason for your sign name.*"

"*H-a h-a,*" I sign as he reaches down to brush some dirt off the backs of my calves. I . . . have not been shaving my legs while at camp, but he doesn't seem bothered.

"*There, all good,*" he signs.

"*Thank you.*"

~

After dinner, we're given time to get ready for the talent show and dance. Our younger girls don't spend too much time dressing up, so we get to the barn early and hang out on the steps. But then some of them decide they want their hair braided, so Mackenzie and I get to work.

"Have you seen Gary at all today?" Mackenzie asks as I reach out to ask a camper for her hair tie to finish off her braid.

"No, I haven't. Why?"

"I overheard him telling Ethan something about donations."

"Huh, we'll have to ask about that later tonight."

Twenty minutes later, Bobby's, Simone's, and Natasha's groups all arrive and head into the dance barn, and Bobby gets to work connecting his phone to play his carefully crafted playlist for the dance.

With the campers' hair done, Mackenzie finishes up her own pigtails. "Want me to do yours, too?"

"Um," I say. "Maybe a half-up, half-down situation?"

"Sure," Mackenzie agrees. "That'll be easy enough."

Jaden's and Isaac's groups are the last to show up. The boys run inside, hoping to influence Bobby's music selection.

Isaac stops on the way up the stairs, watching Mackenzie playing stylist on me. He takes a step back down. "*It looks pretty.*"

"*Thanks.*" I can't hide my face because Mackenzie still has a tight hold on my head. Bobby starts playing some pre-show tunes, and the wooden planks vibrate beneath me.

Isaac takes a seat on the step below me and flashes a smile over his shoulder. "*One, please.*"

He leans back, sitting between my legs so I can grab some hair from the crown of his head. There's enough that I'm able to twist it into a ridiculous little braid that sticks straight up. I pull a spare purple hairband off my wrist and secure it around this absurd updo.

I tap his shoulder. "*All done.*"

Isaac reaches up, then shakes his head from side to side. "*Silly. All right, time to dance!*"

Mackenzie and I laugh as Isaac hops up and heads inside. Once my own braid is complete, we gather our girls into the dance barn. All the campers take a seat, either on the floor or in the few chairs along the wall, for the evening to start with the talent show.

Our group's performance goes surprisingly well. Blake sways along to the music during the verses, but signs the refrain without missing a beat. As we walk back to our seats, she keeps signing the refrain, and Honey joins in. Who would've thought?

Loud, joyful shouts accompany signed applause to fill the gaps between the routines that follow. There's a comedy skit, a couple of dance numbers, and an ASL story, and by the end, the campers are all amped-up.

The show ends with the senior counselors dancing to a song—which they do every year. The lights are dimmed, signaling the final performance of the night. As the staff dance their way to the front, I'm happy to lean on the "junior" part of my role and stay seated with the kids. But Isaac stops in front of me, continuing his goofy dancing with his hand outstretched.

The girls from my cabin are laughing. "Go, Lilah," Blake says, pushing me forward.

Fine. I take Isaac's hand, and we fly onto the stage, jumping and dancing around as Ethan gestures for the campers to hit the dance floor. Simone hands out dollar store glow sticks for everyone to wear around their wrists as they dance or sign along. The moving lights are dazzling, but this is no rave. It's fewer than forty people in a barn that could easily hold three hundred.

Isaac spins me around and twirls me back toward him. Simone holds out green and purple glow sticks for us.

He grabs my hand again, pulling me close and dipping me backward, my hair hanging down over my shoulders. It's summer camp. I'm literally wearing gym shoes and a tank top, but somehow, I feel fancy. I'm sure Isaac and I will have to pull away at some point. But I don't want to. I want to hold on to him tight and never let go . . .

Until my right hearing aid beeps and goes staticky, blurring out the music around me. With the right one gone, the left will soon follow. I stop moving and step back from Isaac, who also freezes, confused. I pull out my right hearing aid and hold it up before running off toward my backpack.

Sure enough, the left hearing aid also beeps. I shove around everything in my bag, unable to find a pack of batteries. Sometime last week I used the remaining ones, and I never got replacements from my suitcase. I don't want to go all the way back to the cabins right now. I could ask if anyone has spare batteries, but everyone's having a great time on the dance floor.

Then it hits me. I go without my hearing aids often lately, every day at the lake or the pool. Or last night around the campfire with Isaac, Natasha, and Jaden. I'm surrounded by Deaf people. If there's ever a place I should feel comfortable going without my hearing aids, it's here. Plus, Isaac is waiting for me on the dance floor.

I pull out my left hearing aid as well and toss them both into the Otterbox. The music is blaring so loud I'm still able to hear the beat.

While I can tell there's a song playing, what I hear is more subdued, faded. Some of the melody, none of the words. My brain is no longer trying hard to search for the lyrics. I'm embracing the beat, which, amplified by the movement of people around me, shakes the floor beneath my feet.

Despite my hurrying back to the dance area, Isaac has been pulled into a circle with a bunch of campers, so I find a spot next to my cabin group. Honey signs something to Mackenzie, who then signs to me, "*Some of the girls need to go to the bathroom. We'll be right back.*"

We communicate despite the loud environment, with no leaning forward, no asking "what," and no hearing aids. To some degree, going without them is a vulnerable experience, but it's also liberating.

Someone taps my shoulder. It's Isaac. He's taken his ridiculous braid down, but I notice he's slipped my purple hair tie around his wrist with his camp bracelets. He reaches for my hand and pulls me close once more. He nods back toward my backpack. "*Okay?*" he asks one-handed.

I turn my head side to side to demonstrate.

He tilts his head, confused. "*You took them out?*"

I nod, unsure what his reaction will be. "*For now.*"

Isaac reaches up and brushes my hair back behind my unencumbered ears.

"I feel strange without them," I say slowly, staring into his dark eyes.

He lets his hand linger at my neck for a moment before bringing it back to his chest to sign with a small shrug, "*Just different.*"

The tempo drops because, of course, Bobby stuck a slow song into the mix. Isaac reaches his arms out to me. I crash forward into his chest for a tight hug. This ballad has less of a beat. The ground beneath my feet is steady, but I lean against Isaac and feel his heart race.

He has me so confused. Would it be too much for him to admit if he likes me or not? This is totally a romantic moment, right? There's no way I'm misinterpreting this. Is it really that hard for him to communicate his feelings? Or at least stop toying with mine?

I'm so absorbed in the moment that it's startling to realize some kids are watching us. No one else is dancing to the song. But my arms are around Isaac's neck, and his hand is resting on my back. I'm not going to let anything ruin this moment.

But of course the next song on the playlist is the chicken dance.

We're immediately torn apart by our attention-seeking campers, while Bobby laughs about his song selection. *Great.*

Isaac gives a wide apologetic smile. "*See you after hours?*"

If nothing else comes of this time with Isaac, at least this will still be a summer to remember.

CHAPTER SIXTEEN

Back at the cabin shortly after the dance, the campers are so exhausted that they crash into bed immediately at curfew. I stifle a yawn myself, but I'm reenergized as soon as I change out of worn-out athletic gear and into nicer shorts and a real bra (outside-world clothes). I wear my hair down, tucking the sides back with bobby pins. And finally, I do my face with light makeup, the usual for a typical day out with friends, much more put together than my standard camp fare.

Ethan catches me on my way back from the bathhouse. "Where ———?"

"Sorry, I don't," I say, pointing to my ears.

"Oh, you don't have your hearing aids in," he says and signs. "Did you get my text?"

"Not yet, my phone is in my bunk."

"All right, we're meeting in the parking lot in ten minutes."

Mackenzie's already dressed and on her way out. I grab my phone to read Ethan's text to all the counselors and hurry so I can catch up.

Ethan: Heeeey everybody, meet in the parking lot for another camp tradition

Jaden: FREDDDDDDDDDDDDDDDDYS

I text Simone as I leave the cabin.

Lilah: Hey Simone, what's all the hype about Freddy's?

Simone: It's a bar down the road. Cheap beer, decent food, the owner loves when counselors come to visit.

Lilah: Oh . . . I'm not twenty-one

Simone: Nah this place won't care, you're good

I've never been to this kind of bar before. At least I'm not the only one underage.

All the counselors stand around the parking lot waiting for Ethan to confirm that Gary and the nurse are all set for duty tonight.

It's jarring to see Isaac with his hair combed back and a casual short-sleeved button-down. But it confirms for me that I'm not seeing him through "camp goggles"—this guy is attractive. I hide my smirk when I catch him giving me a double glance as well.

Ethan finally strolls over and unlocks the camp's twelve-seater van. He takes the driver's seat and turns around to look at us. "Everybody, click in," he says and signs. He turns on the ignition and the radio blares.

I'm squished in the very back between Simone and Bobby. The van bumps along the rough gravel road. I reach out and hold on to the seat in front of me. As Ethan drives, he makes conversation with Natasha in the passenger seat, signing with one hand and looking to his right. Which feels safer than when he signs with Isaac and Jaden using the rearview mirror. But Ethan doesn't swerve a single time on the quiet country road, and we make it to the bar in one piece.

Ethan pulls into a dimly lit lot that's in the middle of nowhere. There's a small brick building, no larger than our dining hall, with nothing else around but trees. Yet a few other cars are in the parking lot.

Simone is visibly relieved when we tumble out of the van. "Thank God ——— any oncoming traffic," she says loudly.

"Maybe I'll drive home," Bobby suggests. "With you guiding me."

She grabs his arm and leads him into the bar through a doorway that's propped open with a brick. A tilted neon sign hanging in the grimy window says FREDDY'S.

I follow everyone into the establishment, wanting to catch up to Isaac, who's at the front of our group with his friends. This place is quiet. There's a bartender, who looks like she teaches third grade by day, and a small table of men with long white hair, which they've tied back into ponytails beneath their trucker hats. On his way to get another drink, one of the guys stops near us at the bar and says something to Mackenzie.

But Mackenzie shakes her head and signs, "*No, I'm okay. Later, man.*"

Does she not realize we're not at camp anymore? Why is she signing to this random guy?

He scrunches up his face, notices everyone in our group is also signing, then shrugs and walks back to his buddies with his drink. Mackenzie lets out a sigh of relief.

"Why'd you do that?" I drag out my sign for the word "why" to emphasize my confusion.

"I've found it's the easiest way to get guys at bars to back off," she explains, obviously proud of her life hack.

But I push back. "How so?"

"They don't think it's worth the effort."

Wow. To Mackenzie, sign language is a skill to get followers on YouTube and use whenever it's convenient for her. She's trying to use it as a deterrent, when in reality a disability doesn't save you from harassment. Rather, it often makes deaf people more of a target for harm or abuse.

There aren't many tables to choose from, so we sit along the sticky bar. The bartender puts three pitchers overflowing with beer in front of us, along with a stack of recently washed cups, not unlike the plastic ones we use at camp, that are still dripping water. Jaden slides the cups across the bar to everyone, but when he gets to me, he signs, "*You drink water.*"

"*Right.*" Even though I wasn't ID'd, I guess we'll still follow the law. Except, Natasha to my right is filling up her glass.

Isaac stops her when pouring his just under the halfway point. "*I have to run tomorrow,*" he signs. They're eighteen. Jaden's only a year older, so nineteen or twenty at most.

Ethan walks up to me. "Hey, you're only drinking water, right?"

"Yeah, but . . ." I point, not too obviously, at the others.

"*But they're not the DD,*" he signs.

"You're driving," Natasha says and signs to me, not beating around the bush.

"I'm *driving*?" I ask. "That thing?"

"*I did it last year. You'll be fine.*" She pulls out her wallet and leans across the counter to hand cash to the bartender. "Wings and a giant pretzel, please. Keep the change."

Her wallet is still open, so I spy a card in the clear slot where a driver's license usually goes. It has the word DEAF in big letters.

"*What's that?*" I ask.

She snaps her wallet closed. "*Deaf ID.*" She takes a long sip of her beer and walks away.

"Deaf ID?" I say and sign to Ethan, who steps up to take her spot. "Do you have that?"

"Nah, I use my phone, but some people go old-school."

"Exactly what for?" I ask, signing "*for-for.*"

"Emergency circumstances, like, if you get pulled over while driving, to show the cop why you can't hear them," he says and signs. "It's especially for deaf people who don't use voice."

"Interesting." I sigh. "I feel like I keep needing Natasha to interpret or teach me about Deaf culture. I worry it bothers her."

"Nah, she can be a little rough around the edges. Very Deaf ———. I mean, you can be, too."

"I'm what?" I ask, not recognizing the sign, either.

"Deaf-blunt," Ethan repeats, holding a flat B-shape perpendicular to his face, then pushing it forward. "Speaking your mind or emotions. Very observational comments because we are very observational people."

Huh. I want to be offended, but I'm proud to have a Deaf trait associated with me. "I guess."

"Natasha doesn't really like to voice most of the time." He holds up a finger, pausing his signing and speaking as he takes another sip. "She went through a rough patch a few years ago. Her dad had a heart attack, and she was with him when it happened. He was unconscious. She couldn't communicate well with the paramedics. When they got to the hospital, the video interpreting service they used instead of a physical interpreter was lagging and impossible to use, so she had to write back and forth with nurses to try to find out what was going on. She felt like the hospital staff wasn't updating her because they found it too difficult to share information with her."

"That is frustrating." Despite my own hearing loss, I've never been in a situation quite like that. People tend to work to communicate with me because I speak. In terms of accessibility, I can sympathize, but I also feel guilty about moving through the world more freely.

"And when she was finally allowed to see him, they called for her from the desk, and she didn't hear it. They knew she was deaf, but no one bothered to go and inform her." Ethan frowns.

"Wait, they didn't even try to get her attention or anything?"

"Nope. After waiting a long time, she went up with a note written out on her phone demanding to see him. And, yeah . . . after that she got the cochlear implant."

"I didn't know she got it that recently." I'd assumed she'd had it since childhood, like most of the kids at camp.

"Yeah, her mom helped her, but her dad wasn't happy. Their whole family is Deaf, going back generations. He thought that by getting the surgery she was turning her back on Deaf culture."

"What? I mean, she's still deaf, even with the cochlear." Most hearing parents run to get their babies surgery as soon as they're deemed candidates for the implant. I understand the situation is more complicated with Deaf parents, but Natasha deciding she wanted it doesn't make her any less Deaf. She's in the corner now, sipping her drink and signing one-handed with Isaac and Jaden. No one would mistake her for hearing, especially seeing the magnet on the side of her head.

"Some Deaf don't see it that way," Ethan says and signs. He refills his drink. "They see it as attempting to fix something that isn't broken. They want people in the community to sign, not speak." He takes a long pause. "It took her a while to recover from the surgery. She almost had to repeat a year of school but was able to do enough summer classes to graduate on time."

"Wow," I say. "That's a lot."

I immediately want to take back every time I've been annoyed with Natasha for sticking with signing when she could jump in with voice. If she doesn't want to, she shouldn't ever feel like she has to. She must've been fed up with the world to want surgery against her parents' wishes. I don't know what I would've done in that situation. But I get why she seems annoyed that with the implant, she's expected to be a go-between.

"Yeah, that's why a place like camp is so important—people can find their own Deaf identities." He takes another long gulp of beer and sighs before muttering to himself, "That's why the money ———."

"We still need to raise more money?" I ask.

"*It's fine, it's fine,*" he signs, taking a sip. "Some donations but still a little short. We're working on it." He smiles reassuringly, then wanders off from the bar.

The bar is crowded, but I don't feel my normal urge to leave a social situation early or hide off in a corner. I don't have my hearing aids in to pick up on headache-triggering noises, since the automated devices would be unsure which sounds to zone in on, cutting in and out while focusing on different things around me. Conversing with Ethan was the perfect balance of lipreading, hearing some phrases, and following along with his casual one-handed signing as he held his drink in the other hand. I may actually get through the night without listening fatigue.

But I'm concerned about what Ethan let slip about the camp finances. We don't have enough raised yet to guarantee next year?

While drinking my water, I notice Isaac looking this way. I stand and am about to head over to my dance partner when two guys walk through the door. I wave to the guy in the gray sweater, assuming it's Oliver, but apparently Ben has borrowed the top for the evening. As Ben beelines to the bar to get their drinks, Oliver rushes over to me. "So . . ." The smile grows across his face.

"So . . . I'm so sorry we haven't had the chance to chat yet." I try to project so the music doesn't drown out my voice. "What's up? I hope you're at least having fun hanging out with Ben. Since the two of you are all alone by the lake."

"Well." Oliver smiles, glancing over his shoulder before leaning toward me, keeping his mouth in clear view as he whispers, "It's precisely that."

"It's what?" I'm not following.

"The two of us ———." Oliver leans forward, eagerly awaiting my response.

"Oh? Wait, you mean . . ." I squeal. Despite our somewhat flirty friendship, Oliver and I have remained platonic. But now it's clear that those nights when I hung out at the lake, Ben wasn't the third wheel—I was.

"It's new. Shh." Oliver motions to play it cool as Ben comes over with their drinks.

"——— looks like a party!" Ben calls out. "Can't get a bloody Uber ———."

"We can ——— ride back ———," Simone offers, leaning away from Bobby at the bar to drop in on our conversation. "Lilah's driving."

Bobby, already bored, walks off, unfolding his cane to navigate to the pool table in the dim light.

"When did everyone decide that I'm driving?" I ask. "Seriously, when did I sign up for this?"

"We'll take any lift we can get," Ben shouts over the noise.

Oliver laughs. "We had to call a taxi company to ———."

"Sorry, it's loud in here and hard for me to hear you," I say. "I'm not wearing my hearing aids."

"No worries," Oliver shouts. "When did you get your ———?"

"My . . . period?" I drop my eyebrows, speaking before realizing I clearly misheard him. "Okay, that can't be right."

Oliver chuckles. "Your hearing aids," he says, enunciating carefully.

"Oh, that makes a lot more sense," I say, shaking off my embarrassment. "I got them when I was a baby. The period was many years later."

"I'd hope so," Ben says, chuckling. "How'd they ——— keep them in your ears?"

"I wore a little bonnet thing." I demonstrate tying it. The headpiece kept my baby hands from yanking out the devices.

"That's cute," Oliver says.

"So did you two know each other before camp?" I ask them.

Ben shakes his head.

"But get this," Oliver says. "Turns out we go the same ________."

"The same what?" I ask.

"University," Oliver says, expanding the abbreviation he'd used. He nods toward Ben. "So, has Ben told you that he knows some BSL?"

"________ so really just the alphabet," Ben says, smiling at Oliver's encouragement.

"Really?" I ask.

"Show us!" Simone chimes in.

Before Ben starts signing, out of the corner of my eye I notice Isaac leaning against the bar, gripping his glass tight. He tries to get my attention.

"*Want to play a game?*" Isaac tilts his head to the pool table, where Natasha and Jaden are getting set up.

I nod several times. "*Just a minute!*"

Ben is holding out both hands, demonstrating the British Sign Language alphabet. "*A, B, C . . .* "

"Weird, it uses two hands," I say. "That's different."

I glance over to the pool table, ready to jump up and play as soon as we make it through the alphabet, but Isaac has already recruited another partner: Mackenzie.

Okay, fine. I'll stay over here.

I nod and take another sip of my water. I'm definitely going to end up with a headache if I spend the whole night with no sign language or hearing aids, trying to lip-read foreign accents.

It's quarter to midnight when we finally get ready to leave the bar. I'm exhausted from third-wheeling the Brits. There's only so long you can have an enjoyable chat about American and British differences, especially because what they were saying started to make a lot less sense the drunker they got.

The bartender leans across the counter toward me as she collects my empty water glass. "I'll be praying ———."

"What?" I'm confused. Does she know I'm about to drive that beast of a vehicle outside?

She speaks up. "I'll be praying you all can get your hearing back."

"Back?" I scrunch up my face. "I never had it," I say bluntly.

She looks irritated by my reply, so I'm relieved when Ethan tosses me the keys. "Here you go!"

"*Really?*" I sign.

"*You're fine. It's not far.*"

But it already feels very illegal, since my Illinois driver's license *technically* has a minor curfew of ten o'clock. Yet no one else appears fit to drive, so I have to do this.

To make matters worse, it starts raining as soon as we exit the door. Ethan swings open the back door of the van for everyone to crawl in.

I climb into the driver's seat and try to psych myself up, gripping the steering wheel tight. "Wait, Ethan!" I turn around and flap my arms to get his attention. "I don't have my glasses!"

His eyes go wide. "Shit. Uh, try these." He hands up the pair he's been wearing. They're huge on me, but the prescription seems close enough. And we have no other options.

"Okay, well. Here goes nothing." I turn the key, and the blaring music picks up where it left off.

"Whoooo!" one of the Brits screams.

"Wait, baby Lilah, I'll help you." Bobby makes his way from the back to the passenger seat.

"What are you doing?" I ask, leaving the van in Park until Bobby settles.

"I'll keep watch for deer." He holds his hands to his eyes like binoculars.

"Shut up, Bobby, you're drunk." Is the whole group really this sloshed?

At first, I drive down the road slower than slow, but I pick up the speed when I remember you can also get pulled over for going below the limit. It's dark and there are no streetlights, so I turn on the high beams, growing nervous with every deer-crossing sign I pass. There are so many trees along the road, something could easily jump out from behind them. And I can't figure out the windshield wipers. They either go too fast or too slow for the fluctuating rainfall. I clench my teeth and carefully watch the road. Yet no one in this party bus seems to doubt my ability to get us home.

Somehow, after what feels like an eternity, I manage to get us back to camp in one piece. The rain has subsided into a drizzle. Everyone jumps out of the vehicle. Adrenaline is still coursing through me as I toss the keys and glasses back to Ethan and climb out of the van. "Never again."

"You did it!" Oliver cheers, wrapping me in a big hug and lifting me off the ground.

"You didn't kill us!" Ben adds.

Oliver puts me down and gives a theatrical bow. "We owe you a debt of gratitude for ———."

"Shh, go to sleep," I say, laughing at his performance. "You have work in the morning."

"Mwah!" He plants a sloppy wet kiss on my cheek, then reaches for Ben's hand. But before the two can walk to their cabin together, Oliver glances at someone behind me. "Whoops, sorry, love. Didn't mean to anger your boyfriend."

"My what?" I turn around and find Isaac, the only other sober one here, standing still in the parking lot. Is he waiting for me? He's fidgeting with his hands, not meeting my eyes.

"Hey," I say, approaching Isaac as everyone else leaves for their cabins.

He shifts around the gravel in front of him with the tip of his sneaker before looking up at me. "*I don't understand.*"

I tilt my head, summoning patience as I wait for him to say something else. But he's taking too long. "*Understand what?*"

"*You.*"

"*Me?*" I ask. He shakes his head and looks down. I wave my hand out and ask another question. "*What do you mean?*"

He takes a deep breath. "*You said you liked me?*" He leaves his hand against his chest while signing with the other. "*But . . .* " He waves, exasperated, in the direction of where I was standing with Oliver.

"*My friend? That I hung out with because you didn't wait for me to play the game tonight?*" My hands are flying. I'm the one who was open with my feelings. He has no reason to be coming at me like this. "*You're confusing me. Yes, I said that I like you. But you never said you like me.*"

"*I'm trying. We hung out with my friends last night. We talked all afternoon.*" He runs a hand back through his hair.

"*I don't know!*" I sign, flinging my hand out from my forehead, unable to think of a more coherent response. It really all boils down to one thing. "*I don't know. You never said it back.*"

"*With action, showing, doing—not words.*" He drops his arms and takes a few steps up the path.

I wipe rain droplets from my face, smudging the little mascara I'd applied back when I'd expected a fun evening with Isaac. I jog after him and tap on his shoulder. "*I don't understand what you want.*"

"*I need to say it?*" he asks.

We're standing close, alone on this dark path, the moon finally shining out from behind the rain clouds. I step closer to him. "*It would help.*" I pull the sign tight to my chest in the small space between us.

He's watching my lips, and this time I'm not saying anything.

Slowly, he leans forward, eyes never straying, but he hesitates and stops a few inches away from me with his mouth slightly open. I can feel his breath on my lips. I drop my hands, my right arm swinging forward to touch his hand. He catches it and laces our fingers together.

I raise my eyebrows in question—is he going to do it or not? I stand on my toes, tantalizingly close to him, until he finally closes the distance between us.

His lips are warm and soft. But they're gone before it dawns on me that I'm kissing Isaac.

My bottom lip sticks to his as he pulls away. He leans back and opens his eyes, a smile widening across his face.

I raise my hand to sign as I mouth the words, "*You still have to say it.*"

He arches an eyebrow and gives a slow nod. "*Yes, I like you, too.*"

"*Really . . . ? Are you sure?*" I tease him. "Hmmmm . . ."

There's a twinkle in his eyes. "*And you still like me?*"

I shrug. "*Maybe you should k-i-s-s me again.*"

He taps his fingers against his chin, feigning deep thought. "*Let me think.*" He wraps his arms around me.

But something is nagging me, so I ask. "*Wait, what's the sign?*"

"*Kiss,*" he demonstrates, using both hands. He presses his fingers against his thumbs and brings his hands together so that his fingertips touch, representative of two people coming together. He pulls me close. "*Your signing was pretty good . . .*"

"*Right!*" A big smile crosses my face. "*That was good? Signing fast, too. I guess we need to fight more.*"

He shakes his head, reaching out for my arms and drawing me toward him once more, for a long, slow kiss this time.

We're pushing curfew, but I don't care, because there's nowhere I'd rather be.

CHAPTER SEVENTEEN

At Sunday morning lake time, we're greeted by two very hungover lifeguards lying horizontal on the beach chairs. Oliver squints up through his sunglasses upon our arrival. He gives the smallest of waves. "Don't drown."

"And don't be too loud," Ben says, pulling his towel over his face to block the sun. "——— if you must drown, do it quietly."

The campers are waiting outside the fence playing games on the grass. Ethan clears his throat, but neither lifeguard moves.

"——— two more minutes," Oliver says. "We'll be ready then."

I suppress my laughter when I notice what's about to happen. Down near the shoreline, Jaden and Isaac have filled two buckets with water and are slowly making their way back up the beach. Ethan holds out one finger and looks at his watch. When it hits nine o'clock, he nods.

A little too eagerly, Jaden and Isaac dump the water on Oliver and Ben, who lunge from their seats.

"Oi!" Oliver yelps, shaking his head and spraying droplets of water on us. "We're ready. We're ready."

As the campers flock onto the beach, Mackenzie pulls our group aside. "Hey, girls," she says and signs. "Line up here. I want to do a quick video."

The girls seem intrigued. Honey waves for Mackenzie to hand over the phone, but Mackenzie shakes her head.

"I'm thinking, like, you all take turns saying your name and one thing you like to do at camp." She holds out her phone with the reverse camera, and signs one-handed. "I'm Mackenzie and I love to dance," she says and signs, followed by a painfully try-hard silly dance.

"*Me! Me!*" Honey raises her hand to go first, but Blake pushes her back.

"No, me first. I'm Blake, and I love to swim." She tugs at Mackenzie's sleeve. "Did you get that?"

"Actually, do that again with ASL," Mackenzie says. "You know how to sign 'swim,' right, Blake?"

"Uh, Mackenzie?" I step forward between clips. "What's this for?"

"A cute post for my story," she answers while gesturing for Honey to repeat her line next.

I'm not sure about this. It feels wrong for Mackenzie to use the young campers to create content for her audience.

I step away and discreetly wave for Ethan. When he's by my side, I ask, "Is it okay for campers to be recorded and put on the internet? Or does that require parent permission?"

"Huh?" Ethan says, busy fastening the straps of his life jacket.

"Parents do sign a release, but that's for the official camp YouTube page, and *that* we haven't used in years. What recording?"

"Oh, well. Mackenzie's making a video with the campers for her personal channel." I'm standing with my weight on one leg and arms crossed like a tattling child.

"That's not okay. Have you said something to her yet?"

"No, I told you first."

"Okay, I'll go talk to her." He ties up his hair. "Just how fast did you run to find me to get her in trouble?" he teases.

"It's not like that." But I uncross my arms and shrug.

"Sure." Ethan just shakes his head. "By the way, we might switch things up a bit, give you a chance to work with the older girls, too. I'm sure Simone could use an extra arm."

"Is that all I am? An extra arm?" I joke.

"Technically, two." He smiles. "I'll get things sorted with Mackenzie and let Simone know you'll be switching to her group starting next week. And isn't that when your brother is getting here?"

"*Right,*" I sign. "Max should be here on the first. Wow, it's that soon already?" I guess it's obvious I've been a little . . . distracted lately. July will mark the halfway point of my time at Gray Wolf this summer.

I see Isaac, towel draped over his shoulders as he helps one of his campers onto the beach wheelchair. He raises his eyebrows and gives me a sweet little closed-mouth smile, reaching out to squeeze my elbow as he walks by, pushing the chair down to the sand.

~~~
~~~

Jaden and Mackenzie are on duty tonight, but Mackenzie is in the staff cabin, so Isaac, Natasha, and I join Jaden around the roaring campfire.

Isaac sits beside me on the bench and reaches into his backpack for his Nintendo Switch. "*Wanna play?*"

I nod, finishing my quick check of my texts and socials, which reminds me of my conversation with Ethan earlier today. "*Also, wait, since when does Camp Gray Wolf have a Y-o-u-T-u-b-e?*" I ask.

"*We do?*" Isaac sets his console down on his lap, searching for the YouTube channel on his phone, then shakes his head. "*One video. Guess what year?*"

"*2012?*" I've never signed a year before, and I hope I'm doing it correctly.

He shakes his head. "*Nope, even older.*"

"*Seriously?*" I raise my eyebrows.

"*All the way back to 2010.*"

"*Wow.*" I think for a second. "*I mean, do you think Ethan knows the password?*"

Isaac slides his phone back into his pocket. "*Maybe he can find out. Why?*"

"Well," I say and sign, "Mackenzie seems to make a lot of money with her YouTube."

"*Yeah, it's awful,*" Natasha chimes in.

Jaden shakes his head. Natasha pulls up Mackenzie's channel on her phone and leans over to show him. "*Shit, that's a lot of followers.*"

"Right," I say and sign. "So, I don't know, maybe we can make a video to get money for camp? And maybe she can share it?"

"*I don't want to ———,*" Natasha signs. I turn to Isaac.

"*E-n-c-o-u-r-a-g-e,*" he quickly spells, and I get the word right away.

"*I understand,*" I sign and shrug, growing nervous that I brought this up. "*It's just a lot of people, and we need money.*"

"*True,*" Isaac signs, deep in thought. "*We should definitely film something, though. And fix the website.*"

"*The website!*" I sign, remembering that horrible nineties setup. "*Even older than that video.*"

"*Sure, I'll work with Ethan to get that fixed,*" Isaac signs.

"*But will enough people see our film?*" Natasha asks.

"*We can try. Have everyone share it, you know?*" I sign. "*And then if that doesn't work, we can ask Mackenzie to share with her followers?*" I sigh and wiggle my fingers arbitrarily to express this frustration while I formulate my next sentence. "*I kinda hate that, but it could work.*"

"I still want her to change this first," Natasha says and signs, pointing to Mackenzie's About page, where she describes herself as an ASL interpreter. "If she wants to sign in her videos, she needs to be clear that she's only learning. Not qualified to teach. It's not fair she gets this many followers when Deaf creators have to work so hard."

We all nod in agreement.

"*We only ask her to share our video if she makes the changes,*" Isaac signs. "*So, who's going to ask her?*" He throws a finger up for nose goes. Jaden follows suit.

Natasha and I lock eyes. "*You are working with her,*" Natasha signs.

"Actually," I say and sign, "Ethan has me helping with the older girls now. But yeah, it was my idea. I guess I could ask her . . . if we find that we really need to."

Isaac gives a thumbs-up, a hint of both amusement and pity in his eyes. "*Game time?*" He picks up the Switch again, offering me one of the Joy-Cons.

"*Yes, please.*"

He slides next to me, and we both put our feet up on the rocks surrounding the firepit. It's so warm I worry the plastic flip-flops will melt onto my feet, so I kick them off to the side.

Isaac side-eyes me. "*Need your glasses? We're driving.*"

"*Driving?*" I ask, shaking my head, confused, until I see his game selection: *Mario Kart*.

While operating our controllers, it's difficult to communicate. But Isaac has fallen so far behind that he raises his right hand to quickly sign, "*I think you win.*"

I grin, turning back to the screen to cross the finish line . . . but I get hit by a shell, and Isaac whizzes by. "What?"

He raises his eyebrows twice. "*Pay attention. Next one is starting.*"

I stay glued to the screen, despite Isaac nudging my shoulder as if he's going to sign something. We jostle back and forth until I cross the finish line victorious.

Isaac bends his fingers and taps them together twice, which looks very similar to another sign I know.

"*Kiss?*" I ask, playing coy.

"*T-i-e.*" He grins and leans forward to kiss me.

CHAPTER EIGHTEEN

The next few days are a happy blur. Before I know it, it's Saturday and time to move to the older girls' cabin, which was a breeze this morning, despite Blake's multiple attempts to hang out with me. Now it's a cloudy lake time, and instead of feeling like Blake's babysitter, I'm getting to relax as Phoebe's new friend. And she's already totally comfortable calling me out.

"Who are you signing with?" she asks, elbowing my side.

We're floating in the lake, bobbing up and down in our life jackets, enjoying the reprieve from the harsh summer sun.

"Just another counselor," I answer while motioning to Isaac, who is atop the inflatable iceberg nearby, that we'll chat later. He nods and jumps down into the water. There are always so many people around. We haven't really had a chance to hang out, just the two of us, since our new development.

"Okay, but, like, who?" Phoebe presses. "You usually also speak when I'm around. Plus, you ——— weird little giggle ———."

"What? No, I didn't . . ." I say, but I can't be sure. "Fine, it's Isaac."

The guy I kissed in the rain a week ago for the first time. The guy I finally got some more alone time with during our on-duty shift last night. The guy who is also swimming over here right now.

"Is that him?" Phoebe asks, hearing the water splashing. "Eh, you do you. Keep flirting. He seems cute."

"Phoebe!" I say, trying not to let my facial expression reveal my exasperation since Isaac is approaching a few feet away.

"*She's funny,*" Isaac signs, clearly picking up on the fact that Phoebe is teasing me.

"*Hi,*" I say, smiling.

He grins. "*I should find my campers. Tell her I say hi.*" Isaac looks around to make sure no one is watching before he gives me a quick kiss on the cheek, then dives back into the water to rejoin the boys at the iceberg. Tonight can't come soon enough.

"Wait," I say, turning back to Phoebe. "How'd you know he's cute? Do you know what I look like?"

She holds out a hand, waving it in an oval. "To me, you are a neutral blob of a person."

"Phoebe, that may be the best compliment I've ever received."

"So what's up with Isaac?" she asks.

"What about him? I didn't say anything about him."

"Uh, yeah, your voice did."

I can't get away with anything around her. "Something's kind of happening there."

"I knew it." Phoebe goes quiet for a second. "Yeah, fill me in on all the counselor gossip. I want the after-hours scoop so I'm ready for next summer."

"You got it."

~~~

Waiting for afternoon game time, some of the staff starts filming counselor and camper testimonials to put in our fundraising video. Isaac's in charge of recording, lest anyone make the mistake of filming vertically. Phoebe helps make sure everyone says something a little different, so we don't end up having to edit clips that all say just "I love Camp Gray Wolf" thirty times. Plus, we keep having to reshoot whenever the wind blows someone's hair over their face.

Jaden's wrapping up his blurb, focusing on how camp is a great support system. But he's interrupted when Mackenzie walks up to us. "Um, Ethan says we can't film videos at camp."

Natasha shakes her head. "*This is for the Gray Wolf page. He already said it's fine.*"

"Yeah," I say and sign. However annoyed I get with Mackenzie, she's still my coworker, so I'm still trying my best to be friendly. "It's to try and raise money for camp next year."

Mackenzie just slowly nods as she walks away, but she turns back to add, "By the way, the audio is going to be horrible with all this wind right now. Just so you know."

"Yeah, that's why we're just doing the ASL ones right now," I say. "We'll delete the audio track."

"Mm," Mackenzie mumbles.

As soon as she turns around out of our sight line, Natasha slaps her hands back and forth to sign "*Whatever.*"

Isaac motions for me to take his phone to record his video. He positions my hands above my shoulders to keep the same height he'd been filming at. "*I'll be fast, don't worry,*" he signs.

I nod, already feeling my arms threatening to shake.
~~~

Isaac pulls his staff shirt from his backpack and slides it over his tank top. In a super-exuberant, flawless one-take, he signs, "*I love Camp Gray Wolf, why? It's the perfect place to be myself, as loud, silly, and confident as I want.*"

Isaac bounds back toward me, grinning wide.

"*Perfect.*" I hand his phone back.

"*You going to do yours in ASL?*"

"Oh," I say, having not really considered it yet. "*Yeah, I think so.*"

He slides off his staff shirt and offers it to me. It hangs a bit long, but the frame is cropped, so that won't be noticeable.

"*Thanks.*" I turn to Phoebe. "I'm going to film mine really quick."

"All right." She tilts her head toward the sky. "Are we still going to play the game? It seems like it might rain or something."

"Yeah, I'm not sure."

I stand in the spot at the edge of the field, with the gravel path and cypress trees behind me, capturing all the vibes of a summer camp location. But as soon as I'm in position, I realize that I don't know what to say.

"*Ready?*" Isaac signs one-handed.

I nod. "*I love Camp Gray Wolf, why? Because . . .* " But I drop my hands back down to my side and shake my head. "*Nope, again. Sorry.*"

"*It's fine! Need help with a word?*" Isaac asks.

"*Yes, please. S-p-e-c-i-a-l.*"

He demonstrates the sign and waits until I'm ready to start again.

"*I love Camp Gray Wolf, why? This is a place to learn ASL and experience Deaf culture and make friends like me. It's amazing to have this special place away from the hearing world, where I met some of my first Deaf role models. Now I can be one for the campers myself."*

I felt confident while signing, but after a big smile at the end of the take, I drop my hands and shrug. "*Was that okay? Should I try again?*"

Isaac shakes his head. "*That was great!*"

When I walk back to give him his staff shirt, he gives me a side hug. "*You'll definitely have one of these shirts next year.*"

"*I hope so.*"

So much needs to happen before then. I need to be hired as a senior counselor. And camp needs to have enough money to still exist.

Ethan waves for everyone to line up at the end of the field he sectioned off in a rectangle with tiny orange cones, which the wind keeps blowing away. A couple of campers chase them down for him. Ethan stacks them up, not bothering to try to set them up again. We can play the Elves, Wizards, and Giants tag game with natural landmarks rather than the markers.

"Are you ready to play the game?" I ask Phoebe.

"Wait, quiet." She pokes her nose up and turns her head. "Do you hear that?"

"Hear what?" The sky has gotten dark. A recognizable putrid shade of green. "Oh . . . shit."

"The tornado siren," Phoebe says. "It's getting louder."

I don't hear it yet, but I know she's right. I jump and wave for Ethan, who is about to announce the game instructions. Instead, he runs over.

"Is everything all right?" he asks.

I point up. "Phoebe hears the tornado siren."

"Shit, that has gotten bad."

At the same time, Gary tears toward us on the golf cart. He speaks loudly but calmly. "Everyone get to the dining hall basement."

Ethan runs back toward the field, relaying the message once more, adding, "Counselors, do a head count and get all your campers to the dining hall."

"Lilah, Simone, get your kids on the golf cart," Gary says, jumping out of the driver's seat.

"Do you mean?" I nod toward the golf cart.

"Yes, drive your campers up."

I rush Phoebe toward the passenger side while Simone guides her girls to squeeze onto the back. We zip across the grass to the dining hall while everyone else walks quickly behind us. Small chunks of hail fall from the clouds, starting to pelt us from the side.

I can vaguely hear the sirens now. Phoebe must have heard the ones from the next town over. Is this a watch or a warning? Even when it's just my family hanging out in the basement for a few hours, the possibility of a tornado always gets my blood pumping. There's a reason for the cliché of Midwesterners standing at the window trying to get a glimpse before hurrying down to the basement.

Phoebe is mumbling something.

"What's that?" I shout, peering out of the corner of my eye to watch her response.

"A tornado ——— destroyed my school."

"What? Really?"

“It was before I was born.”

Obviously, they do touch down sometimes. But that’s not what I want to be thinking about right now. “Was everyone okay?”

“Um, no . . .”

Honestly, I wasn’t that worried until she said that.

I park us in front of the dining hall and shout, “Let’s get to the basement!” Then I turn to Simone. “Shoot, the lifeguards. Should I drive down to the lake?”

“We’re here, we’re here!” Oliver shouts, out of breath, running toward the dining hall from the opposite direction.

The rest of the staff and campers are approaching now, too. Gary finds the door at the back of the dining hall, opening it to reveal a dark wooden staircase. Leaving the wheelchair off to the side, Isaac carefully carries one of his campers down the stairs. Gary does a head count to ensure everyone is here.

“There’s no rail,” I tell Phoebe, moving her hands to my shoulders. “Follow me.”

The basement is a third of the size of the dining hall. It’s a tight squeeze to fit us all in, and there’s one light barely illuminating this space. The floor hasn’t been swept in years. Gary is the last one downstairs after the lifeguards and kitchen staff.

Phoebe and I find a spot to sit along the wall. As we crouch to the floor, the single light bulb hanging above us flickers and goes out. Phoebe says something to me, but it’s too dark for me to lip-read what it is.

“Hold on,” I say, fumbling around in my backpack, trying to find my phone or mini flashlight. Some of the other counselors have already turned theirs on, casting eerie shadows on the wall. “Crap, no service.” I lean back against the cold concrete wall, pulling my legs to my chest and resting my phone between my knees with the flashlight pointed upward.

I turn back to Phoebe. "You were saying?"

"Never mind." She's already pulled a book from her satchel and is running her fingers across the pages.

And then we all sit here . . . and sit, and sit, and sit, waiting for the sky to clear and Gary to release us from this cramped and overcrowded basement. Mackenzie tries to lead a hand-clapping game, but none of the campers are in the mood, preferring to just talk among themselves.

Honey crawls over to sit beside me and Phoebe. She points toward Phoebe's book. "*I want to learn.*"

"Hey, Phoebe," I say. "Honey is right next to you and wants to learn Braille."

"Cool." But Phoebe keeps reading.

I give a smile and shrug to Honey. "*One second.*" I press Phoebe. "Maybe you could show her some? We've got nothing else to do."

"I'm reading, isn't that something?"

"This would be a very junior-counselor-worthy thing to do . . ."

Phoebe slowly nods. "Okay fine, ———, and only if she teaches me sign."

"*She wants you to teach her ASL, too,*" I sign. Look how far my skills have come this summer, interpreting to facilitate communication between a deaf and a blind camper. Sometimes there's purpose to being in the middle.

Honey nods eagerly. "*That's fun.*"

Phoebe holds out her novel, scanning the bumps with her finger until she comes across the letter *A*. She nods for Honey to reach out and examine the letter. After which, Honey reaches out for Phoebe's hand and presses the sign *A* into her palm, using the tactile approach. It's a touch-based method of signing that I've seen Deafblind kids use before.

"Does the letter move?" Phoebe asks.

"Oh, she's actually signing the word 'yes' now," I say.

Blake is lurking off to the side, and I can tell she's interested. I nod for her to come over here, too.

"What are you doing?" she asks.

"Learning Braille and ASL," I explain. "Want to join us?"

Blake sniffles, wiping her nose with her sleeve. "Sure." She cuddles beside me and, to my surprise, follows along with the alphabet as Honey demonstrates it for Phoebe.

"——— longer are we going to be here?" Phoebe asks, moving on to the next letter. "I'm starving."

"Same," I agree. It's already dinnertime, but the storm has derailed our schedule. I should've stocked my backpack with snacks. "Maybe it's clearing up already."

"Nope, it's louder," Phoebe says.

"There's food right upstairs. Should I make a run for it?" I ask.

"I'll speak kindly at your funeral," she says. "My stomach is growling; can you hear that?"

"That loud?" I ask.

"Yep. You might need to prepare words for mine, then."

Gary pulls the door open and runs upstairs. He comes back a minute later, waving his phone. "It says there hasn't been any touchdown nearby, but the storm is still going strong, so we need to stay here." Ethan jumps up, biting his flashlight between his teeth to spotlight his hands as he interprets.

I'm jealous of Isaac, who's looking snug in his Yosemite hoodie. It's getting cold down here, even with everyone crowded together.

A Fruit Roll-Up lands in my lap. There's only one person this could be from, as I've noticed it's his go-to snack. I look up and catch Isaac grinning mischievously.

Off guard and glad for the snack, I give him a big smile back, showing way too many teeth, so I pretend I was trying to make a silly face.

"*I hope we're not here all night,*" he signs.

"*Same,*" I sign back across the room. "*I'm cold.*"

Of course, he takes off his hoodie and tosses it to me. I catch it, but when I start to shake my head and hold it back toward him, he insists. "*I'm fine. I'm not cold.*"

I put it on without further hesitation, ignoring a glance from Natasha. Has he told his friends about us? I mean, we were pretty obvious last night around the campfire.

"*Thank you. Now I'm only a little cold . . . and a little tired . . . and a little hungry—so thank you.*" I hold up the Fruit Roll-Up in gratitude.

Isaac raises his eyebrows. "*Hungry, or . . .* " He keeps his hand at his chest, suggestively recalling my signing mistake from our first day of camp, but not daring to repeat the motion with so many campers around.

I smirk. "*Wouldn't you like to know.*"

He drops his jaw in mock astonishment. "*Lilah, there are children here.*" But he bites his lip and smiles.

~~~
~~~

Any nervousness or excitement from the tornado siren is gone as we enter hour three sheltering. Campers are slouched over one another, fast asleep. Simone has some of the craft supplies in her backpack, so I weave together a few bracelets, including one for Isaac, to try to keep myself awake. Phoebe gets a paper cut, which means I have to get yet another accident report to log her bandage usage. Every time we use something from the first aid kit, we have to write it up, no matter how minor.

The longer we're trapped down here, the less likely it is that Isaac and I will get any time to hang out together before curfew. Summer days are limited. I don't want to miss a single evening together.

Gary checks upstairs again and is gone for over thirty minutes. When he returns, he passes around small boxes of cereal for everyone to munch on dry. Better than nothing.

"The storm has passed, so it looks like we'll be free to go soon. But hang on for a little longer!" Gary says and Ethan interprets. People start to stretch out, eager to get out of this cramped basement. "Counselors, quick meeting in the stairwell."

We squish together into the small stairwell. Since we're along the wall where no one will notice, I reach for Isaac's hand.

"Okay, first," Gary says and Ethan interprets. "A question: Are your kids more tired or hungry?"

"Definitely tired at this point," Mackenzie says. Honey and Blake used up so much focus during the Braille and ASL session that they've been out for at least an hour.

"All right, if anyone needs more food, let me know. Now, the more pressing issue. This was a messy storm. I drove around to check things out. The paths are a wreck, and a couple of trees got knocked over by the wind. More specifically, two of the cabins were hit."

There's collective gasping as we take in the news. Gary raises his arms to calm us as we barrage him with questions.

"The damage is fairly minimal, aside from, well, a hole in the roof." He sighs. "Fixing all this is going to be costly."

Of all the trees and places around camp to fall, there had to be damage to our cabins? Are we going to need to get this fundraiser video up as soon as possible to even make it through this summer, let alone next year?

"But that's not tonight's problem," Gary continues. "Everyone should be able to get their belongings—just watch out for wood shards."

"Which cabins?" Bobby asks.

"Right. The oldest boys'," Gary says. "And the older girls' cabin, shared by Natasha's and Simone's groups."

And me. Because all my stuff was just moved to that cabin.

"The staff cabin?" Ethan suggests.

"That's my thought," Gary says. "There are some spare bunks in the other four cabins to divide some campers up, and anyone else can go to the staff cabin. I'll quickly reconfigure cabin assignments, and we can get out of here."

What exactly does the roof damage look like? I was really hoping to trudge back to the cabins and pass out, not have to deal with all this.

"Thank you all for toughing out a difficult night," Gary says. "We're past camper curfew, so let's see if we can handle these arrangements as efficiently as possible."

CHAPTER NINETEEN

The tree through the roof? Yep, that fell directly above my bed. That's what I get for choosing a top bunk. Even after shaking out my sleeping bag several times, there's still debris.

Gary helps move our belongings with the golf cart, but it still takes a while to get everyone settled in the new room assignments. Jaden's group is split into the extra bunks over with Isaac and Bobby. Meanwhile, Natasha's group, as well as Simone and two of her girls, are in the staff cabin, but there aren't enough functioning bunks, so Phoebe and I take the spare beds in Mackenzie's.

"You're back with me!" Blake exclaims as I'm trying to roll out our sleeping bags as quickly as possible.

"Just couldn't stay away," I say, unsure if I'm really channeling the "counselor cheer" right now.

Phoebe is hangry, which makes this all even more stressful. "I need food," she says.

"Yeah, Gary's gathering up some stuff for sandwiches."

"It's been forever. I need a real dinner."

"I need more cereal," Blake adds, holding up her empty carton, licking her finger to scoop up more of the sugary dust. That'll help her fall asleep . . .

"And I need to brush my teeth," Phoebe whines.

"Don't you want to wait until after eating?" I ask.

"Or a shower . . ." Phoebe continues.

"It's late tonight. We can shower tomorrow morning." I also really want a shower, but Gary advised that we wait until he can make sure everything's running properly. I rarely can tell the age difference between Phoebe and me, but right now, our different roles mean that she gets to complain while I have to put on a happy face.

"I'm not going to be able to sleep," Phoebe whines.

"I promise you will; you're exhausted," I say. "You'll be out as soon as you hit the pillow."

And when the time finally comes, she is. Fast asleep. I, on the other hand, am tossing and turning because I have to use the bathroom. I've mostly avoided leaving the cabin by myself in the middle of the night. That's the stuff horror movies are made of. But my need to go overpowers my fear.

I fish around in my duffel bag for my glasses so my vision is as clear as possible in the dark. I throw on Isaac's hoodie before stepping out into the cold night. It's not that long of a walk to the bathhouse, but I'm coming at it from a different cabin and angle now, careful of the storm debris beneath my feet. With every step on the muddy ground, my eyes dart away from the path my flashlight illuminates and up to the woods. It's not less creepy when I reach the bathhouse, among the flickering lights and moths.

Wanting to get back to the safety of my cabin, I'm in such a rush—speeding from the stall to the sink and out the door—that I nearly have a heart attack when I exit and crash into Isaac. We'd been texting earlier, so I knew he was up, too, but I didn't expect to see him here.

"*I gotta go. But wait here,*" he signs, and then he emerges a minute later. "*Hey, nerd, I like your glasses.*"

I reach up and adjust the frames from the bridge of my nose, signing "nerd" while sticking out my tongue.

Isaac smiles. "*Can't sleep?*"

I shake my head.

"*Me either. A little scary today.*"

I nod. He reaches for my hand, and I instinctively curl into his chest for a hug, not embarrassed at all to be caught still wearing his hoodie. Now I'm still tired, but also wide-awake. And I remember what I have in the pocket of Isaac's hoodie: a green duct tape bracelet with a stripe of purple.

"Here," I whisper, holding it out for Isaac. I hope it'll fit. The woven tape is pretty rigid but still has enough flexibility to scrunch up and let Isaac's hand slide through.

Isaac holds up his wrist victoriously. The bracelet stands out from the rest of his camp collection. "*It's perfect.*" His eyes dart to the ground as he reaches into his own pocket, retrieving a very loosely woven strand of string, in matching purple and green. He looks it over in his hand. "*It's not very good . . .* "

"*No, it's great.*" I hold out my wrist expectantly.

Isaac attempts to tie the string, but it's too dark. He steps back and purses his lips. The only lights are in the bathhouse and the nearby lanterns of the dance barn. But that's the opposite direction of the cabins.

Yet we walk together to the porch, which is damp and littered with debris from the storm. Underneath the bright light, Isaac reaches for my wrist and ties on the bracelet. I stand on my tiptoes and kiss his cheek.

"*I wish we could go somewhere,*" I sign.

"*Me too.*"

We're already somewhere we're not supposed to be. The bracelet is already around my wrist, but Isaac's hand is still there, and he runs his fingers across my palm. The lamplight flickers above us as I watch the reflection in his eyes. We really should be getting back now.

But the only direction either of us moves in is to each other. My back's against the wall, yet I want him closer. He leans toward me slowly, and the back of my neck tingles in anticipation until our lips meet, and we melt into each other.

It's as if we've paused time to kiss in a way I've never kissed before. With no one around, being together is almost entirely brand-new again.

The taste of his mint toothpaste. My fingers through the curls of his hair. His arms wrapping around my back and reaching beneath the oversized hoodie to directly hold my waist. The certainty that he wants me as much as I want him—and that the storm, the miscommunication, the chaos, the confusion—all of it got us to this moment.

~

Several bright flashlights are coming our way. I jump back from Isaac, withdrawing my arms into the sweatshirt sleeves. How long have we been out here?

A voice shouts from behind one of the lights. "What the hell, Lilah." It's Simone, along with Mackenzie.

"I was so worried." Mackenzie wraps me into a suffocating hug. "A girl going missing from her bed doesn't usually end well. According to true crime podcasts, that is."

"What?" I ask, still standing several feet apart from Isaac, knowing we've been caught. But if it's just Simone and Mackenzie, hopefully it's all right?

"Gary's on his way," Mackenzie says. If the director is heading over from his small cabin near the front entrance, then something is *really* wrong.

Simone walks forward, shining her flashlight right in my face, then pulls out her phone and holds it to her ear. I take a step toward her, my brain racing through ways I could possibly sneak back to my cabin and make like this never happened.

"What's up?" I ask nervously. Isaac is also fidgeting beside me. I guess there are worse states we could have been found in, but I have no idea what to expect for being caught out and about after curfew.

Through the darkness, I see Ethan up ahead, waiting outside the cabins. *Shit.*

"Yeah, no, we found her," Simone says on the phone. "Turns out someone else was missing, too. Uh-huh. Yeah. M'kay."

When Simone hangs up, Mackenzie finally answers my question. "One of the campers was sick," she says and signs. "They tried to wake you up, but instead they woke me, and I panicked when you weren't there and I couldn't find you."

"Who was sick?" I ask, but Mackenzie is already walking back to the cabin. Isaac gives me an apologetic shrug and follows her lead.

When I turn to Simone, she looks mad. "Phoebe ———."

"Phoebe?" I ask, concerned. "Is she all right?"

"Yeah, she should be. I mean, she threw up and was looking for you." Simone saunters back to the cabins. She has some things she wants to say to me first. "Then Mackenzie gets me from the staff cabin, and I go over to find Phoebe anxiously avoiding a pile of vomit, the little girls complaining about the smell, and you nowhere to be seen."

"Shit." I twist my fingers together, feeling the exhaustion crashing over me.

"Mackenzie made a whole production out of it, straight up assuming you were abducted or some shit."

"I'm so sorry." I've been up nearly twenty-four hours straight at this point. What time is it even? "I just stepped outside for a minute and then—"

"Lilah, that was irresponsible."

"But . . . I mean, come on. Haven't you and Bobby kind of been encouraging this? As my friend, can't you be a little understanding?"

"This? No, I have not been 'encouraging this.' You have a break from nine thirty until midnight when you can do whatever you want if you're not on duty. Otherwise, we're on the clock. It was a stressful enough day already without all this. So yeah, sure, tough break or whatever."

"For sneaking out?"

"Getting caught." She nods up ahead. "——— so guess who gets to clean up the vomit pile."

Oof, that's easy enough to assume. "Me."

"Yep."

I'm directed back to the cabin, where Ethan is still waiting outside, shaking his head disapprovingly. "Gary will be having a talk with you two."

I hurry inside, immediately hit with the smell. Most of the young girls are still awake but quiet in their bunks. I shine my phone flashlight, discovering the puddle of puke in front of Phoebe's bed, as colorful as the cereal we had for dinner mere hours ago.

"Hey, it's me. Are you all right?" I ask Phoebe. She rolls over and takes a sip from her water bottle.

Mackenzie steps inside with a handful of paper towels and Clorox wipes. "Simone said to give these to you."

"Ah, Lilah," Phoebe says. Her voice is hoarse and low, and her lips are moving slowly. "You've missed all the fun. My stomach certainly had a night."

I finish the sanitizing job and meet Gary outside the cabin. I dare a quick glance at my phone. It's almost four in the morning. *Fuuuuck.* I join him outside and wait in uncomfortable silence while he checks his phone before looking up at me.

"I'm very disappointed," he says loudly. "Can you hear me? That was immature behavior and not why you're here this summer."

"I'm sorry. I—"

He puts up a hand. "Now is not the time for this discussion. Honestly, with everything that happened tonight, ——— at the bottom of my priority list. ——— first and only warning.

You enjoy considerable freedoms as a junior counselor, but you are still a trainee. Don't slack on your job responsibilities. Or else, since you're not yet eighteen, I'll have no choice but to call your parents."

So much for feeling grown-up this summer. I can only imagine how my parents would react if I got fired from this job for sneaking out late at night to see a guy.

"And I doubt they'd be keen to hear why," Gary finishes.

"It won't happen again," I assure him.

"Good. Ethan already interpreted my conversation with Isaac, too. So you're not being singled out here." Gary looks around to the two damaged cabins and slides a hand down his face, stifling a yawn. "What a night."

"Yeah." I'm not sure if I'm allowed to go to sleep yet.

"Okay," he says, nodding. "Go on. If Phoebe needs extra rest tomorrow, you two can hang out here for a little while. Just coordinate with Simone."

I finally crash back into bed a few minutes later. I lie on my stomach and stick my face into my pillow, muffling a groan.

"Lilah," Phoebe calls out in a tone that suggests she's called my name a few times and no longer cares if any other campers hear her.

I hold out my phone and light her face with the screen. "Yeah, sorry. You okay? Gary said we can sleep in if you need to."

"Good. Are you in trouble?"

"No, I don't think so." I ponder this for a minute. "But it was a close one. You know—"

Phoebe drops her head back to her pillow, apparently already fast asleep, and a text from Isaac pops up on my phone.

Isaac: sorry :/ tonight was fun until we got in trouble.
see you tomorrow.

Since I've been so worried about camp not having enough funding and proving myself as a junior counselor, I never even considered being sent home early was a possibility. We'll have to stick to hanging out during official break time. I really like Isaac, but I can't jeopardize my time at camp again.

CHAPTER TWENTY

Natasha shakes me awake in the morning. She climbs up and sits on my bunk uninvited. Mackenzie and the other girls are already on their way to breakfast.

"What are you doing here?" I sign and say through a yawn.

"*Why are you not up yet?*" she signs.

"Simone texted me earlier to stay here with Phoebe." I look through the wooden slats to confirm that Phoebe is still asleep in her bunk. "*What's up?*" I ask Natasha.

"*We need to talk.*" She looks mad. Great. It has to be about last night. What's it to her? Her signing is too fast for me to follow, especially this early in the morning.

I hesitate, trying to recall any of her motions to figure out what she just signed, but I end up having to ask, "*Again, please.*"

She rolls her eyes and adds voice to her signing. "Don't hurt Isaac. He's not really as confident as he seems here."

I shake my head, eyebrows narrowed, questioning what she's talking about.

"You don't know him in the real world. He's had to deal with a ton of jerks at school, always fighting his way out of messed-up situations. And girls have tried to date him, but they don't actually bother to try to communicate with him or really get to know him, so he's got a lot of trust issues, especially with hearing people. So as his best friend, I'm telling you—be careful."

This explains why Isaac would be cautious around relationships. It puts into perspective his hesitation earlier this summer and what he said about wanting to make sure he really knows someone before he dates them.

"Okay, but that's not me," I say, feeling defensive and a little tired of having to prove myself. "And you know that. I wouldn't be part of that problem. I like him, and he clearly likes me, and you two are friends, and I was kinda hoping that you and I were getting to be friends, too. So why don't you trust me instead of threatening me? Isaac can take care of himself."

Natasha shakes her head. "I'm not threatening you. I'm warning you."

"Warning me? About what?"

She climbs down from the bunk, considering her words. She stops on the ladder when her head is almost beneath the top bar and says, "He searches for reasons to shut people out. When relationships get hard, he distances himself. Just know that."

It's strange to hear this from Natasha, because she's incredibly guarded herself and Isaac's close friend. How many of those other girls had a similar confrontation with Natasha? Is she telling me all this because she's rooting for my relationship or against it? I'm not sure, and I'm too exhausted to process all this right now. "*Okay,*" I sign, nodding slowly before collapsing back onto my pillow.

I guess I'm different at camp, too. Sometimes it seems like my friends from school don't really know me or how to communicate with me. But at the same time, have I been open enough with them about what I need? I've never really asked them for support or accommodations.

As much as I roll my eyes whenever the hearing itinerant teaches me to "advocate for myself" in class, which puts the burden on me, maybe a little bit of advocacy within my own relationships wouldn't hurt.

~

At lunch, Ethan waves me over. Worried it'll be about last night, I motion that I need a minute and fill up my water bottle first, taking a deep, stabilizing breath.

I approach Ethan's table, apologies already pouring from my mouth. But he gestures for me to stop. "Hey, you heard from Gary, you know what's up and what not to do going forward. We don't need to go over it again," he says and signs.

"*Whew.*" I'm so relieved that Ethan can still be friendly and hasn't reverted to boss mode. Honestly, out of the whole ordeal, Simone seems to be the only one still mad about it. She's barely talked to me despite spending the entire day with me and our group.

"Actually, I just wanted to see how soon we could get that fundraising video up." He notices the concerned look on my face. "Yeah, the numbers aren't great, and we need to prioritize these cabin repairs."

"Of course, we recorded a bunch yesterday. Wouldn't take too much to finish up a few more clips today and get it edited tonight."

I stop by Isaac's table to tell him the plan and go back to my group. "Hey, Simone, should we have the girls do the recording after lunch?"

"Yeah, sure," she says flatly.

"I mean, we can do it whenever, it doesn't have to be now."

Simone shrugs. "That's fine."

"Anything I can do so you're not mad at me about last night? Can I say I'm sorry again?"

"Lilah, just give me some space. It's fine."

"Hey," Phoebe calls out. "Can I do a video now?"

After lunch, we meet Isaac and his campers by a small grove of trees to switch up the backgrounds. Phoebe volunteers to go first.

"Hey, everyone," she says in a cheerful but commanding tone. "Camp Gray Wolf is this amazing place for the deaf and the blind. But we almost got hit by a tornado! Empty your pockets as fast as you can to help us fix our cabins and save this incredible camp! I would really like to have the chance to be a junior counselor next year."

I hold my laughter until Isaac stops recording. "Are we allowed to mention the tornado?" I say and sign. Isaac shrugs.

"Don't cut the tornado!" Phoebe calls out. "People respond to honesty."

~

Monday morning, we post the fundraising video and try to do a push on socials. I'm sneaking a glance at my phone during arts and crafts to check the number of donations we've received so far. It's crawled to a couple hundred dollars, which is a great start, but we'll definitely need to reach a larger audience to raise the money we need to save Gray Wolf and keep it free for everyone.

"Hey, Lilah." Bobby approaches, putting a hand on the back of the folding chair I'm sitting on. "Feels like I never see you anymore. I'm no longer the most important man in your life."

I let out a dramatic gasp. "Oh, Bobby. Never!"

"Well, that's all about to change, because guess who's arriving today and got assigned to my group."

"Max is in your group!" How has June passed so quickly that my brother is already here? "That's great. You're going to get along so well."

"Why exactly is your brother getting here so late?"

"Ah, you just came to me for the scoop. I'm not really sure. My mom mentioned some doctor appointments and a school sports thing. It was just easier for him to miss June."

"He's never been here before?"

"This is his first summer. But he's only . . ." I count the age down from my own. "Eleven."

"We'll get him up to speed in no time." Bobby nods. "And how's the video doing? My post has gotten a ton of likes already, so tell me that I'm single-handedly saving camp."

"You're single-handedly possibly helping us fix one cabin. Possibly."

"Well, I'm not made of money. None of us are. How do we get it in front of more people?"

Ugh, I know how we could get more engagement. "There might be a way, but what if it's pity money?"

"Eh, money is money." He shrugs. "We gotta do what we can to get by."

"All right, well, wish me luck."

"Right now?"

"Yep, before I lose my nerve. Be right back." I walk over to the other side of the craft area, where Mackenzie is sitting with her group. I wave hello to the girls and take a seat on the empty chair beside her. "Hey, how's it going?"

"Great! Look at our pinecone decorations!" Mackenzie says, gesturing to the glittery mess in front of her.

"Nice. Hey, I have a question for you," I say.

"Oh, is it serious?"

"Well, kind of." I debate how to ask this. "If you had a chance to help save camp, would you do it?"

She wipes her hands on the already glitter-covered washrag beside her. "I don't have that kind of money lying around. Wish I did, though!"

Does she seriously think I'm asking her to finance the whole thing herself? "But you do have followers," I say.

"I see." She's inquisitive but waits for me to explain.

"So the fundraising video on the Gray Wolf channel is doing well! But that page has, like, seven followers. We could use a boost." I didn't think I'd have to spell it out this much. I wave Natasha over so that she can come help, and I notice this makes Mackenzie tense up.

Mackenzie takes a deep breath. "I thought I wasn't really supposed to use camp in my videos anymore."

"This is different," Natasha says and signs, coming to my rescue. "We've been sharing it and just need more reach."

Mackenzie hesitates but regains her composure, speaking in an extra-cheery tone. "Of course, I'd be happy to help! I'll mention it at the top of my next video."

"Before you do," Natasha adds, and Mackenzie stiffens again, "um, your About page says you're an interpreter."

"Right, I do need to update that to include 'student.' I forgot, whoops!"

"You can use sign in your videos," Natasha explains. "I'm glad you're learning, really. I wish more people would. But I don't like that you position yourself as someone qualified to teach ASL, because you're not. Lessons should come from within the Deaf community in order to be accurate and properly reflect Deaf culture, not from hearing people, especially not those who are still learning."

Mackenzie looks around nervously. "Right, but the people who watch my videos are mostly hearing, and it just inspires them to learn. Then they can go find other teachers." She shrugs, then quickly adds, "Who are Deaf."

"How are they supposed to know to search elsewhere if they think they can learn it from someone with a large platform like you?" Natasha asks.

"And maybe not all of your viewers are hearing," I add. "Deaf and hard of hearing people don't magically know ASL from birth. There are a lot of barriers to learning. Like, I've been trying to use the internet as a resource, but it's so hard to weed through the incorrect stuff out there. Not saying that your stuff is totally wrong. It's just that you're still learning, too."

"Um, okay," Mackenzie says. She grabs the rag to wipe her hands again, which only covers them in more glitter. "That's something to think about. I'd be lying if I said I hadn't gotten any comments like that on my videos before."

"It's an opportunity to rebrand," I say.

She considers this, nodding slowly. For a while, I think this is the end of the conversation, but Mackenzie speaks up again. "Okay, I'll put some thought into it. But for now, I'll change my About page and go ahead and boost the camp video."

"Thank you, Mackenzie," I say, impressed with how civil her reaction is. We did just approach her out of nowhere and ask for a favor, and we kind of critiqued her entire platform.

Now let's see if this gets us closer to our fundraising goal.

CHAPTER TWENTY-ONE

Later, everyone is gathered in the dining hall, thrilled that today's lunch is pizza. I asked Phoebe to save me a slice since Bobby and I have to go get Max in a minute once Gary gets here.

Isaac waves me down. "*Your brother?*"

"*He's almost here.*"

"*I'm ———— to meet him,*" Isaac signs. I tilt my head, and he spells out, "*C-u-r-i-o-u-s.*"

"*He's, like, this tall.*" I hold my hand below my shoulder. "*And people say we look alike.*"

"Lilah, where are you?" Bobby calls from the dining hall doors. "We can't be late. I need to make a good impression on your parents. Show them that, unlike a certain someone, I'm responsible."

"If you dare mention even a peep about the other night, Bobby," I say, my eyes wide, "I swear."

We meet Gary at the golf cart and zip down to the parking lot, arriving right as my parents' minivan pulls onto the gravel.

The back door slides open, and Max jumps out. His Bears jersey nearly comes down to his knees. For his small stature, he usually packs a lot of personality, but right now, he seems nervous.

"Hey," I shout. "Welcome to Gray Wolf!"

"Ugh, you're not one of my counselors, are you?" he says, rolling his eyes and looking at our parents as they get his duffel and sleeping bags out of the back.

"Nope, that'd be me. I'm Bobby." He steps forward and holds out a hand, which probably makes Max feel grown-up, since he immediately straightens his shoulders, eager to impress.

"Nice to meet you," Max says, shaking Bobby's hand.

Now it's my turn to roll my eyes. "Yeah, Bobby's all right."

"Hey," Bobby says. "I'm more than all right. Just 'cause you're biased toward a certain other counselor—"

"Hey!" I nudge Bobby with my elbow. "Seriously, don't."

Gary gives my dad a clipboard with the arrival paperwork he needs to complete. Meanwhile, my mom walks over and tells me something that I don't hear.

"What?" I ask loudly.

Immediately, she looks at my ears. "Is it pool time?" she asks, speaking up.

I shake my head.

"Lake time? Bedtime?" She narrows her eyes.

I shake my head again, frustrated, knowing exactly where she's going with this. "My hearing aids are back in my suitcase. It's fine. Gosh."

She purses her lips and shakes her head. "Your audiologist ________."

Is she still lecturing me about my hearing aids?

"I said, your audiologist says hi."

"Yeah, I got that. Were you there recently?"

"Max had an appointment with her. And with the otologist. He had a sharp decline in his left ear."

"Oh." I watch Max to see what his reaction is, but he and Bobby are chatting away like old friends. My mom's being very serious about his hearing loss.

"So we're seeing if he's a candidate for a cochlear implant." She stares off toward the trees.

"I guess. Well, tons of kids here have one." To me, CIs kind of seem interchangeable with hearing aids in some ways, but they're definitely more involved, especially the setup.

"It's a major surgery," my mom says, presumably wondering why my reaction isn't bigger. "Well, it's supposed to be 'minimally invasive,' but it would still take at least six weeks for his head to recover before they could turn it on."

"Can he just stick with two hearing aids, then?" My brother and I both had a dip in hearing at our annual exams. I'd hope this would get my family to take learning ASL seriously. But instead, my parents are jumping right to surgery.

"The hearing aid isn't working well enough for that ear anymore."

"Then he could go without it?"

She shakes her head. "He needs it to hear us."

I can tell that this is the end of the discussion, which tracks. While Max and I are free to attend Deaf camp, we do live in the hearing world. Our school accommodations are based on using speech and hearing aids. They do not include services using ASL and interpreters. I'm sure the doctors are pushing for the surgery as the next logical step, proclaiming it's the best option.

But maybe it is? In some ways, surgery could be seen as the simpler option, since it's unlikely that everyone around Max would learn an entire new language to communicate with him. Especially since he'd have to also learn the language himself.

I can see both sides of the debate, and it's not an easy decision. I know what my own preference would be, but it's him going under the knife, not me.

So what does Max think?

~

After hours, I wait for Isaac at the firepit. Mackenzie is there by the picnic table with her laptop, editing her latest video.

She waves me over. "Would you mind taking a look?"

"Sure." I move to sit beside her. "Oh, you included captions this time! That's great. Having captions for both the speaking and sign portions makes it accessible all around."

She seems eager for me to hit Play. "It certainly takes longer to get content up . . . but it's worth it."

This video must've been filmed during Mackenzie's afternoon break, because she's standing against the wooden wall of the dance hall with the sun shining brightly in front of her.

"Hey, friends!" she says in her typical cheery opening. "This is a short update to let you all know that I'm still alive and loving life at summer camp. If you have the spare means to do so, I really hope you'll check out this fundraiser." She points up to the left, where I assume she'll be adding the link to our video. "Help us save this incredible place.

"Now, I also have some news. There are going to be some big, exciting changes coming to my channel soon. I can't wait to share more, but for now, keep an eye out for this very special update. And if you have any suggestions about what you'd love to see on my channel, feel free to drop them in the comments. Love you all! And remember to like and subscribe!" Of course, she ends the video by waving the ASL "I love you" sign toward the camera.

"That looks good," I say. "What are some of the other changes you're going to do?"

Mackenzie shakes her head. "I'm not sure yet. Buying some time, and kind of hoping there'll be some good feedback in the comments."

"That'd be nice." I notice that the tab for the fundraiser is open. "Have there been any updates?"

"We're almost at the smaller summer repairs goal. Hopefully my followers can push us over that one at least."

"Yeah, fingers crossed!" But I fall short of excitement. We still need more money in order to meet the main fundraiser goal and ensure that Gray Wolf can continue to exist. Repairing the cabins is helpful only if we're able to house campers in them next summer. "Yeah, one step at a time, I guess."

"Oh, by the way, it seems like Blake has a new friend," Mackenzie adds.

"Really? Does that mean she and Honey are officially besties?"

Mackenzie laughs. "I meant your brother. We were paired for small-group activities with Bobby's boys this afternoon. Blake and Max dominated in the obstacle races."

"Interesting," I say, drawing out the word. "Well, I'm glad he's fitting in at camp."

It makes sense that Max would gravitate toward other speakers at camp, but I want him to experience ASL this summer, and I'm not sure he'll be getting that from Blake. And with Bobby as his counselor, he doesn't have to work with the communication barrier on a daily basis, as he would if he were with Jaden's or Isaac's group. I'll have to see how I can encourage him to give ASL a try.

~~~

Tuesday is sports day, so for the afternoon activity everyone hangs out on the big open field with footballs, volleyballs, soccer balls, baseballs, Hula-Hoops, and a whole assortment of other playground staples. Phoebe wants to sit in the shade and make more bracelets, and I'm happy to oblige.

I'm tying a bracelet around Phoebe's wrist when Isaac walks over and asks, "*Where's your brother?*"

I search the field and point to the baseball area. Max has picked up the Wiffle ball bat and is swinging it through the air.

"*He likes baseball,*" Isaac says, nodding approvingly. "*That's my game. So you wanted me to talk to him?*"

"*Yes, please.*"

At the firepit last night, I told Isaac how frustrated I am that Max doesn't seem as interested in learning ASL as I am. I guess a part of me is being selfish—I want him to learn so that I have someone at home to sign with once camp is over. But I also want him to know his communication options, especially with a big decision about a cochlear implant coming up.
~~~

"You good for a minute?" I ask Phoebe. "I'll be right back."

"Yeah, no hurry, I could do this for hours." Phoebe has decided against making her string bracelet-length, so she keeps on braiding what looks like a long woven snake now.

I follow Isaac over to Max. "*Want to play catch?*" Isaac asks my brother.

Immediately Max looks at me. "What'd he say?" I shake my head and point back toward Isaac, who repeats his question. "Come on, Lilah," Max whines.

Isaac breaks it down, one word at a time. "*Play?*"

"I don't know what he's saying," Max says. "Lilah, just tell me."

"What do you think he's saying? What is everyone doing right now?" I ask.

"I don't know." Max paces a few steps, looking around. "I don't know, playing?"

"Right," I say and sign. "*Play.*"

"*F-l-y?*" Isaac signs, picking up one of the Wiffle balls and nodding toward the bat.

"Come on," I say. "I know you know the alphabet."

"D?" Max asks.

I shake my head. "*F-l-y.*"

"Fly?"

"Yes, thank you."

Isaac reaches out for the Wiffle bat. He nods for Max to run out farther into the grass.

"Oh, fly balls?" Max jogs back into position. He gestures throwing a ball high into the field.

"*I think he figured it out,*" Isaac signs to me with a grin. He tosses the ball into the air beside him, effortlessly swinging the bat to lob the ball in Max's direction. Max runs to get it but misses. He chases after it and throws it back to Isaac, who catches it one-handed.

Isaac puts the bat beneath his arm and signs to Max. "*Again?*"

"What?" Max shouts, holding out his hand with one finger up. "Throw it again!"

"That's the sign," I say, repeating the word. "*Again.*"

"Oh, yeah," Max says. "*Again.*" He tacks on another gesture to indicate throwing, and repeats a few more signs he knows. "*Yes, again, throw!*" But he tries to go too fast, and in all that waving, what he ends up with is mostly a jumble of nonsense.

"It's okay to go slow," I say. "You have to make sure that the clarity is there first. Speed will come with time, I promise."

Isaac hits the ball directly in Max's direction for an easy catch. Max throws it back, eagerly signing, "*Again.*" Then he points up to signal "higher next time."

Isaac looks at me proudly and nods toward Max, as if to say, "Look at that."

"*It's a start,*" I sign. "*Thank you.*"

"Hey, are you talking about me?" my brother shouts.

"Yep," I say, smiling.

CHAPTER TWENTY-TWO

Before wandering off with Isaac after hours today, I want to clear the air with Simone. Bobby had a headache and went to bed early, so she's alone at the firepit, reading one of her books.

"Hey, you're not mad at me about the other night still?" I ask, diving right in.

"I don't know." She keeps running her fingers across a page, but I wait expectantly, so she pauses and looks up. "Like, I know you're primarily hanging out with Phoebe, but sometimes it feels like I have an extra camper in my group now, not an extra counselor."

"Oh. Sorry, I should've been more helpful. Working with the older girls has been so much easier than the younger kids, I guess I was treating it too much like a break. Or like the last few summers I missed being here as an older camper myself."

"And I get that," Simone says. "But that's why I was angry that night."

"That makes so much more sense. I knew it couldn't possibly be about sneaking out, 'cause I'm convinced you and Bobby have done that before."

I thought this would break the tension and make Simone laugh, but she just looks away. "I don't know, that's all complicated right now."

"Again?"

"Well, it's like he wants to come back next summer—if there even is a next summer—but I just got into this program at school to be an aide, and I need the credit to graduate. I'm definitely not coming back. I actually have to move to Minnesota for a full year, so there's a lot to figure out."

"That *is* a lot. I'm sad that you won't be back next year. I'll miss you. Congratulations on the program, though. Are you excited?"

"Definitely." She waves a hand. "The timing of it all isn't great, but the program is definitely a good thing."

"That's good. I'm glad," I say sincerely, but I understand the Bobby piece is complicated. "Oh—hey, I meant to ask you if you want something from the store. Isaac and I are gonna grab some snacks."

"I'm fine, thanks." She goes back to her book, so I just stare at the fire while I wait for Isaac. He finally walks over from his cabin.

"*Ready to go to the store?*" I ask him.

"*Of course,*" Isaac signs. Natasha and Jaden are both approaching the fire, scrolling through their phones. Isaac cups his hands around his mouth and hoots for their attention.

"*What?*" Natasha signs.

"*Can you drive us to Super Mart?*" Isaac asks. They'd driven to camp together, and I've learned that their friendship goes back even further than I would've guessed. Apparently, Isaac's hearing mom met Natasha's Deaf parents through a support group for families learning ASL when Isaac was a toddler.

Natasha frowns, gesturing toward Jaden. "*We're on duty. Can't you wait for tomorrow?*"

I tap Isaac's shoulder. "*I have my car, remember?*"

"*Oh right! Let's go.*" He hops up and retrieves his wallet from his backpack, leaving the bag on the bench next to Jaden.

"*Need anything?*" I ask them.

"*Whatever snacks you both get will be fine,*" Jaden signs. "*If you wanna share.*"

"*I got you,*" Isaac signs.

Isaac and I make our way to the parking lot. I catch him giving me a silly look. "*What?*"

We're walking down a dimly illuminated path, so I watch Isaac's hands signing in the moonlight. "*You have to wear your glasses to drive,*" he says with a smile.

"*Right, I almost forgot.*" I sling my backpack around and get the glasses out of their case. It's really so much more comfortable wearing them without also having hearing aids in. Both can be a lot of weight on my ears.

The stars shine bright through the tree branches. We cross the small footbridge in the forested area before the parking lot, making the transition back toward the real world. There's a thrill to be leaving camp with Isaac, and only Isaac—like the whole night is full of possibilities. I breathe in the fresh, crisp air . . . and swat away a pesky mosquito.

"*Or we could drive this.*" Isaac points at the camp van.

"*Never again.*"

There are only seven or eight cars in the parking lot. I manually unlock the car doors and climb into the driver's seat, quickly grabbing an old water bottle from the passenger side and tossing it in the back before Isaac gets in.

"*Awesome that you have your own car.*"

"*Yeah, it's only because my parents can't drive me to school.*" I've never considered this car awesome, especially since all of my classmates drive much nicer ones, but I guess it is for a city boy who gets to use public transportation. "*I'd rather have a bus to take.*"

"*Yeah, I take the train.*"

We both click in our seat belts, and I turn on the car. Isaac reaches a hand to the side door, feeling for vibrations. "*No music?*"

"*What do you want?*"

I usually prefer when the instruments don't overpower the vocals, so that once I've looked up the lyrics, I can sing along to the majority of the song.

"*I love h-e-a-v-y m-e-t-a-l.*" He mimics putting on headphones and banging his head back and forth. I offer him the cord to play whatever he wants.

I try to set up my phone's GPS, but the service is spotty. "*Where do we go? I can't remember.*"

"*I think this way. Go out and to the right.*"

I glance over at Isaac as he directs me for the next few turns, and thankfully, twenty-five minutes later, we arrive at Super Mart.

I pull into the parking lot, conscientiously using my turn signal since there's a police car in the corner. Its lights are off, so it's probably empty, but I make the turn slowly just in case.

"*How is it ten thirty already?*" I turn off the car and shove my keys into my backpack.

"*Let's hurry and get back to camp,*" Isaac signs.

Leaving Gray Wolf with just Isaac was fun, but now that we're at this middle-of-nowhere Super Mart, I'm realizing how much I'd rather be sitting together around a warm campfire. Plus, the unspoken truth is that neither of us can afford to be caught after curfew again.

Outside the car, I'm struck by how quiet it is. Sure, I've been off camp grounds without my hearing aids already—at the bar and for snack runs—but those were with several people and felt like an extension of camp, where things are still loud and accessible.

But here we are, late at night in a store parking lot. Maybe I should put my hearing aids in, since they're still in my backpack. Judging by the few cars around us, there are other shoppers in there. Going without the devices that I'm so used to wearing to function in society, I feel like I'm naked in public. Isaac must sense my hesitation. He grabs my hand as we walk inside.

Super Mart is such a depressing place, with its fluorescent lighting and warehouse scent. There are more people walking around here than the nearly empty parking lot suggested. We go left, walking along the registers to get to the food section on the opposite side of the store, dodging a few customers with carts who don't make room for us.

We move swiftly. "*I'll find the cookies,*" I sign.

Isaac nods, turning into the next aisle, on the hunt for his Fruit Roll-Ups.

Meanwhile, there are way too many kinds of Oreos for me to choose from. Five shelves of them, to be exact. I'm debating trying something other than the classic Double Stuf when I sense someone else standing near me. I turn and see a man moving suspiciously slowly. There's no strolling around at this hour. It's the time of day for quick in-and-out purchases. But instead, he walks up to me.

I snatch the bag of Oreos directly in front of me, without confirming what kind they are, and walk to the end of the aisle, but the man takes a few more steps and blocks me. "Do you ————?" he says.

I can't tell what else he's saying. Every polite societal instinct in me wants to lean forward, shake my head, apologize, and ask him to repeat. But I don't owe this strange man any of my time. He takes another step, backing me into the shelf. I shake my head.

He mutters something else. When I shake my head again, he gets louder but not any clearer, until I recognize the familiar phrase on his lips. "What, are you deaf or something?"

"*Enough, I can't hear you,*" I sign.

At first, he leans back, startled. I briefly consider how Mackenzie told me she fakes being deaf to get creepy guys to leave her alone—but then the man in front of me curls up his lips into a narrow, unsettling grin, stepping even closer. I can smell the alcohol on his breath.

I push past the man and run to the end of the row, where I find Isaac rounding the corner. Isaac immediately takes stock of the situation and stands still, jaw clenched and eyes narrowed, looking as intimidating as he possibly can while holding four boxes of Fruit Roll-Ups.

Isaac wraps his arm around me, and the man backs off and scurries out of the aisle.

"*Are you okay?*" Isaac searches the emotions on my face.

"*Let's go.*" I look down at the Oreos in my hands and discover they're Birthday Cake. "Oh wait, ew."

Isaac nods in agreement, holding my hand as we walk back to the Oreos. "*My favorite is M-i-n-t,*" he says, as I'm already reaching for that very flavor.

"*Same!*" I'm relieved to be far away from that drunk man and back at Isaac's side.

We hustle to get out of the store and back to camp. Unfortunately, three of the four self-checkout lanes are closed, and there's a line for the only available one, with none other than that creepy guy at the end of it.

"*This one.*" I point to the regular lane, where an old woman behind the counter hands a customer their receipt. There's no line.

Isaac winces and tenses up, bobbling his head indecisively. But when he notices the drunk guy in the self-checkout line, he leads the way to the cashier.

After putting our snacks down on the belt, I unzip my backpack to find my wallet, but Isaac nods that he'll get it. The lady quickly bags the items on the circle platform beside her and spins it around for us to grab our stuff on our way out.

Isaac goes to stick his card in the chip reader, but half of the machine is covered in duct tape, and a sign indicates to swipe instead. I wrap my hands around his left arm, leaning into him as a way of saying thanks. I love the smell of campfire smoke on his clothes. If we hurry, maybe we can get back in time to cuddle around the flames.

After Isaac puts his card away, I notice that the lady behind the register is saying something. Isaac looks at me, but I don't catch what she says, either. He reaches for his phone, probably to use the Live Transcribe app. But she must've been asking if we needed the receipt, so I go ahead and respond, "No, thanks."

Outside the store, I pause to dig out my keys while Isaac takes a few steps with our bags, looking for the car. I'm about to hold his hand when I realize someone behind me is yelling.

I cringe. Is it that guy?

But it isn't. It's some other man, dressed in all black, who runs past me and straight at Isaac. "Hey!" I shout at the man while lunging forward to alert Isaac—but the man beats me to it.

He grabs onto Isaac's shoulder and tries to spin him around. Isaac glances back—first, at the man holding onto his shoulder and shouting in his face, then at my petrified stare. In the next instant, Isaac throws his elbow back, knocking the man in the nose.

It's only as the man stumbles back, raising a hand to his bleeding nose, that I realize there's a patch on his chest.

On his uniform.

Oh no. He's a security guard.

The guard curses loudly. Isaac tries to step toward me, but the man grabs him by the shirt. The guard hasn't tried to identify himself, and Isaac must not have noticed the patch, since this guy grabbed him from behind and closed in too fast this time. The two grapple with each other on the sidewalk. Isaac's shock is now pure anger as he drops the two bags full of snacks. They fall to the ground, boxes of Fruit Roll-Ups spilling out.

"*Stop!*" I realize I signed the word, slamming my right hand perpendicular onto my left palm.

Isaac attempts a punch. The guard swerves out of the way to land one of his own. Isaac raises a hand to clutch his eye. As he does, the guard sticks out a leg to trip Isaac to the ground. Isaac falls, sprawling onto the concrete, scraping his cheek and palms against the curb.

The flashing lights arrive then. And I find the strength to step in.

"Stop it!" I yell at the guard. "You hurt him. Stop it!" The automatic doors keep opening and closing behind me. I'm planted in the sensor's range. "Get away from him!"

But the guard pins Isaac to the ground as the police car parks in front of us. The officer gets out, thoroughly unamused. He's clean-shaven with a buzz cut. He walks leisurely up to the guard and Isaac, holding his belt with both hands. "What's going on here?" he asks in a deep drawl.

"Can you help us?" I try to keep my voice level, but it wavers. "That guard grabbed him. Isaac can't hear what you're saying since he's deaf."

The officer squints toward me, holding up his hand. "Stay ________." He motions for the guard to step back, then helps lift Isaac off the ground.

Isaac stands and carefully raises his scratched hands to his head, the bundle of friendship bracelets sliding down his arm. His face is pale, except for the red lines on his cheek. His brow is furrowed. There's a gash above his left eye that is starting to bleed. His teeth are clenched tight, and his eyes, blinking rapidly from both pain and the nearby emergency lights, start to water.

The guard is saying something to the officer, but I can't tell what. Or why he attacked Isaac. I get closer.

"Young lady," the officer's voice booms sternly.

"Excuse me," I say, taking another step closer. Isaac gives the slightest head shake no, but I ignore him. "What is—"

The guard raises his voice to talk over me, but at least I can kind of tell what he's saying now. "They ——— and then stole ——— when I called him to ———."

"We didn't steal anything," I protest, but I am ignored.

The officer sizes up Isaac and his worn camp clothes. Isaac raises a hand to his forehead and brings it in front of his eyes to inspect the blood. He slowly wipes it on his sleeve, then holds one finger toward the officer.

"Why are you pointing at me?" the officer barks. The security guard slinks back toward the wall.

Isaac points toward his pocket. "*My phone,*" he signs cautiously, mouthing the words along with his signs to try to help the cop follow what he's saying.

"He can't hear you," I tell the officer. "He's deaf."

"I've told you ———," he shouts back, still not paying attention to me.

"*I'm deaf and need to grab . . .* " Isaac slowly signs, bringing his hand down and motioning to the pocket with his phone.

"What are you doing?" the officer says. He reaches forward and pushes Isaac's back against the patrol car, preparing to search him.

"I'm trying to tell you that he's deaf!" I shout. While I know exactly what Isaac was signing, the officer must have no idea. Nor could he read Isaac's lips.

"He's what?" The officer pauses the pat-down and turns to look at me.

"*Or if you have paper to write—*" Isaac signs carefully.

Taking Isaac's movement as a threat, the officer grabs him by the arm, spins him around, and handcuffs him behind his back.

"I'm telling you he's deaf!" I shout again.

"Stand back." The officer reaches to open the door of the police car, shoving Isaac, with his arms and primary method of communication bound behind his back, toward the seat. Isaac doesn't step forward.

"He hasn't done anything," I say, my voice hoarse.

The officer pushes him again.

Isaac stands, frozen. He looks at me, tears in his eyes, lips quivering.

"*I don't know what's happening,*" I sign to him, trying not to cry. I feel so helpless.

The officer scrunches up his face and watches skeptically as I sign. "He's deaf?"

"Yes, he can't hear you," I explain. "And he's hurt because that guy grabbed him and—"

"Tell him ——— in the car then while I ———," the officer says.

"*He wants you to get in the car,*" I sign, my hands shaking. I'm so terrified of messing up right now, because the last thing I want is the officer to suspect that we're bullshitting. I turn back to the cop. "But really, he didn't do anything."

"I still need to do some questioning inside," the officer says. His voice softens. He says something else, but I can't understand any of it now.

"But he needs a bandage or something," I insist.

The officer's voice is gruff again. "Then stop ———. Right now, he needs to ———. I don't have all night."

"He didn't do anything wrong. Please."

"I saw him assault the security guard," the officer says, tired of this back-and-forth. He holds Isaac by the head and sets him inside the vehicle.

After shutting the door, the officer looks back at the guard, who is standing along the wall next to the store entrance, still wiping his bloody nose with a paper towel. "——— get the cashier for me?"

The guard hurries inside. He grabbed Isaac. Jumped on him. Started this whole thing. He's the one who should be sitting in the car right now.

I approach the car door so I can try to sign to Isaac through the tinted windows, but the cop points to the pillar behind me. "Stand there against the wall and don't move until I come speak to you." I reluctantly take several steps back.

The security guard returns to the door with the cashier. The officer huddles with them for only a few minutes, jotting notes on a little pad of paper, before the cashier walks away. The security guard comes outside, picks up the snacks Isaac dropped, and carries them back inside. The officer returns to me.

"The card ———," he says.

"What?" I quickly remember how Oliver told me this question can come across as confrontational, so I hold a hand behind my ear to capture as much sound as possible while nervously asking, "Sorry, can you repeat that?"

"The card didn't swipe correctly," he says.

"It didn't?"

"When the cashier told you two, your friend grabbed the bag and walked off without paying."

"I—" Shit. But that's not the question cashiers always ask—it's usually the receipt. Shit. Shit. Shit. "That's my fault. I thought she asked if we needed the receipt. I assumed because—well, I couldn't hear her."

"I thought he was the deaf one. You don't look deaf."

I frown and try another phrase. "Partially deaf. Hard of hearing."

"Sure."

Does he think I'm lying? This would be a lot easier to prove if I was wearing my hearing aids right now. I should have put them on. Isn't that what they're for? To help me avoid shit like this in the real world? I'm not in the safety of camp. And now it's my fault Isaac is injured and held in a cruiser.

"My hearing aids are in my bag. We're from Camp Gray Wolf. We can go back and pay for the stuff now. I can—" I swing my backpack around, but the officer holds out his hand with the pen, motioning for me to stop.

He holds up the notepad. "Your name?" It's the first of many questions. My name, Isaac's name, why we're at Super Mart so late, where our summer camp is, and so on. He rolls his eyes every time I ask him to repeat a question.

I answer everything as best I can, even though I'm distractedly staring at the back seat of the police car. "Please, we can run the credit card again. Just let him out of the car."

The officer checks his notes and returns the notepad to his pocket. "All right. We're going now."

"But why do you have to take him? It was all a mistake."

"Was ——— mistake that he assaulted ——— guard?"

"That guy grabbed Isaac from behind. He didn't know what was happening," I say. The officer walks away toward the driver's seat of his car. I walk after him, insistent. "He needs an interpreter."

"——— drive along behind us."

"Me? I— I'm not an interpreter."

"You were signing with him, weren't you?" The officer gets into the car. I squint through the flashing lights.

Isaac needs a certified interpreter who can explain any complexities of what's said at a police station. While I'm better than nothing, I'm not *that*. Plus, I'm pretty sure that legally he needs to be provided with a legitimate interpreter in a situation like this. I doubt whatever small station he's being taken to will have one on call.

"*I'll get help,*" I sign, hurrying after the car. I don't even know if Isaac can see me through the window.

Shit, I'm supposed to be driving behind them. The cop pulls away and drives off without waiting for me. I scramble to grab my phone and take a picture of the vehicle, cursing myself for not recording anything earlier. I run to my car, but I've already lost sight of them.

CHAPTER TWENTY-THREE

Gary answers the phone sleepily, and I babble something incoherent about Super Mart, Isaac, and the police. He asks a question I don't understand, so I say, "Text me. I can't hear you," and hang up the phone. I can't stay at Super Mart. I'm too jumpy. There aren't many places to go, so I drive a few minutes down the road to Mackie's, park, and look at Gary's text.

Gary: Stay where you are

Lilah: I'm in the mackie's parking lot now

I couldn't stay there

I text Isaac, though I know it's unlikely he'll see the message.

Lilah: I'm so sorry. It's going to be okay, I promise.

We're gonna come get you. I'm so sorry.

The radio is off. I choose to sit in absolute silence. It's late enough that the Mackie's indoor seating is closed. There's still a car or two going through the drive-through. I count eleven cars before Gary's jeep pulls in next to me. I wipe away the tears in my eyes and try my best to stop sobbing.

Gary gets out, along with the nurse and Ethan. I should go to meet them, but I can't summon the energy to move from the car. Gary walks up and knocks on my window. "Lilah."

I nod, still stuck in my seat. I have to tell him what happened. I have to tell him it was my fault. I have to tell him that Isaac is beat up and alone and needs our help. He knocks again. I find the strength to hit the unlock button, letting Gary open the door.

He crouches so he's at my eye level, like I'm a third grader about to be reprimanded by her teacher. "Hey, Lilah." His voice is softer now but still urgent. I was expecting him to be angry. Somehow this is scarier. This means things are bad. "Where's Isaac?"

Ethan and the nurse stand closely behind him. I clear my throat but find my breathing growing shallow. "The police officer took him." I hyperventilate. "He's hurt."

"Okay, Lilah," Gary says, speaking slow and clear. Ethan stands to the side, interpreting for me. "Why did the officer take him?"

"The security guard grabbed Isaac because he thought we didn't pay," I say. "But we did pay. But the machine didn't work. But we didn't know. And the guard was fighting with Isaac. He pushed him so hard. And Isaac fell and was all scratched up."

Gary looks back at the nurse and Ethan. I'm worried that I've left out too many details.

I stare down at my hands as I describe the next part. "That's when the police came. When Isaac was signing and asking for paper to write things down, the officer handcuffed him."

Gary nods toward Ethan. "——— report for Lilah to fill out?"

Ethan grabs a folder from his backpack and pulls out an accident report. I cringe at the sight of this form. Ethan hands me the empty sheet and a pen. This situation is so tense my instinct is to make a joke. "Seen my fair share of these," I mumble.

Gary doesn't crack a smile. "It's important that you write exactly what happened." Ethan nods solemnly as he signs "important" twice.

"Right now?" I ask.

"Ethan will stay with you and drive you back to camp," Gary says. "We'll go find Isaac."

"Shouldn't I go with you?" Ethan asks.

"It's fine," Gary says. "I'll ———. Get Lilah back to camp. And ——— call her parents."

Ethan's face falls, but he stays by my car while Gary and the nurse drive off. Gary can't sign, and while the nurse can, she's not as fluent as Ethan. Gary wants to sort things out at the police station, but Isaac might be more comfortable with Ethan there. And me. Or—maybe he wouldn't want to see me.

But I need to see him.

"We need to go with them to get Isaac," I say and sign.

Ethan holds the door open for me to get out of the car. "Here, I'll drive," he says and signs.

"Where are we going?" I don't want to go anywhere other than to Isaac.

"Let me drive," Ethan says more firmly.

Instead of getting out, I crawl over the middle to the passenger seat, pushing my backpack to the ground and curling into a ball.

Ethan gets in, sliding the seat back so his legs can fit. "Fill out the paper."

I hold it up. "Now? Can't it wait until we get Isaac?"

Ethan takes a deep breath. I can tell he's shaking. But his voice is steady when he says, "Now."

So I write, trying to keep my words legible. In fine print, I cram in every detail I can recall. The number of times I told the officer that Isaac is deaf. That Isaac would need an interpreter. That the security guard jumped Isaac without identifying himself first. I don't write on the lines because they're spaced too far apart. I'm writing so fast I can barely read my own handwriting, but several minutes later, I've covered the entire front and back of the page.

I hand everything back to Ethan. He gives the paper a quick glance before shoving it into the folder and sliding it into his backpack, which sits on the gearshift between us. He stares ahead, tense.

Ethan turns the key. Nothing. He tries again and again to no avail. Apparently, I'd left the lights on, and now the battery is dead. "Shit." He slams his hands against the steering wheel. I should've known this old car would cause trouble this summer.

"I'm so sorry," I say, so quietly that I'm not sure he hears me. With the events recounted in a written record, it all feels so real now. Isaac must be terrified. And he's all alone. I cry. Warm, ugly tears that I've been struggling to hold back roll down my cheeks. "I'm so sorry."

He turns to me, reaching out to grab both of my arms. "You're fine. Lilah, it's all going to be fine." He pulls out his phone and texts a lengthy message.

I get my own phone out of my backpack to text Isaac again.

Lilah: Help is on the way. I'm so sorry. I hope you're okay. They're coming to get you.

Ethan and I wait. Camp is at least twenty minutes away, but exactly twenty-two minutes later, a car comes speeding into the parking lot.

Jaden, Mackenzie, and Natasha hop out. Natasha runs right to my window. "Why did you let this happen?" she signs and shouts. "What did you do?"

I recoil back toward Ethan, who signs to Natasha. "*Stop.*"

Jaden grabs Natasha and walks her back to the vehicle. Ethan joins them, so Mackenzie takes his place in the driver's seat. She stares at me. Even though it's Mackenzie, I wish she'd reach out and pat my arm. The way hearing people stare without touching now feels unsettling.

"Are you okay?" she asks me.

"You know what happened?" I ask.

"Ethan gave us a brief version. I'm here to talk if you need to." Mackenzie expects me to say something.

I wait until I find her staring unbearable and then I sign, "*I don't feel like it.*"

Out the window is Natasha in Jaden's car. She's sitting with her arms crossed while he signs to her. Ethan gets the jumper cables from the trunk and connects the cars. Jaden joins him.

"She's mad at me. She probably hates me," I say. Any hope for a friendship there feels lost. And I don't blame her.

"She doesn't hate you. She's scared," Mackenzie says and signs. "I'm sorry this happened to you."

"It didn't happen to me. I'm sitting right here while Isaac is hurt and alone. And I said I don't want to talk about it." I cross my arms and turn away.

~

Once my car is running again, Ethan stops by the window. "Are you good to drive her back?" he asks Mackenzie.

"Yeah."

"Where are you going?" I ask.

"We have to take your statement to Gary," he says, walking away to get in the back seat of Jaden's car.

I fling open my door. "Then I need to come with you."

Ethan turns around, jaw still tight, brow narrowed with concern. "Lilah, what I really need is for you to go back to camp. Okay? Go with Mackenzie and wait for us to get back. It's just Bobby and Simone there right now covering the duty shift, so we really need you both back with the campers. Can you do this for me?"

"Why do they get to go?" I point to Jaden and Natasha, who both avoid my gaze.

Ethan doesn't have an answer. "Sorry, Lilah." He climbs into the car, and they speed away.

Mackenzie comes and gently pulls me back to my car, where my eyes finally run out of tears. I kick my feet against the glove compartment. "Everyone hates me. And I should be there for Isaac. But he probably hates me, too."

"Lilah, no one hates you. I promise. They're concerned. You're very upset." She backs the car out and drives away. "Plus, they need us back at camp. That's an important job they're trusting us with, you know."

I don't like Mackenzie driving my car and coming up with pathetic things to say to try to make me feel better. I don't like Ethan treating me like a burden. I don't like the way Natasha and Jaden looked at me. I don't like the way I keep seeing Isaac's face as he got into that police car.

"Your idea is the worst," I say, gritting my teeth.

"My idea?"

"To pretend to be deaf. You don't understand." I shake my head.

"I don't." Mackenzie says this loud and clear.

"You don't." I'm shouting now. "You don't and it makes me so mad. That everyone assumes they know, but they don't. And they make it so difficult. Sometimes they make it all so difficult." Then I curse, loudly.

We sit in silence the rest of the way back to camp, and for a few more minutes in the car once we arrive.

"Lilah, I can't imagine how awful tonight was," Mackenzie says and signs one-handed. "You're right. And I hope you'll forgive me. I didn't know as much as I thought about Deaf culture, and I might have used that to my advantage. That was wrong. But I still want to learn and be better."

Part of me wants to pick a fight. How dare she not give in to my argumentative frustration. "You don't understand. This place is so important to me. Before coming back this summer, I didn't realize just how important it was. And now, what if he never gets to come back? What if I never do? What if none of us do?" I struggle to speak through hiccups from my shallow breathing. "But no matter how hard I try, I feel like I can't do anything right. And after tonight . . ."

"Lilah, what exactly are you talking about?"

I don't answer. Instead, I cover my face with my hands and sob gently. This summer was supposed to be the best one yet, not the worst. And at this rate, I won't get the chance to have a better one next year.

"Lilah," Mackenzie starts to say, and I can sense the uncertainty in her voice. She signs as she speaks, "Isaac is going to be okay. He has to be."

I don't respond, so we sit in silence for a while. "Let's get back to the cabins," Mackenzie suggests.

"I want to wait here for them to get back."

"It's almost midnight," Mackenzie says and signs. "They might be a while, and you need to get some sleep."

"I won't be able to sleep. I need to wait for Isaac."

"You can try. Come on."

I drag my feet, following her on the path until we reach Simone and Bobby at the campfire.

"I'm sorry," I whisper, apologizing to everyone as if it'll take away what happened tonight. I'm not sure if I'll have to explain everything, but the look on Simone's face tells me she already knows. News travels fast.

Simone throws her arms around me and hugs me tight. "I'm so glad you're okay."

"Of course I'm okay. But Isaac . . ." There's a catch in my voice at the mention of his name.

Simone squeezes me tighter. "I've got you."

"They took him, even though it was my fault." I sob into Simone's shoulder. "It was all my fault. I should've asked her to repeat. I shouldn't have said no when I didn't know. They should have taken me."

CHAPTER TWENTY-FOUR

When I wake up the next morning, I'm alone in the cabin. I immediately clutch my phone, but it's dead. I crawl over to the wall and plug it in, waiting in agony for it to power on. By my watch, it's nine thirty. Did they just let me stay here? Am I supposed to go join everyone else now?

There are no texts from Isaac when I turn on my phone. There's only one text from Ethan asking me to let him know when I'm up. I guess this means that no one has called my parents yet. I get back to Ethan before sending another text to Isaac.

Lilah: I hope you're okay. Please Isaac let me know that you're okay.

A few minutes later, I get a text, but not the one I want. Instead, it's Ethan responding to the reply I'd just sent.

Ethan: I'll be right there

Lilah: Where's Isaac

Ethan: One sec I'll be right there.
Don't worry, Isaac's home.

That leaves me with more questions than answers. Isaac's home? Does that mean he's okay? Why hasn't he responded to my texts yet?

I grab my backpack to find my hearing aids. Except instead of putting them back in, I grab my car keys.

Last night might never have happened if I'd been wearing my hearing aids—if I had abided by the wishes of the hearing world. They want us to adapt to them so that they don't have to adapt to us. I wanted to try to embrace my hearing loss, but last night I saw why I shouldn't.

Ethan's on his way to find me. I might as well pack my things and go home before he gets here.

I scramble to my feet and start going through my stuff. Why did I bring so many things? Forget it. I don't need this sleeping bag. Or these old camp clothes. I shove the essentials into my backpack and book it. My parents can get the rest of my belongings when they come to pick up Max. My parents, ugh. I'm going to have to explain this all over again, aren't I? I can already see the disapproval on my mom's face when she asks if I was wearing my hearing aids last night.

I'm headed to the parking lot when Ethan pulls up in the golf cart.

"Where ———?" he asks, confused.

I turn around, not catching the rest of his signing. "I'm going home. Bye."

"Lilah, get in, please."

"No, thanks."

Still puzzled, he slows to a roll beside me, at my pace. "Where's the rest of your stuff?"

"Don't need it. Bye," I repeat.

He hits the brake. "Lilah, get back here. I need to talk to you." I keep walking until he shouts, "You're not leaving!" But when I turn around, his voice is soft and he moves his hands calmly. "Unless you want to, that is . . ."

I pause, then walk back to the golf cart, staring at the ground. "Really?"

He lifts a plate covered with a napkin that's on the seat beside him and nods for me to climb in. "Here's some breakfast."

There are two plain slices of toast. "Uh, thanks?"

He reaches into the backpack at his feet and pulls out a jar of Nutella.

"Oh," I say. "*That's better.*" I tear the bread in pieces and dip it into the chocolate-hazelnut spread.

"I thought so."

Ethan drives to the cabins while I eat in silence. Once I finish, I take my hearing aids out of my backpack and shove them into my ears, only to be met with plugged silence. I don't have any spare batteries with me, either. "Ugh. Dead."

"Orange ones? Check my backpack," Ethan offers.

I dig around in the front pocket until I locate the pack.

"You good?" Ethan says and signs.

"Where are we going?"

"Around." He waits for me to get my hearing aids back in before we drive off, following the path around the outskirts of the campgrounds.

I can hear more sounds now. The rumble of the wheels over the gravel. The loudest birds in the trees. The snap of my fingers as I stretch out my hands to crack my knuckles. The world is noisier, but I'm not sure I really missed any of it.

I ride along, silently at first, until I can't hold back the question I've been dying to ask. "So, Isaac's okay?"

"He and his mom are going to sort some things out," Ethan explains. "He went home last night. I think his mom's also talking to a lawyer to see what their options are. She was grateful for the statement you wrote."

"The statement? You mean the accident report?"

"Yeah."

If I'd known it was going with Isaac and his mother, I might have paid more attention to what I was writing. I thought it was going to be shoved into a folder somewhere for camp records. "Well, it was my fault. I should've been wearing my freaking hearing aids. Then this never would have happened."

"Hey." He stops the golf cart and turns toward me. I'm staring at my shoes. He waves his hand to get my attention. "Look at me," he says and signs.

"What?"

"When you are wearing your hearing aids, can you always tell what people at the register say?"

"Well . . . no."

"It's not crystal clear, right? Aren't you often guessing what you think you may have heard?"

"Yeah."

"So how would it have been any different? Maybe you'd have heard, but it's also still very likely you wouldn't have."

"But maybe I would have—"

"Did the cashier point at the card reader? Or wave her hands frantically as you walked off? Should you have announced your hearing loss to the random service worker at Super Mart? Should Isaac have to wear a pin on his shirt that screams to the world 'I'm deaf' everywhere he goes?"

I shrug, unsure what he's getting at exactly.

"This was a shitty situation, Lilah. It happens." He takes a long, deep breath. "Miscommunication is a fact of life. We just have to deal with it more often than most people."

"Sure. And now Isaac hates me. I'll probably never see him again."

"I promise, Lilah, the person he's mad at the most right now isn't you. Or the cashier, or the guard, or even the officer. It's himself."

"But he didn't do anything wrong."

"I know." We don't have anything else to say until Ethan adds, "He might come back."

"I wouldn't."

"Do you want to go home, Lilah?" Ethan asks gently. "I'd love for you to stay, but only if you want to."

I shrug. Of course I want to stay. But I want to stay at a Gray Wolf where last night never happened. One where we can all enjoy our Deaf haven and not give a second thought to the dangers of the outside world.

But Ethan wants me to stay. Max would probably be mad if

I left early. And staying here is maybe my best chance to see Isaac again.

"I'll think about it," I tell Ethan.

"Okay. We do have to call your parents, though, to let them know what happened. Do you want to come with me and do it now?"

Yeah, I'm sure they'll be *thrilled* to learn what happened. "Let's get this over with."

CHAPTER TWENTY-FIVE

The rainy day suits my mood. Phoebe can tell something is wrong and sits with me in the dance barn, stringing together friendship bracelets.

I didn't give my parents all the details during our call, knowing they'd be mad to learn I hadn't been wearing my hearing aids out in public. They asked if I wanted to come home after everything that happened, and honestly, I thought I did. I was going to take the day to decide, but I made up my mind as soon as I saw Max this morning. Our time here is important. I'm going to stay.

Ethan shows a movie on the projector. The Disney film is playing with both closed captioning and audio description. There are also card games and friendship bracelets and crayons to keep the kids entertained. Meanwhile, all the counselors are walking around like zombies. It was a late night.

Max walks over and stands, with his arms crossed, in front of Phoebe and me. "What's wrong?" he asks me.

I don't want to answer. I put the string aside for now, blankly staring around the dance barn, watching the various activities. I already have too many bracelets.

Is Isaac still wearing the bracelet I gave him?

"Are you mad because Isaac's gone?" Max is perceptive.

"How do you know?"

"Because at breakfast some campers were asking where he was, so Gary and Ethan announced Isaac had a family emergency and went home for a little bit. So . . . what happened?"

"You're nosy," I say. Phoebe chuckles beside me. I'd never really heard her laugh clearly without my hearing aids in.

"Sure," Phoebe agrees. "Well?"

"Um. What Ethan said—an emergency. Hopefully he'll be back soon." I don't want to get into it with my younger brother right now. So I tell Max, "I think Bobby's looking for you."

"Is he gone?" Phoebe asks as Max walks away. "Now can you tell me what really happened?"

"Okay, fine." I push a button on my hearing aids to lower the volume and reach into my backpack to look for some medicine. Phoebe must hear the rattling from the small plastic container.

"Are you taking pills or something?" she asks.

"Yeah, my head is killing me." I wash them down with a sip from my water bottle.

"Is it 'cause your hearing aids are bothering you? Why'd you put them back in?" she asks. "It's raining, after all."

"Because I should, I guess. Wait, how could you tell I'm wearing them?"

"You haven't needed me to repeat as much today," she explains, as if it were obvious. "But if they're giving you a headache right now and we're just sitting here—"

"I don't know. Because I feel like I should, honestly."

"That's not a good reason," Phoebe says.

"Okay, maybe because I'm scared." In as few words as possible, I explain what happened the night before.

Phoebe, for the first time all summer, doesn't have a quick response. After thinking for a minute, she asks, "Did I tell you I want to go to college in the city?"

A little surprised by what she says—but happy for the change of subject—I say, "No, I don't think so."

"My parents don't want me to because there's a lot to navigate, like city streets and being on my own for the first time. So because they're scared, I can't admit that I am, too."

"You're afraid?" It usually seems like nothing can faze Phoebe. She's not the kind of person to throw a vulnerability out there.

"Of course—everything that is new has the potential to be terrifying. But with change, we adapt. Like disabled people have done for, you know, all of human history. Modify, adjust, transform, innovate." She pauses. "Do you need me to keep going?"

"Create a more accessible world so that we can thrive," I say in agreement, understanding her point.

"We wouldn't know our limitations if people didn't keep telling us."

One of Natasha's campers approaches, peering at the pile of string in front of Phoebe. "Can I look for a color?" she says and signs. I nod. After she takes her pick, the girl looks back up at me. "Oh, we match!"

We do? She's not looking at my bracelets, and I can't find a single piece of apparel we're wearing in common. That is, until she lifts a finger and points to my ear.

"You have purple, too!" I say, realizing what she means.

"It's my favorite color." She holds up her wrist full of friendship bracelets, all varying shades of purple.

"It's a cool color."

Out in the real world, I always notice whenever someone else has hearing aids. Usually it's someone old, with a tiny in-the-ear device or a hidden mold with very thin tubing running up the ear. But it never escapes my glance. Especially when it's someone young like me. That's usually easier because we get a wider variety of colors to choose from.

I'm always tempted to walk up to strangers and be like, "Hey, I've got those, too!" But what if they don't have the same reaction? What if they want to keep their hearing aids hidden and are upset that I see through their disguise?

Camp Gray Wolf needs to stay alive. It's here that we can find our community—a place where we can be ourselves, unapologetically.

~~~

I take my time getting to the campfire tonight. I'm not eager for my Friday on-duty shift without Isaac. It's been a few days with him gone, but time feels like it's moving in slow motion. In the bathhouse, Simone and her girls are brushing their teeth. Natasha walks right past me toward the showers. I've been avoiding her, which is easy because I'm pretty sure she's avoiding me, too.
~~~

Back at the cabin, I change into my pajamas and linger on Isaac's sweatshirt, still sitting in my bunk. Will I get to give this back to him? Would he be mad if I kept it?

I put on my raincoat in case it pours again and grab my beach towel so I can sit on the damp benches around the firepit. For a few minutes, I'm sitting there all alone. I can't stay in the staff cabin since it's still housing campers after the storm. I stare at my phone that still has no new messages. Nothing from Isaac.

I'm startled when someone walks out of the darkness to stand beside me. Mackenzie gives a small wave before spreading her beach towel on the nearby bench. Simone and Bobby arrive as well.

"Want to play a game? I'm pretty sure I brought UNO," Simone says after sitting by my side. "Or borrow a book? I've got some non-Braille ones."

"No." I can't really stomach entertainment right now. "But thank you for joining me."

She leans against my shoulder, and we sit together in comfortable silence.

Yet time crawls. A minute, or maybe an hour later, I jump when my phone buzzes.

It's just a message from my mom, and I don't feel like replying. The only person I really want to be texting with right now is Isaac. So I do.

Lilah: Hey I know you don't feel like talking
but I just wanted to make sure you know
I'm here when you're ready

I nearly jump out of my seat when the three little dots dance at the bottom of my screen. I hold my breath as Isaac types a response. But he stops writing and the ellipsis disappears.

I wait a few minutes, hoping he might still send a reply—but nothing.

~~~

Saturday evening, I get a message from Oliver asking me to hang out, so I wander down to the lake. He's lounging in one of the beach chairs, staring up at the stars, when I take the seat beside him.

"Ben's doing some artwork on his laptop, so I'm all yours for the night," Oliver says. "How can I distract you?"

I look at the sky, watching clouds drift in front of the moon. "I don't know. I don't really feel up for much of anything."

"Are you hungry?" he asks.

"Not really."

"Well, I'm starved, so you can sneak some bites off my plate."

"Bites of what?" I ask, wondering if I missed something he said.

But Oliver jumps up, grabs his bag, and starts walking up the path. I jog after him, curious. I can't sit here lost in my thoughts right now.

"Where are you going?" I ask when I've caught up to him. "I really don't want to leave camp."

"Leave camp? Nope, we're doing something even better."

We turn at the edge of the path, and Oliver walks straight up to the dining hall's side door.
~~~

"Are we allowed to be in here right now?" I ask, staring through the dark entryway.

"Nope, we're breaking in." Then he finds a key on his lanyard and unlocks the door. "We got a spare as lifeguards, since we don't always eat at your normal mealtimes."

It's eerie being in this building after dark. Oliver flips on only one of the lights in the kitchen, leaving the rest of the building haunted by shadows. Our footsteps echo across the empty space, since all the tables and chairs are folded and put away each night during cleaning.

Oliver peers into a small pantry. "I'm going to make you my famous macaroni cheese."

"You mean mac *and* cheese."

"Nope, unnecessary word." He fills a large pot with a tiny bit of water, enough for a meal just for the two of us. He leans against the counter. "You're keeping those in now?" He points toward my ears.

"Yeah." I lift myself up to sit on the counter. "Doesn't that make it easier for you? You don't have to put up with me saying 'what' a million times."

"I never actually minded that."

"Really? A lot of people do."

"I just want you to feel comfortable doing whatever you want," he says, still making sure to face me as he talks.

"Thanks, Oliver."

He dumps the dry noodles into the pot, searching in the big industrial-size fridge for some cream, butter, and cheese.

"Otherwise you're doing all right?" he asks, turning to make sure I still have a clear view of his face when he speaks.

"Yeah, I guess I just felt like I made so much progress figuring myself out this summer, and it all got erased in a single night."

"No, don't think of it that way."

"It's hard not to," I admit.

"There's still plenty of summer left," he says. "And a whole life ahead of you. You can keep finding yourself again and again. The important part of all of that is just being true to what your heart tells you."

"Dang, that's poetic."

"I have been reading a lot of Ben's poetry collections lately." He leans back to stir the boiling water.

I consider what he said. Up until this summer, wearing my hearing aids was nonnegotiable. I diligently put them in every morning without question. I never would've thought I'd go without them for most of the last month. But I can do that. I have that choice—and so many choices ahead of me. A multitude of ways I can explore my identity and decide how to exist in this world.

Oliver drains the noodles and assembles the ingredients. "All right, hop down, grab us a couple bowls, and get ready for the best meal of your life."

We take our cheesy snack and sit outside on the dining hall porch, staring out at the slumbering campgrounds waiting to come to life again the next morning. I bask in the cool evening breeze, finding peace in this moment, especially as I take a bite of the delicious meal.

"*This is good,*" I sign, nodding as I chew. Before I can say it out loud, Oliver jumps in.

"That means 'good,' right?" he says, smiling. "I knew it."

CHAPTER TWENTY-SIX

Natasha waves at me across the fire. It's a very cold Tuesday night, but our staff cabin is still housing campers, so the options for gathering after hours are limited. From my bench on the opposite side, I watch her across the flames.

"*Hey, I need to talk to you,*" Natasha signs. I'm nervous since we're not exactly on the best of terms right now. "*I want to say sorry.*"

I shake my head. "It's fine."

"*No. About that night.*" She looks away for a second before adding voice. It's been exactly one week since Isaac left camp, and we'd been avoiding discussing the subject until now. "I was just scared. Isaac explained more about what happened, so I wanted to apologize."

"It's okay, really," I assure her, fixating on the fact that she's gotten messages from Isaac. But I'm relieved that, even if he doesn't want to get back to me, at least he's in touch with his friends. "I probably would've reacted the same way."

"Yeah," she says and signs. "I noticed you haven't been signing as much lately."

"Oh, I don't know. I guess since I'm working with the blind campers mostly right now." But as I talk to Natasha, my hands stay by my side, like they're too heavy to lift. "Yeah . . . so you've heard from him? Is he doing okay? I sent him a message, well, a few messages."

Natasha gives me a pitiful, knowing look. "I'm sure he'll respond to you soon."

Ethan walks up, with a very enthusiastic Mackenzie and Jaden by his side, and waves to get everyone's attention.

"Do you have the staff here?" He looks around the firepit to confirm. "Let me text Simone and Bobby real quick."

"What's up?" I ask Ethan.

"Let's wait for everyone to be here," Ethan says and signs.

Mackenzie sets up her laptop on the picnic table. Gary pulls up on the golf cart as Simone and Bobby arrive. Everyone's seated and waiting for Ethan's announcement.

"Which do you want first, the good news, or the great news, or the best news?" he asks.

"All of them!" Bobby shouts.

"Okay, we'll build," Ethan says and signs. "To start, the initial donations received, thanks to all your families and friends, as well as Mackenzie's boost to her followers"—Mackenzie nods, having been waiting expectantly for this shout-out—"have officially secured us enough funding to get started on repairs to the storm damage!"

"We can get our staff cabin back?" Simone asks. "No more hanging around in the cold?"

"It'll take a while to mend the roof of both cabins, but they'll be looking better than ever in no time!" Gary announces proudly.

"Now, the great news. I'd argue this is tied with best," Ethan says and signs. "It's not one hundred percent yet. But I've heard from Isaac, and he should be returning to camp soon!"

My heart races with excitement and despair. He's returning to Gray Wolf? But he's been in contact with seemingly everyone but me?

"And last, but certainly not least . . ." Ethan gestures for Jaden to take the next part, voicing his signing.

"*So I shared the fundraiser, then my cousin shared it, then my cousin's friend shared it, and last night ———— made a huge donation!*" He fingerspells too fast, and I'm so overwhelmed by the news that I don't catch the name when Ethan interprets it.

Simone nods toward me. "She's that famous Deaf actress, right?"

"Dang, the Deaf community is small," Bobby says.

"And her sharing it also got us even more donations," Ethan says. "And so much interest in the camp. Thankfully, Isaac had rebuilt our website with a contact box and sign-up form."

"Yes, it's a very good thing there will be more money," Gary chimes in. "Because it looks like we're going to need more cabins and staff for *a ton* of new campers."

More staff? More campers? So that obviously means we're back next year, right?

"By my calculations," Gary says, with Ethan still interpreting, "we're set for hopefully at least the next ten years." He continues, sharing details of all the renovations he and Ethan have in mind for the campgrounds, such as clearing additional hiking trails and adding a basketball court or volleyball net.

"And we're also definitely coming up with some sort of end-of-summer outing to celebrate," Ethan adds. "We'll do something even bigger and better than we've ever done before."

~~~

I sit out today's pool time, keeping an eye on the campers from the comfort of a deck chair, sneaking glances at my phone as often as I can manage. If you'd told me when I was a camper there would come a time that I'd voluntarily pass on swim time, I wouldn't have believed it. But I've swum so much this summer that I can use a break.

I feel my backpack vibrate on my lap, so I pull my phone from the mesh side pocket. I squint to read the screen through the harsh sunlight, imagining I just got a text from Isaac. But it's just an irrelevant notification. It's been two weeks since he left, and I'm desperate to hear from him, but I'm starting to think I never will. My hopes have been dashed so many times that I almost don't believe the message that pops up on my screen then.

Isaac: Hey

One word. That's all I get. One single word—no exclamation mark or anything. What am I supposed to do with that? Is he upset, angry, tired, relieved, or what?

Lilah: How are you?
~~~

My heart flutters and my stomach twists into a nervous ball of anxiety while I wait.

Isaac: I'm okay. How are you?

Lilah: Okay

I'll hit him back with a single-word text of my own. Except, he doesn't respond. After a few minutes of waiting, I cave.

Lilah: I miss you

He types for a very long time. I'm clutching my phone, even though I should be more discreet, as texting during work hours is frowned upon. Each second I wait, I grow certain that he's going to say he never wants to see me again. But then I receive a paragraph that I have to read three times to process.

Isaac: I'm sorry I hadn't replied to your texts yet. It's been . . . rough. I was mad at everything and everyone. It's really frustrating when this shit happens, and no matter what I do, I feel like I react the entirely wrong way. Especially in miscommunications. I need space to calm down and think.

He needs space? He's been gone for so many days already. I'm guessing that means he's not coming back to camp after all, but does it mean he doesn't want to talk to me, either? All I got from that answer is that he doesn't miss me.

I watch the minutes pass by, knowing that I need to put my phone away and keep an eye on the campers. My thoughts are racing when Ethan walks over and taps my shoulder. I blink rapidly to hide my tears and drop my phone in my lap. "Sorry," I say. "I'll hop in the pool with the campers now."

"Actually, come with me real quick," he says, gesturing toward the golf cart outside the pool gate.

"I know I shouldn't have been on my phone, but—"

"Lilah, relax," Ethan says, picking up my backpack for me. "You're not in trouble, I promise."

He drives us to the cabins, and sitting there at a picnic bench around the firepit is Isaac. But he's wearing a casual button-down and pants, not summer camp attire.

"Is he back?" I ask.

But Ethan only smiles. "We'll meet you at the dining hall for lunch. Don't be late."

"*I've been waiting for you,*" Isaac signs. "*Before seeing everyone else.*" There's a bandage over his left eyebrow. The scratches on his cheek are fading but still noticeable. It must be painful. He looks like he was in a fight. Because he was.

"*Why are you here?*" I stop a few feet away from him, planting myself firmly on the ground but not moving closer. I lower my eyebrows and fold my arms across my chest.

"*I'm back.*"

I narrow my eyes and lift one hand to sign, "*For good?*"

He nods, but he notices I'm looking at his outfit skeptically. "*My mom and I had breakfast earlier.*" Isaac gestures toward his phone. "*Get my text?*"

I nod, looking at my feet. He had good reason to leave, but he cut me out and sent this scary text. I'm not sure where we stand right now, so I fight the desire to rush to hug him. "*Do you not want to see me?*"

He shakes his head fast and walks over to stand beside me. "*I'm not mad now,*" he signs.

"*But you were mad.*"

He nods solemnly.

My eyes water again. "*At me?*"

Now it's his turn to stare at his feet. He barely lets his finger drift in my direction when he signs, "*At you. At myself. At everyone.*" He keeps his head bowed but lifts his eyes to look at me. "*My mom was really sad.*"

I'm embarrassed about how upset I've been with him. He's been dealing with some real shit the past few days. Still, he cut me out. All I needed was a single message letting me know that he was okay. "*I was sad, too.*"

He scrunches up his face, and the bandage on his forehead creases. I don't like seeing him like this.

"*It's my—*" I take a deep breath, frustrated that my sign language is still too shaky for this conversation. "*F-a-u-l-t.*" I spell it out slowly and purposefully, not wanting to repeat it if my hands shake too much.

But Isaac waves his hand. "*No. Not yours. Not mine, either.*"

"*Okay.*" I still don't know what he wants. I can't tell if he knows, either. "*Should I go?*"

His eyes are wide and confused. "*Go?*"

"*You said you need space?*"

He shakes his head and pulls out his phone. He frowns at his message and types again.

Isaac: When I get mad I need space to calm down but I'm not mad anymore. I came back because I want to spend the rest of the summer here. With you. But I understand if you're still mad at me.

He hits Send, but I'm sitting close enough to read over his shoulder. I lead him back to the bench, where we sit side by side. "*But I'm not mad at you,*" I sign. "*Never was.*"

He smiles and sits back against the table, so I scooch next to him, leaning in to gently kiss his cheek, careful to avoid the scratches.

"*Did your mom help?*" I ask.

He nods and leans in close to me, but I hold out my hands to sign some more.

"*It was wrong. We should share the story o-n-l-i-n-e,*" I sign. "Or something," I say, shrugging. I don't know how to take action in this situation.

"*Online? No. Never,*" he signs. "*People like to watch me. One time someone took a video of me and my mom signing. When I go places, they watch like I'm an animal at the zoo. I don't need people knowing about this. I'm not their sad story. And I'm not their* ———." I tilt my head, so he spells out the word. "*I-n-s-p-i-r-a-t-i-o-n.*"

"*I understand.*" And I really do. Who knows how the internet would react? They'd probably find a way to place the blame on us. Often, when people are inspired by disabilities, what they're really thinking is *Wow, I'm so glad that's not my life.*

"*And we have the fundraising video. People would find that and my social media and everything about me, all because of the worst night of my life. I don't want that."*

I reach over to hug Isaac. This time, he's the one to pull away.

"*I almost forgot. I got you this.*" He reaches into his left pocket, pulls out a bag of strawberry cheesecake jelly beans, and hands it to me. "*Not easy to find.*"

"*My favorite! You remembered.*" I turn to my backpack, grabbing the green bracelet I made during rainy day activities. "*I made you another one.*" I shrug, glad I have something to offer in return. I'd offer a million of them if I could.

He immediately holds out his wrist for me. "Your official welcome back," I say as I tie the string.

"*Perfect.*" He smiles, pointing to the bag of jelly beans in my lap. "*Can I try one?*"

"*You didn't eat one yet?*"

He shakes his head and opens his mouth.

I roll my eyes, laughing. I place a few jelly beans in his hand and lean forward to kiss his lips. "*I'm glad you came back.*"

He nods and brings the candy to his mouth. "*Okay.*" He shrugs.

"*Okay? Only okay?*"

"*They're good, but they're no M and M chocolate.*"

"*If you say so.*" We sit in a comfortable silence, huddled together. "*Should we go to the dining hall?*" I ask reluctantly, but I'm sure he wants to meet up with the others.

"*In a minute.*" He wraps an arm around me, and we stay right where we are. "*I missed you, too,*" he signs finally.

CHAPTER TWENTY-SEVEN

To celebrate Isaac's return, the entire staff gathers to make s'mores at the campfire after hours.

With things smoothed out with Natasha, I realize there's still something important I need to ask her about, since she's the only counselor with a cochlear implant. I need more insight into what it's like to have one before Max needs to make the decision.

Ethan already told me some of Natasha's experience, but I want to learn from her why she got the implant. It seems rare that her entire family is Deaf, but she chose to have the surgery. Deaf families are usually excited when their children are like them, but often they give birth to hearing children, like Mackenzie's college friend, who is a CODA. So most of the kids I know with implants have hearing parents.

Natasha is standing opposite the campfire from me. I inch my marshmallow farther into the flames and wave to get her attention. "Can I ask . . ." I say, then make my way around the fire to sit with her. "Why did you get your cochlear implant?" I say and sign one-handed. I'm immediately terrified of the look on her face, so I quickly add, "My parents think my brother needs one."

"*No one needs one,*" she signs, with the emphasis on the word "needs." She pulls back her stick to inspect her marshmallow.

"Take a video of Max when he tries it on!" Mackenzie chimes in. "Have you seen those 'baby hears for the first time' videos?"

"I hate those," Natasha says and signs, wanting to make sure we follow her crystal clear. She takes a deep breath. "A cochlear implant doesn't fix everything. It's a surgical procedure after which I had to train my brain how to hear the world. My hearing isn't magically restored the same as a hearing person's."

Mackenzie slumps forward, letting her marshmallow burn. "When you put it that way," she says and signs. "I should have assumed as much, honestly. If you dislike it so much, why did you get it?" I'm glad Mackenzie's here to ask the tough questions for me.

Natasha takes a deep breath. "A few years back, I got really fed up with the world. My entire family is Deaf—mother, father, brothers, sisters, aunts, uncles, cousins, grandparents. Everyone. Some could use hearing aids, but they don't often wear them and communicate only with sign. Very proud to be Deaf, as they should be."

She pauses and looks at me. "*Right,*" I sign, not wanting to interrupt her story.

"But I was so frustrated everywhere I went," Natasha says. "How I was so dependent on interpreters. How people treat us differently. And when my dad had to go to the hospital . . . that was the last straw for me."

Isaac returns from assembling his own s'more. "*Talking about your implant?*" he asks Natasha. I take his appearance as an excuse to step over to the supplies and quickly put together my s'more as well.

Natasha resumes. "I wanted greater independence and at the time thought this was the way to get it. But when I decided to do it, my family got mad—my dad, especially. He said I'd no longer be Deaf enough. Always going on about 'we can do anything but hear.' To him, my wanting something to help me hear was a betrayal."

"But you're still Deaf," I say and sign. I know I'm constantly worried about not feeling "Deaf enough," but I don't understand how it's possible that Natasha does as well.

"*You're still Deaf,*" Isaac signs at the same time.

"I know," Natasha continues. "And even with the cochlear, I need interpreters. Sure, I can 'hear better' now, but still not well enough to go without my other resources. And recovery was difficult after the surgery. I was worried it had failed. Sometimes these implants don't work. It could still potentially fail. But I recovered from the procedure, and my dad got nicer about my decision, although still very 'I told you so.' I've gotten used to hearing a bit more of the world around me, but I don't wear the processor all the time, preferring the quiet. But until this world gets a lot more deaf-friendly, I guess I'm glad I have it as an option."

I know exactly what she means. "So does that mean you're glad you got it?"

She scrunches up her mouth. "To be honest, if I could go back and do it all over again, I don't think I would get it."

"Really?" Mackenzie asks.

Natasha shrugs. "I've got it now, so I might as well use it when I want." She looks at me. "I don't know. What does your brother think?"

"I'm not sure," I say and sign. "I need to talk to him about it."

Natasha agrees, signing emphatically. "So many kids are implanted super young, without consent."

Isaac turns. "*Your brother?*"

"*His left ear could use a cochlear implant now,*" I sign.

"*Teach him ASL,*" Isaac signs. "*Like we did with baseball.*"

"*I'm still learning myself,*" I sign.

As much as I'd love for my family to be fluent in ASL, the possibility of that seems a long way away. It's difficult to imagine sign language as part of my real world, rather than just existing at camp.

"S'mores!" Ethan joins our huddle at the campfire, finished with his paperwork early this evening.

"Not turning in early?" Mackenzie asks.

"Nah," Ethan says and signs, grabbing a marshmallow and a seat by the fire. "How could I miss this celebration?"

"Do you think I should tell my brother he shouldn't get the cochlear?" I ask Natasha.

While she ponders, Ethan chimes in. "For Max? Why not? My twin has one and loves it."

"Really?" I didn't know he had siblings, let alone a twin.

"Yeah, she got it when she was pretty young," he says and signs one-handed. "I've got the two hearing aids, but she's got one cochlear. Her other ear has full hearing."

Ethan stands to make his s'more, so I wait for him to sit again. Natasha is curious as well.

"But doesn't your family sign?" Natasha asks.

"Oh, no." Ethan shakes his head as he takes a big bite. "Only me. I went to Deaf school all my life, but my sister wanted to be mainstreamed."

"Interesting," I say and sign. "My brother hasn't picked up much ASL yet. I'm trying to teach him as I learn."

"*And I'll help you,*" Isaac offers once more. He slides closer to me on the bench.

"Hey, you're wearing your hearing aids again," Natasha says and signs, pointing to my ears.

"Yeah." I turn slightly toward Isaac but look at the ground in front of his feet.

"*You are,*" Isaac echoes the observation. "*I love the purple.*"

I shake my head while Natasha rolls her eyes. "You're only now noticing?" Natasha asks. "How is that possible?"

She's about to chastise him further, but Jaden shows up and sits next to her. Bobby and Simone are heading our way, too. I snuggle next to Isaac and share another smile with Natasha across the circle. It's an "entire staff around the fire" kind of night. I've missed these.

CHAPTER TWENTY-EIGHT

The sun hasn't begun to set yet, but we're preparing a Friday night campfire down by the lake, complete with ASL story time, most likely Jaden's retelling of the Deaf King Kong joke. Gary is sitting on the golf cart going through some paperwork and waves me over.

"How've you been, Lilah?"

"It's been a wild summer. But things are good." Nervously, I stretch out my arms, watching as the cart's headlights cast a long shadow behind me.

"Glad to hear it. So I've been crunching the numbers after our new fundraising success. Any idea what your plans are for next year?"

"Well, not yet."

"Would you be interested in being a senior counselor?"

"Yes!" I blurt out. "I mean, if I'm allowed. I'm not sure I was exactly the most stellar junior counselor this camp has ever seen. And I'm still working on my ASL."

"Are you kidding? You've done great. Helping put together this fundraising video, for one. That's some brilliant leadership. We're not going to let you go that easily. You've done great with the campers, especially helping those who also aren't fluent in sign. I have complete confidence that with a few more summers working here, you'll be fluent. It'd be impossible not to be. Heck, even Bobby and the lifeguards know a bunch of signs now. Meanwhile, I've managed to get by using the staff as interpreters." He pauses to scratch his beard. "Now, don't think I've forgotten about a certain curfew incident."

"Never again," I say, shaking my head solemnly. But I did it! I managed to secure the senior counselor job. Even though it was a long, sometimes difficult summer, I did it.

"The way I see it, you'll be Ethan's problem," Gary says. "I won't be here next summer."

"Why not?"

"Time to hand over the reins. Plus, Ethan's more than ready to take over." Gary seems nonchalant about it.

Ethan knows Gray Wolf inside and out. He's been a camper since he was six, a junior counselor, a senior counselor, and now the assistant director. He deserves it, and we'll have our first ever disabled director.

"I'm sure he's excited," I say. "We'll miss you, though!"

"I'll find a way to stop by and see how all the renovations are looking. I'm excited for you all." Gary beams at me. "Any questions about the gig?"

"Oh, I don't know." I wasn't expecting this conversation right now.

Gary glances at his papers again, then smiles back at me.

"If you think of any, just let me know. Ethan will be in touch with the particulars next spring."

"Do I still have to interview, or . . ."

"This was the interview. I've already talked it over with Ethan. He'll be thrilled to know you're on board."

"Awesome."

"Now, do you mind sending Phoebe my way? I've got a question for her as well."

I weave through some of the younger kids running around and head back to where Phoebe is waiting for me at the benches. "Hey, so, Gary has something to ask you."

"Oh, do you think it's about next summer?" She's already shaking with excitement.

"Possibly. Ethan asked me a while ago if you'd be interested. Deep breaths," I say, reaching out to steady her shoulders. "Want me to guide you over?"

"He's just right there?" She nods ahead, unfolding her cane. "I'm on it."

I wait patiently while Phoebe walks over and chats with Gary for a few minutes. She's beaming when she hurries back. "All right! You're looking at next year's junior counselor!"

"Yes!" I crash into her with a hug. "They better assign you to my group."

~

I reapply some bug spray before heading to my second-to-last on-duty shift of the summer. When I arrive at the firepit, Isaac's already got a flame going. He's sitting on the rocks, poking the kindling with a long stick.

"*You look happy,*" he signs as I walk over.

"*I got some good n-e-w-s earlier.*" I toss my backpack on the top of the picnic table, not caring that the surface is still damp from a light smattering of afternoon rain.

"*Can spell n-e-w-s, or similar to 'inform,'*" he signs for me, bringing his folded hands from near his head to extended open palms. "*What is it?*"

"*Guess who's a senior counselor next summer?*"

"*You are?*"

"*Yes,*" I sign, doing a little dance as I walk over to him, wearing his hoodie, putting my arms up and flapping the sleeves around with excitement.

"*That's awesome! I'm happy for you.*" He offers a hand to help me take a seat on the rocks beside him. My feet are warm by the flames.

"*What about you?*" I ask, looking up at him.

"*What about me?*" he signs, bobbing his head. "*I'm excited!*"

"*Are you coming back?*"

He tosses more sticks into the fire. "*I can't.*"

I expected this response, but that doesn't make it easier to digest. "*Why?*" I hold the sign for a few seconds, even though I have a good guess. But if he came back for the rest of this year, why wouldn't he want to come back for next summer? "*We could be together all summer again.*"

"*I've got baseball,*" he signs. "*For college. It was already hard to make this year work.*"

"*Oh.*" I hadn't expected this, but I knew he played. I try to think of some way he can come back. "*Maybe you can come back and visit camp for a week.*"

"*Maybe.*" He doesn't look sure.

"*You leave for college soon, right?*"

"*On the last Sunday.*"

"*Like, the last day of camp Sunday, Sunday?*" That's barely any time together left. Is he leaving straight for the airport? I thought we might be able to find a way to see each other a few more times after camp was over.

He scrunches up his mouth and nods slowly. "*But!*" His eyes widen with excitement. "*Ethan's planning an end-of-summer surprise in the city for that Saturday night.*"

"*Yeah, I remember he said that.*"

"*Yeah. It'll be awesome.*"

I lift my head and gaze at the dark night sky. I wish summer wasn't so short. "*Where are you going to school? RIT, right?*"

"*No.*" He shakes his head. "*Gallaudet.*"

"Oh," I say, having assumed because that's where a lot of counselors had gone before. "*I thought you were going to be in New Y-o-r-k, but Gallaudet is in DC, right?*" Either way, it's far away from me.

He nods, reaching back into his backpack to grab something. He nudges my shoulder, so I sit back up and notice that he's holding two Fruit Roll-Ups.

"*Where from?*" I ask.

He smiles. "*My mom.*" He holds up the backpack. It's crammed with snacks. His mom made sure he didn't have to go on any more food runs.

"*That's a lot. You'll never finish it all.*"

He takes a bite and shrugs. "*More for the plane.*"

"*Right after camp.*"

"*Right after camp,*" he repeats.

The fire starts to dwindle, so Isaac reaches forward and tosses in another log. I watch the flames engulf it. Isaac's off to college after this. I always knew this was coming. I can be realistic. Our days are numbered.

"*That's so soon,*" I sign.

He wraps his arm around me. I stretch out my legs until my feet are near the fire. I lean against Isaac, finishing the Fruit Roll-Up that'd been dangling from my mouth.

I'll miss him. I'll miss the person I am around him.

He can sense my apprehension and leans forward, planting a soft kiss on my forehead. We spend the rest of the night wrapped together in front of the fire as I count the hours we have left together.

~~~

Knowing I'll be back next year, I try not to be too sad as this year winds to a close, but it's hard not to get nostalgic as everything turns into a last. Last time at the beach. Last time hiking along the path. Last time playing large-group games on the grassy field. Last time at the pool. Last time the chef serves some sort of sludge for dinner. Last night Isaac and I dance together in the barn, forgetting the world around us.

No matter how repetitive some things seem after an entire summer's worth—the same songs performed at each talent show, the same cannonball jumps at the lake, and soon, the same tearful farewells that inevitably plague every camp at the end of the season—it's hard not to be upset that this season is almost over. Saying goodbye to Gray Wolf will never be easy.

And just like that, another week passes, and the final Friday is here. Isaac and I are supposed to be on duty, but Gary and the nurse offer to keep watch near the cabins, letting us roam
~~~

the campgrounds with the rest of the counselors. Isaac and I wait at the firepit for Ethan, Jaden, Natasha, Simone, Bobby, and Mackenzie to join us.

"Let's do the lake again!" Ethan says and signs.

"Not the bridge." I don't think I could manage a second leap this summer.

"*We could jump from the d-o-c-k,*" Isaac offers.

"That's what I was thinking," Ethan says and signs. "Just a casual night at the lake. I already told the lifeguards. Let's go!"

We take our time walking down to the water. This path is so familiar now that I can anticipate every turn and sign without looking where I'm going.

Oliver and Ben are waiting for us at the fence. "Ethan gave us a heads-up this time that you all would be coming," Oliver explains.

"So you can join the fun," I say.

"But unfortunately, it can't go too late," Oliver says, frowning. "We've got an early train to catch tomorrow morning."

"How early?" I ask.

"Like, five o'clock," Ben says.

"*Very* early. Wow, is this the last time I'm going to see you?" I'm sad to see them go.

"Nope, because we'll still be around," Oliver says. "Traveling the States for a while before our international flight departs from Chicago. We'll be back in the area in a month, and you should meet us for dinner."

"Yes, that's perfect! So you can tell me all about your trip. Even though I'm sure I'll see it all on Instagram first."

"Are you coming back next summer?" Oliver asks.

"I am—senior counselor!" I say. "Are you?"

"That's the plan," Oliver says. "For me, at least."

Ben gives a noncommittal nod.

"What a relief! It seems like so many people aren't coming back. I'm very glad you'll be here again," I say. Isaac is waiting for me near the water, so I wrap up my goodbyes for now. "I'll catch you later before we call it a night!"

I rejoin Isaac, who leads us to the edge of the dock. "*Scared this time?*"

"*Only a little,*" I sign, thinking about the end of summer rather than about the physical short leap into the water, but happy to be holding tight to his hand all the same.

He leans forward and kisses the tip of my nose. Then we jump.

After I pop back up, Isaac and I wade over to the shallow area near the other counselors. It's still too deep for me, so I bounce on my tiptoes to keep my face above the surface. Isaac reaches out to hold me afloat. Facing him, I rest my arms on his shoulders and wrap my legs around his waist.

An hour or two passes, and eventually it's time to get back to the cabin. The rest of the counselors get ready to leave.

But Isaac doesn't move to emerge from the lake yet. "*I don't want to go.*"

"*Same.*"

"*Why is it the last night of camp?*"

I reach for his neck to draw him in for a kiss. One that hopefully conveys how glad I am to have him here and how much I never want to let him go.

"*I'll miss this,*" I sign.

"*Me too.*"

CHAPTER TWENTY-NINE

It's a chilly, overcast morning after breakfast, but everyone is making the most of the final hour before camper pickup. In the grassy area outside the cabins, kids are exchanging contact information, finishing up bracelets, and playing games in small groups. This might be the perfect time to finally pull Max aside to talk. Better late than never. But it's more of a struggle than I expect, because he wants to run off and spend the rest of the remaining time with his friends.

"Max?" I shout, waving for his attention.

"What?" he asks, turning to face me, annoyed.

"So, Mom said you might be getting a cochlear implant?"

He shrugs and takes a step backward. Did he hear me?

I put my fingers to the side of my head. "The cochlear implant?"

"Yeah," he says, knocking his hand forward to sign "yes." "Mom and Dad want me to get it."

I dig my heels into the ground. That's exactly what I was worried about. "Do *you* want it, though?"

He shrugs again. "I need to be able to hear, don't I?"

Max is only eleven. He's still a kid. Of course he's going to do whatever our parents want him to do, especially if a doctor has lectured him on how this is a way for him to have a "normal" life. What kid doesn't want to be normal?

"There are other ways, though," I say. "You can stick with your hearing aids and learn sign instead."

"Nah, that won't work." He signs, "*No, no, no.*"

I grin, shaking my head. "See, you're learning it! It will help."

"It won't." He looks away from me and walks toward his friends sitting in a circle on the grass.

I follow and tap his arm so he looks at me again. "Why not?"

"'Cause I can't remember it! And no one uses it outside camp." He shakes his head like he doesn't understand why I'm even bringing it up.

"You'll practice," I reassure him. "We can all learn and use it together as a family."

"I talk to other people. Like at school. How would I sign to them? They wouldn't learn."

"You don't know that."

But I do. I get why he's angry, enough so that I can ignore his cheap insult. Maybe his friends would learn a handful of words, or at least Google some swear words for a laugh. Heck, maybe their parents would sign them up for an ASL class. But would the kids actually stick with it? Since they'd expect the boy with hearing loss to lip-read anyway.

I guess studying a new language can be a lot to ask of people. I understand why they might think it's too much effort—but this makes it feel like their lack of interest in learning is really a lack of interest in you.

I tap Max's arm again. He shrugs me off but at least turns back to face me.

I tilt my head as I speak. "I'm just saying, you don't have to have the surgery if you don't want to."

"But I have to." He clenches his teeth, annoyed by my persistence.

"No, you don't."

"Yes, I do. You don't understand," he says, scowling at me.

"Why wouldn't I understand?"

"Because we're not the same." He crosses his arms and looks away again. "Because I'm more deaf than you!"

He's got the same look I'd seen on Natasha countless times. If Max had shouted this at me even a few weeks ago, it would have cut deep. I reach out and grab his shoulders, turning him back to me.

"Hey. We are in the same boat. Yes, your hearing loss is a little bit more severe than mine, but not much. We still go through the same exact things. We're in the same family. You're going to the same schools with many of the same teachers I've had before. I'm your older sister, so I'm the one who has to struggle through everything first. You get to learn from my mistakes and benefit from the fact that I've already educated some people in our lives along the way."

He rolls his eyes, but he unfolds his arms. "Fine."

"Promise me you'll think about this. It's okay if you want one. Really. I only want to make sure it's your decision."

"I said fine."

He's several feet away from me now, and I know I won't have his attention much longer.

"Don't do it because the doctors want you to, or even because Mom and Dad want you to. Do it because it's what *you* want to do. What you think will make things best for you."

"Okay," he says plainly.

"And take time to think about it. You don't have to rush into anything."

"*Okay-okay,*" Max signs with a cheeky smile, trying to make a joke to end my lecture.

"Promise me?" I ask, needing to be sure I've gotten through to him.

"Yeah, whatever." He steps away. But, wide-eyed, he turns back to look at me. "I promise."

~

It's time to head to the parking lot and say our final goodbyes to all the campers. Phoebe lets me roll her bag up front. The departure window is still a few minutes away, yet her parents are here early, already waiting.

Her dad takes the suitcase, while her mom gives me a smothering hug. "Thanks for helping our girl out," she says.

"Nah," I say, unsure how to respond. "It was fun."

"I got an audiobook for the drive," her mom says, returning to the passenger seat.

"Keep in touch, kid," I say to Phoebe.

"I'm your age in, like, three months."

"Well, I'm eighteen in, like, one month," I say. "I'll see you next summer. Don't forget to tell your parents the great news."

"You bet," Phoebe says.

"Add me on Instagram or Twitter or whatever. If you—" I hesitate, unsure if she's active on social media.

"Yeah, I use them. Screen readers are a thing, you know? Make sure you add alt-text to describe your pictures for me."

"I'll add a 'hi, Phoebe' at the end."

She extends her arms wide into the air. "Hey, I'm trying to give you an awkward hug goodbye here."

I tackle her. "We don't live too far away, you know."

Once she's gone, I hang around the parking lot for a while, feeling largely unneeded. The younger kids are bursting with energy, while their parents were clearly hoping for exhaustion instead.

Honey and Blake come to find me for goodbyes. "Maybe I'll be your counselor next year," I say and sign to their delight.

Since Honey's parents have arrived, I give her a big hug and am pleasantly surprised when Blake approaches her to do the same. "*See you next year,*" Honey signs to Blake.

"What'd she say?" Blake asks, nudging me.

I'm happy to relay the message. "'See you next year.'"

"That's what I thought," Blake says, waving goodbye as Honey walks off.

Despite her late arrival, Blake isn't the last camper to be picked up. Her dad climbs out of the truck and scratches his head. "Huh, not late this time."

"Hey, Daddy," Blake says, waving to him, using the sign for "father" against her forehead.

"I learned some sign language, too," her dad calls out. He makes a thumbs-up, peace sign, pats his head, and taps his nose. Real amusing stuff. I'm proud that Blake doesn't laugh.

"I know none of that is right," she says.

"Toss your stuff in the back," her dad calls out. "Long drive here and even longer drive back."

Ethan helps Blake put her stuff in the truck bed. She opens the front passenger door but runs back to hug me and Mackenzie one more time before she leaves.

Max is one of the last campers to be picked up, since my parents probably wanted to let him have as much time at camp as possible, given that he missed an entire month.

"Are you driving back today?" my dad asks me while we wait for Max to say his goodbyes.

"Tomorrow. We're going to Chicago tonight for an end-of-summer celebration."

"That's fun," my mom says. "And I see you've got your hearing aids back in."

I ignore that comment, seeing as I don't plan on wearing them all the time now. Especially when I'm relaxing at home, I've learned it's nice to be able to tune out the world around me. But she doesn't need to know that right now. "Mom, I've been thinking, and you should wait a little while before Max gets a cochlear. Give him time to think about it."

"But the doctor says—" my mom starts, but I cut her off.

"Max needs a better reason to have the surgery than 'my parents want me to,'" I say before reassuring her. "I think he might go for it. And that'll be fine. Just give him more time to think. From what I've heard, too many kids get them because their parents want them to, not because they want it."

My mom is quiet for a while. "You know, when he was born, one of the doctors told us he might never speak."

"Would it have been so bad if he didn't?" I ask. "Being deaf isn't something that needs to be fixed."

"I know, sweetie. Hindsight is much clearer," my mom continues. "But it can be scary as a new parent. You got your diagnosis at a couple of weeks old."

"I thought I failed the newborn hearing screening."

"On one of the follow-up checkups," my mom says. "I already knew you were responsive to my voice, at least when I spoke loudly. I knew it would be a challenge, but I felt more prepared, somehow. I'd already gotten to know you. And sure enough, once we had you fitted with hearing aids, you did well. But with Max, they told us all this as I held him in my arms for the first time. And as he grew up, he didn't make it all seem as easy as it was with you."

"It wasn't easy for me," I say.

"I know." My mom considers her words. "But I was never too worried about you."

"Would you have been more worried if I had a profound loss?"

My mom hesitates. I can only imagine the concerns she had at the time—all a distant memory now. "Probably. But we would have figured it out."

"I wish I'd been able to learn sign language." To make myself clear, I add, "That our whole family had learned."

"It wasn't something you needed."

"There are varying levels of need," I say. My family has always treated hearing aids like glasses—the difference is, glasses are a corrective device, while hearing aids are only assistive. "I'm picking up sign pretty well now. It helps a lot. It'll help Max, too."

My mom nods. I understand it must have been scary to have not one but two deaf kids, especially since they'd never met anyone with hearing loss before us. I don't fault her for wanting what she thought was best for us, raising us as hearing-passing.

That's what ableism has shown as the "best move." But I want to use sign language.

It seems like my mom is about to say something else when Max comes running to us. "Can we stop and get Portillo's for lunch?" he asks my parents. "Oh, Lilah's gonna be a senior counselor next summer," he says, breaking my news to them before climbing into the van.

"You got the job?" my dad asks.

"Yep."

"That's exciting," my mom says. "Looks like you'll have to keep practicing your sign."

"That's the plan." Then, as he has all summer, Isaac appears by my side. He nudges my arm for an introduction. "This is Isaac," I say and sign. "Isaac, these are my parents."

"Hi, Isaac," my mom says.

Isaac signs as my dad reaches out to shake his hand. "What did he say?" my dad asks.

"He says nice to meet you," I say. I demonstrate each sign for my parents to copy, "*Nice. To meet. You.*"

Isaac grins at their attempt. "*Have a safe drive home,*" he signs to them, noticing another of his campers' parents are here for pickup. "*See you later,*" he signs to me with a smile before jogging away.

"What'd he say that time?" my dad asks.

"Oh, drive home safe," I translate.

"He seems nice," my mom says, smiling. "I see why you're extra eager to improve your sign language."

I blush. "One of many reasons."

CHAPTER THIRTY

Ethan gathers us around after the last of the campers leave. "All right, it's almost one," he says and signs. "We need to clean and pack up. But I wanted to announce our plans for tonight." He pauses for dramatic effect. "We got donations specifically for our counselor celebration fund, so we're bringing back the end-of-the-season reward night. To thank you for all your hard work this summer, we've got tickets for the concert at Wrigley Field."

"*Awesome,*" I sign to Isaac, who nods enthusiastically.

That afternoon when we board the Amtrak train, Natasha flips one of the pairs of seats so she and Jaden can sit directly across from me and Isaac.

"*I hate this shirt,*" Jaden signs. He's wearing one of Natasha's #44 Rizzo T-shirts that she usually wears as a large pajama shirt, but it's a little snug on Jaden.

"*You have to wear it,*" she signs. "*We're going to W-r-i-g-l-e-y.*"

"*I don't like the Cubs,*" he signs. "*None of you are wearing Cubs shirts right now!*"

"*I like the Cubs,*" Isaac signs.

"*Me too,*" I sign.

"*And you're already in the shirt,*" Natasha signs.

Some of the other people on the train are watching us. It bothers me for a little while, but soon I'm so invested in our conversation that I don't notice them anymore. It's nice not having to struggle to hear above the noisy train.

With Isaac nearby, attuned to my comprehension, I'm confident. I never feel lost in the conversation when he's by my side.

The skyline finally comes into view. I love going to Chicago. The tall buildings, the elevated train, the old historic bridges, and the cool breeze blowing in from the lake. The only thing better than the view from the train ride into the city is driving down Lake Shore Drive at night, when the whole view is illuminated by city lights while the lake is an expansive darkness to the east.

We get into Union Station with a few hours to kill before the concert and take the L to Wrigley. I feel like I'm really holding my own in the real world with the older counselors—until they head to a bar with bouncers posted at the door.

Natasha and Jaden keep conversing in sign while handing their fakes to the bouncer. Is the goal to distract him enough so he doesn't notice the IDs are fake? Or do they want to make him think that communicating with them would be too much of a hassle so he doesn't bother turning them away? Either way, it works.

I realize I'm not positive if Mackenzie is twenty-one yet, but she makes it into the bar as well, along with Ethan, Simone, and Bobby, leaving me and Isaac alone on the sidewalk.

"*I don't have a f-a-k-e,*" I sign.

"*I don't have a fake, either,*" Isaac signs.

"*What do we do?*"

"*I know a place,*" Isaac signs.

"*You two okay?*" Ethan asks. When Isaac nods, he pulls out his own ID and goes inside.

Isaac grabs my hand and we cross the intersection. Wrigleyville isn't as busy as on a game day—at least not yet. There's still time before the concert opener, though the crowd is slowly gathering. The noise and chatter are overwhelming. I'm still readjusting to wearing my hearing aids, which I'd considered leaving at camp. I'll be signing with Isaac all night, and they won't make much of a difference when it comes to hearing the loud music. But it felt like the best choice for tonight to put them back in.

Isaac leads me over to a two-story brick building decorated with baseball iconography on the outside. The restaurant has a large bar, but Isaac heads upstairs, straight toward some batting cages.

"*Oh, fun,*" I sign when he lets go of my hand.

"*I'll get baseballs, you get sodas?*"

I turn to go get our drinks, but he grabs my arm. "*Later. Play first.*" He steps into the box and selects some settings on the pitching machine. He's just about to put in the money when he turns around and notices I'm waiting outside. He waves for me to join him.

"*No, no. That'll be a w-a-s-t-e of money.*"

"*Not a waste,*" he signs, waving for me again. "*Come on.*"

I reluctantly open the gate and join him. He picks up a bat from the back and hands it to me, helping me find my stance at the plate.

"*Ready?*"

"*I guess.*"

The first ball lobs toward me. I'm grateful he set the machine on slow. I make contact, sending the baseball dribbling down the cage. I take a few more swings, getting a few hits, while also entirely missing a couple other times. I step out of the box back toward Isaac.

Another ball flies at the plate, bouncing once and landing with a thud against the backdrop. "*No, no,*" Isaac signs. "*I'll help you.*"

He carefully turns me back toward the plate, standing behind me so I don't step too far into the path. His arms wrap around me as I lift the bat, and he places his hands over mine. Though we've been entwined for much of the last few weeks, my skin still tingles at his touch.

When the next pitch comes, he pulls the bat back and gives the ball a soft tap, swinging our arms forward and sending it soaring through the cage. He does the same for the next few baseballs until the machine powers down, signaling the end of my turn.

His arm is still around me, so I turn to hug him. I lean away, signing, "*Okay, your turn. Go ahead and show off.*"

Isaac grins wide. He cranks the machine up to a faster setting. "*Safer to wait outside.*"

I step out of the cage and watch. He's cautious, not wanting to risk additional injury this summer, but sends every single baseball soaring with a loud clang. A small line of sweat forms on the side of his face, but he wipes it away with the back of his arm without missing a single hit. His jaw is set, serious while he concentrates, but his body is loose, making it look effortless.

Isaac finishes the set and joins me. He pushes back a small curl of hair that had fallen to his last remaining bandage on his forehead. "*I see why you have to do college baseball camp next summer.*"

He shrugs, but I can tell he's pleased I'm impressed.

We get some sodas to drink, and by the time we leave, it's no longer scalding hot, since the sun has begun to set behind the buildings. We make it through security, show our tickets, and walk into the crowded concourse. Isaac interlaces his fingers with mine, so we sign one-handed. "*Where are our seats?*"

"*This way.*"

Isaac and I weave through the crowd, reaching a gate that leads into the field where the stage is set up. We wait in a short line to show our tickets again. I check my phone and see recent messages in my group text with Kelsey and Riley.

Kelsey: Lilah, are you back home yet? Or still at camp?

Lilah: Actually, downtown at a concert right now with the staff for an end of summer celebration! I'll be home later tomorrow.

Riley: Didn't know deaf people went to concerts . . . ?

Followed by a second message a few seconds later.

Riley: Sorry, that's not rude, right?

I chuckle and hold up the message to show Isaac. "*They want to know why deaf people would want to go to a concert.*"

Isaac shakes his head, also finding this amusing. "*Because we like music?*"

"*Right.*"

The rest of the counselors are on the other side of the baseball diamond at the opposite gate. Isaac waves across the field to them. "*We'll meet you up front,*" he signs at a distance.

He stands close to me again. The scratches on his cheek have faded, but I remember exactly where they all were. I reach up and gently brush my fingers over the area around it. "*Does it still hurt?*" I sign one-handed.

He shrugs. "*It's fine.*" He gets a mischievous glint in his eyes and guides my hand to his forehead. He lowers his arm and signs, "*Remember when you hit me there?*"

Tug-of-war. The first few weeks of camp feel like a lifetime ago. "*It's not purple anymore, I promise!*"

He raises his eyebrows and bites his lip. "*Kiss it and make it better?*"

I stand on my tiptoes and wrap my hand around the side of his head to draw him closer. I peck his forehead, his cheek, and his lips.

"*Much better,*" he signs.

"*Good.*"

We're let onto the field a few minutes later, guided to the row of gates at the very front, practically at the stage.

"*Excited?*" Isaac asks.

"*Yes! I've never—*" I'm not sure how to sign the rest, so I gesture dramatically to the stage. "Been this close!"

We're at the front of the fenced area, right behind where the sign language interpreter will be. There's no interpreter for the opening band playing right now, but we're so near the stage that it's still fun to watch even if I can't understand a single word.

The other counselors join us. We stand around, chatting and watching the opener. There's a buzz in my pocket, and I open my phone to an Instagram notification from Kelsey. It's a photo of her and Riley hanging out at a backyard firepit, surrounded by a bunch of our classmates, and I'm tagged in the caption because they're "missing me" at this party.

Isaac notices me holding the image open a few seconds longer than I mean to. He turns with his back to the stage and gestures for us to take a selfie. I reverse the camera and smile. Isaac leans in toward me and I snap a couple of shots. I hesitate over what to caption it, so I show the picture to Isaac for his thoughts.

"*Maybe 'Deaf pride,'*" he signs. I type it out all lowercase, but he nudges me. "*You can do ———, Deaf,*" he signs, holding his thumb and index against an outstretched finger on his other hand.

I'm unsure I understand what he's signing, so I give him my phone and he makes the change, capitalizing the *D* in "Deaf."

"*Can I use that?*" I stare at the word. Then I let slip the question that's been in the back of my mind all summer. "*Am I deaf enough?*"

Do I need his affirmation? Have I been searching for approval to claim the word "Deaf" or even "deaf" as my own, worried I didn't meet some specific criteria—not having a profound loss, not being fluent in sign language, not facing some of the same obstacles in life because I speak?

Isaac looks at me and nods encouragingly. "*There are different levels of deafness: m-i-l-d, m-o-d-e-r-a-t-e, s-e-v-e-r-e, and p-r-o-f-o-u-n-d.*" He shakes out his hand a little bit after all that fingerspelling. I smile.

"*It's your choice. People think different things. Some prefer capital* D, *Deaf,*" he signs, demonstrating by holding up an index finger and bringing the other hand to it in the same shape as the uppercase letter. "*Or just deaf, or hard of hearing.*" He shrugs. "*But whatever way, all deaf, all belong.*"

"*That's nice to know. It's just, sometimes, it feels like not everyone thinks that way.*"

"*People think different things. It matters what you think. Your ________, your choice. I-d-e-n-t-i-t-y,*" he signs, to make sure I understood the letter *I* tapped against his open palm.

Because that's just it—I've been deaf since birth, as simple as that. And the older I get, the more my hearing loss will become a joke to some people, the way the elderly are ridiculed for needing hearing aids. I need to take pride in my identity, in whatever way I choose to share it with the world.

"*Belong.*" I smile at Isaac, linking two F-shape hands together to repeat one of the signs he used earlier. "*I like this sign.*"

He grins and retrieves his own phone. "*Let's take another picture.*" He presses a kiss to my cheek and captures the moment.

Meanwhile, my phone commands my attention, with plenty of likes and comments on my picture rolling in. Maybe it's because I haven't really posted anything all summer. My friends' replies all basically sum up to "How are you so close to the stage?!" and "Who's the guy you're with?!"

Finally, it's time for the main show. The sun has gone down, the opener has finished their set, and the interpreter has taken her place in front of us. Our entire group cheers and waves in ASL applause. "*Thank you!*" Natasha signs to the interpreter.

"*She's a C-D-I,*" Isaac quickly explains to me. "*Deaf interpreter.*"

"Oh," I say. "*Like, she's Deaf?*"

He nods and quickly looks around, pointing out the hearing interpreter off to the side, relaying information to the certified Deaf interpreter on stage. "*More style. Better ASL.*"

Lights flash along with the heavy vibration of the music, signaling the band's arrival on stage. We're right next to a gigantic speaker that forcefully shakes the ground beneath our feet.

The stage is high in front of us, so I find myself craning my neck to watch the performance. Toward the end of the show, there are some people to our right who have climbed onto each other's shoulders to get a better view. Simone shouts something to Bobby, who helps her hop onto his shoulders.

Isaac taps me. "*You too?*"

I nod eagerly. He hunches over and offers a hand to help me up. He slowly stands upright, lifting me high into the air. He's steady, without wobbling in the slightest, wrapping his hands around my shins to hold me tight. This is the best possible way to experience a concert.

The interpreter's been moving nonstop this entire show, breathing as much life into her signs as she can.

And when a song I know well comes on, I sign right back at her, letting my hands fly, careful not to move too much so Isaac won't lose his footing beneath me. For some of the other songs, a lot of the ASL went over my head, but as I sign along to this one, I think I may be getting the hang of this. Just maybe, I'm finally figuring out this whole hearing-loss thing.

CHAPTER THIRTY-ONE

I can't believe it's the last morning already. Didn't I arrive at Gray Wolf just a week or two ago? How is it possible that the entire summer has gone by? I'm not ready to leave this place, these people.

We have to be off the grounds by ten, so Ethan instructs us to meet at the footbridge to the parking lot. "There's something we want you all to see," he explains.

"As I'm sure you've all already noticed, my construction guy is here this morning to attend to some quick cabin repairs," Gary says. "But I had him put this together first. This used to be a staple of our camp's former glory."

We exit the wooden area into the parking lot, where above us is a brand-new, towering entryway arch, with a proud and friendly wolf front and center. Written in both English and ASL lettering is CAMP GRAY WOLF.

My eyes water. "I love it. And I know all of our campers, new and old, will love it next year, too."

"My thoughts exactly," Ethan agrees. "Let's all get a photo underneath it."

We gather to document our final moments of the season, smiling wide at the camera that's propped up against the side mirror of the camp van, waiting for the flash to go off.

Then Gary runs back to set up another shot, just in case. What summer camp will Gary end up at next year, since he's passing on the mantle to Ethan? Or will he hang up his tie-dye for a season? I'm sure Ethan's de facto uniform will be a whole closet of Deaf-pride attire.

"Let's take a silly one!" Mackenzie says and signs, because of course she does. She already told me she'll be back and offered to video call with me so we can "practice our ASL together." I'm not sure I'll take her up on it, but I appreciate the offer.

Unfortunately, Simone and Bobby aren't planning to come back—at least, not for a full summer. Maybe they'll pop in for a visit, or volunteer for a few days . . . or stop by to drop off wedding invitations. Who really knows with those two?

Natasha and Jaden will still be in town for a few weeks before heading to college. They've invited me to hang out in the city with them and Ethan. I'm so relieved they don't think I'm slowing them down anymore, or at least I've endeared myself to them enough that they no longer care.

If only Isaac had more time before school. He's standing beside me, putting bunny ears behind my head, but soon he'll be over a thousand miles away at Gallaudet University in Washington, DC. When we finish taking pictures, Isaac wraps his arms around me.

"*I'll miss you,*" I lean back and sign, willing myself not to cry.

"*I'll miss you, too.*" He hugs me tight but doesn't say anything else.

Our future seems so up in the air. Is this a breakup? Were we ever really "dating," or was this just a summer romance? I want so badly for this to not to be the last time I see him.

"*You'll text me?*" I ask, barely conveying the whole range of emotions I'm experiencing right now but hoping he'll read my facial expression.

He squeezes me tight. "*Of course.*"

He bends down to kiss me. I reach up to pull his face close to mine, not ready to let go. We've been through so much together this summer. It's not fair that time is now tearing us apart. I want another month here, or a week—heck, even a single additional day. Anything to sit near the fire under the stars with Isaac by my side.

But life has to move on.

CHAPTER THIRTY-TWO

I've been home for a month, but it's taken a while to settle back in with Kelsey and Riley after an entire summer immersed in Deaf culture.

On our way back from hanging out Friday after school, I finally decided to speak with them about what I need. "You can tap me to get my attention. Like, instead of calling my name a million times."

I had to address this mainly because I've been instinctively tapping them, and they were getting annoyed. But it opened up the conversation, and I dove into other accommodations, such as letting me sit in the middle. Putting captions on without complaining when we watch TV. Rephrasing things that need repeating, rather than just dropping the subject and leaving me in the dark. Some basic stuff that would be a huge start to a more accessible friendship.

At first, I was nervous, because Kelsey and Riley sat quiet in the front seat, staring straight ahead. But Kelsey broke the silence. "That all makes sense. I'm sorry it's been so difficult before."

"Yeah, things like the cafeteria at lunchtime are just always going to be impossible," I say. "So sometimes I'll be quiet and not really engaged in the conversation, but that doesn't mean I'm, like, ignoring you all or being rude. And keeping the radio down while we're driving would be nice," I say, nodding to the stereo ahead of me.

"All the time?" Riley complains, but I'm quick to reassure her.

"We can definitely blast it while we're singing along to something. Don't worry."

"Perfect," Kelsey says, smiling as she slows to a stop in front of my house.

They drop me off at home, and I head inside right on time for dinner. We're two weeks into the fall quarter, which is also a couple of classes into the ASL course my family has started taking.

"Plates on the table, please," my mom says and signs as I enter the kitchen.

"*Are you gonna help?*" I ask Max.

"*No,*" he signs. He flips through a stack of note cards, practicing the words we learned this morning. "I'm busy studying."

Hopefully it's a glimpse of what's to come. For sign to fully work for me, the people around me actually need to use it.

However, I'm under no illusions. Learning a language is difficult; it takes time and commitment. One intro class doesn't mean we're all on the path to being fluent. But this is what I want, so I'm going to stick with it and encourage them to do the same. This is how I want to embrace my disability and the access I need. It's not hearing loss—it's Deaf gain.

Max has already decided to go ahead with the cochlear implant, so that procedure is scheduled for the start of next summer so he has ample time for recovery, as well as time to retrain his brain with the new device, before classes start back up. He'll miss a season of sports, and a month of camp again, but not much school, which was obviously our parents' idea. To play it safe, he's decided that he only wants to get it on one side, even if his other ear ever becomes eligible in the future. "Part cyborg," he said with a grin when sharing his decision.

After dinner, we sit around the table. My dad waves for my attention. "Your phone," he says and signs.

"Oh." I hadn't realized it was vibrating, but I'm even more surprised when I see why. I'm getting a video call.

From Isaac.

We sent a few messages back and forth after camp, but I mostly haven't heard from him, since he's likely busy getting settled into college. Yet, now he's calling me out of nowhere? I rush up to my bedroom and take a deep breath before answering.

"*Oh, hi,*" I sign, holding the phone out in front of my face.

"*I thought you might need someone to practice your ASL with.*" Isaac smiles. He's calling from his laptop, sitting cross-legged in his new dorm room, with a Cubs poster on the wall behind him.

I grin. "*I don't know, Mackenzie did offer.*" I shake my head as I take a seat on my bed, leaning back against the wall and propping my phone up between my knees so I can sign with both hands.

"*Don't worry, we'll sign and have your ASL perfect, everyone will be amazed at camp next summer. And maybe soon you could come tour Gallaudet, too?*" He raises his eyebrows questioningly, and I can sense his anticipation for my answer. "*It'd be great to show you around.*"

"*I'd really like that.*" I smile, leaning back against the wall and settling in for our conversation. "*So what's up?*"

My hands fly effortlessly, and I can tell that, even though it's not summer and I'm back to reality, who I was at Gray Wolf is still at my fingertips. It's not just the fluency, but the confidence. I know who I am. I don't need to be more hearing or prove my deafness.

I can bring both worlds together. Just being myself, I'm complete.

AUTHOR'S NOTE

Growing up, rather than struggling through spoken conversations, I'd hide away from interactions. You could find me in the corner, devouring a book and seeking comfort in the clarity of the written word.

Yet I was often disappointed with the representation I found there. In the rare references to hearing aids, the devices were typically worn by elderly side characters, whom the protagonists would trick or ridicule. Or if a young character was disabled, they only existed in the story to be pitied or helped by the hero. Why didn't a kid like me get to be the main character? Why didn't our experiences get to stand on their own?

The majority of deaf kids have hearing parents. From birth, the odds are against us ever getting access to language or community. In fact, the history of signing itself is fraught with obstacles. Oralism continues to stand in the way of early language access for children. And leaders of eugenics movements, including Alexander Graham Bell, have long wanted to prohibit deaf people from marrying or socializing or even being born.

Therefore, it's a point of pride that through everything, Deaf culture exists.

Like Lilah, some of my earliest involvements with the community and ASL came from going to a deaf summer camp. *Give Me a Sign* is by no means representative of all those with hearing loss, since no single novel could possibly encompass our variety of backgrounds and stories. I simply hope it gives readers a glance into the depth and complexities of Deaf culture, as well as an understanding of why I and so many others are proud to be Deaf.

To all my deaf readers, I hope you know your deaf experience is valid, however you identify or communicate. And if you want ASL to be part of your life, it's never too late to learn. With all the hurdles we face, it's no wonder that so many of us struggle to understand our place in this world—but I promise, you belong.

ACKNOWLEDGMENTS

Getting these words from my brain to your bookshelf was all made possible by many wonderful people:

My incredible agent, Kari Sutherland, who checked more boxes than I'd thought possible during my representation search. I appreciate your editorial eye and willingness to share personal experiences. Thank you for being such a passionate advocate for my work. I can't wait to see what the future has in store.

Of course, my fantastic editor, Polo Orozco. From our very first chat, immediately, your feedback just *clicked*, and I knew you would truly elevate this story. Thank you for your enthusiasm and brilliant insights.

I'm also so grateful for everyone whose hard work and dedication helped make this the final book you're reading today: Cindy Howle, Ariela Rudy Zaltzman, Misha Kydd, Laurel Robinson, Kaitlin Yang, Christina Chung, Amy White, Natalie Vielkind, and Elsa Sjunneson. And for all the support from Penguin, especially from Jen Loja, Jen Klonsky, Shanta Newlin,

Elyse Marshall, Felicia Frazier, Emily Romero, Christina Colangelo, Alex Garber, Carmela Iaria, Helen Boomer, Kim Ryan, and their teams.

Shout-out to Signed Ink and my fellow Deaf writers and artists—thank you for helping brainstorm signs that would work simultaneously so that both characters could be utilizing ASL on the cover art. (For those of you who are curious, it's "right!" and "interesting.") Thanks also to the community within Disabled Kidlit Writers and the encouraging Lillie Lainoff.

Aiden Thomas, thank you so much for seeing the potential in this story. Without your mentorship, this book wouldn't be where it is today. And thanks to all those who read versions of this draft, especially Briana Miano, Brighton Rose, Gigi Griffis, and AJ Cosgrove.

Rebecca Johns, your class was a turning point in my life. I'm eternally grateful that you showed me I was capable of writing enough words to fill a novel. And to all my professors and classmates at DePaul, thank you for being there at the start of this publishing adventure, especially Ava Tews and Savy Leiser, who read materials, and Jane Fox, who initially sent me down the right path by saying that my concept was "definitely a YA story."

My Slack'ers, we've weathered so much together. I'm eternally grateful for your friendship and support. I don't know what I'd do without our internet home. And Alexa Landis, thank you for always being a quick message away.

Camp Lions, thanks for many transformative summers and always welcoming my brother and me with open arms. I promise my time there was never quite as eventful as Lilah's. Ms. Joy and the team at Children's, thanks for fostering community and making appointments a delight.

To my parents, thanks for all the library trips, the reading aloud, the book-themed twelfth birthday party, and so much more. And to my grandparents, I'm so glad I got to share this accomplishment with you all. Your love and encouragement mean the world to me.

To @Cara.toons, you're my number one critic. To Mark, thank you for a favorable ranking in your pool-shift reads. To Luke, sorry there are no cryptids—maybe next time!

Mika and Zuko, for always curling up by my side during late-night editing sessions.

Most importantly, Gabe. I couldn't have anticipated all the impossible hurdles life would throw at me during the journey to this book's publication. Without you, I never would've made it to the finish line. Thank you.